P9-BBQ-010

On that awful day, the chambermaid had witnessed a fierce quarrel. That very night, the beautiful refugee model, whose sad eyes gazed from the covers of the top magazines, was found dead, her famous face mutilated beyond recognition.

Franz, her handsome patron . . . Lise, her selfish friend . . . Madame Braun, the owner's French wife . . . Fitz-Marley, the faithful friend who never hid his sympathies, only his passions . . . any one of them could have done it. It was up to Detective Capricorn to find the killer and the terrible secret hidden behind the ornate doors of . . .

THE BRANDENBURG HOTEL

Murder Ink.® Mysteries

DEATH IN THE MORNING—Sheila Radley
THE BRANDENBURG HOTEL—
Pauline Glen Winslow
McGARR AND THE SIENESE CONSPIRACY—
Bartholomew Gill

Scene Of The Crime™ Mysteries

A MEDIUM FOR MURDER—Mignon Warner
DEATH OF A MYSTERY WRITER—Robert Barnard
DEATH AFTER BREAKFAST—Hugh Pentecost

A Murder Ink.® Mystery

THE BRANDENBURG HOTEL

Pauline Glen Winslow

A DELL BOOK

Published by
Dell Publishing Co., Inc.
1 Dag Hammarskjold Plaza
New York, New York 10017

To Ray, with love

Copyright © 1976 by Pauline Glen Winslow
All rights reserved. For information address St. Martin's
Press, Inc., New York, New York.
Dell ® TM 681510, Dell Publishing Co., Inc.

ISBN: 0-440-10875-6

Reprinted by arrangement with St. Martin's Press, Inc.
Printed in the United States of America
First Dell printing—October 1980

A NOTE TO THE READER

Scotland Yard and its Criminal Investigation Department are too well known to need explanation, but the Special Branch, perhaps, is not. Originally the Special Irish Branch, formed to counter Fenian activity in London, it is now involved more broadly in the defense of the realm. It is separate from SIS (Secret Intelligence Service) and MI5 (Security Service), which are Great Britain's intelligence and counterintelligence services, respectively, and which are also separate from one another. And although MI stands for Military Intelligence, in fact it is not a military organisation, the military having their own services, for instance, Naval Intelligence Department (NID). During World War II there was a certain rivalry between SIS, which was the descendant of the Secret Service of gentlemen amateurs, and the more newly formed MI5, composed mainly of bureaucrats. Some of the glamour of SIS was tarnished after the exposure of Burgess, Maclean, and Philby, but all that was long after the time period covered by this book, the events in which, of course, are purely imaginary. . . .

Curtain Raiser

Many people were to lose their sleep over the Brandenburg affair. In Buenos Aires two young men arose after a sleepless night and decided to forgive their erring father and consulted a lawyer as soon as his office opened. In the Welsh mountains a small group of men met in a place they had abandoned in 1940 and argued unhappily until the dawn. In London a writer who had been with Naval Intelligence was inspired with the idea for a marvellous plot, but by morning, mindful of the Official Secrets Act, regretfully put it aside. A woman in Germany was visited by memories and regrets and stared all night at the ceiling, afraid to lower her light, remembering she no longer had a child, or loving husband, and she was growing old. A woman in the Midlands cried all night because this had happened just when it seemed she had a future. But the man in Spandau prison, when he heard of it at last, merely shrugged his shoulders. Because nothing was going to help or hurt him ever again.

Except for the parties directly involved, the first to be disturbed was Nora, the youngest chambermaid at the Brandenburg Hotel near Illwood village, and that was before the disaster had happened. Nora was romantic and was deeply intrigued by the events of the day before. She had always been fascinated by the

German guests and that day they were having a row.

Nora watched from the corner of the cocktail lounge, where she was not supposed to be, clutching an armful of linen, fixed to the spot with curiosity. The guests were at tea on the terrace that was divided from the cocktail lounge by a wall of glass, and Nora was hidden in the heavy curtains that were drawn across at night. Although she could see well enough, her curiosity was not likely to be assuaged—they were arguing in German, of which she understood not a word—but the scene was certainly exciting.

The Brandenburg was a luxurious hotel, very expensive, and all the guests had the appearance of riches, at least to Nora, who came from Illwood and was the postman's daughter. The Germans, though, had a special interest for her, not only because most of them were good-looking, and all of them well-dressed, but because of their strange story.

'Like—like something in the pictures,' she had remarked to the head chambermaid and housekeeper, Mrs Dermott, usually known as Scotchie, but Scotchie had merely sniffed and told her not to be foolish and to get on with her work. Still, it was true, Nora thought. For all those elegant people had been arrested as enemy aliens near the beginning of the war and kept in camps, and even real prisons, for years and years—just like Bertie Postle from Illwood who was no good and had been caught twice breaking into people's houses. Why, it had only been last Christmas, when Nora herself had come to the Brandenburg, that Mr Diener had been released, although the war had been over for simply ages.

Her eyes round, she watched the quarrel progress. Carry, who was serving, had taken care of them quickly and kept out of the way. Mr Diener had not even noticed his tea was at his side, he was so angry. Carry could have given him a fresh cup, Nora thought, because she liked Mr Diener. He was tall and fair and striking, not young, of course, but, well, important-looking. He was important, too: Nora's father said the Diener works had made guns for the army all through the war.

But now he looked red and perturbed and unlike himself. He was really shouting, his voice rising above the others and going on when they stopped. Some of the other guests looked at the Germans, surprised, because they were usually quiet and kept to themselves. That Lady Cecily was raising her eyebrows—she would, Nora thought, the old cat, as Lady Cecily felt she had to tell everyone how to behave and was always complaining that Nora had not left her room in the state her ladyship considered it should be.

Mrs Roth noticed Lady Cecily's look and she didn't like it. She put her little hand on Mr Diener's sleeve and he bent down to hear what she had to say. Mrs Roth never had to speak in a loud voice; she was tiny and very pretty and all the men stooped to listen to her. She was the prettiest woman that Nora had ever seen, and as elegant as—words failed her, for she had known no elegant woman in Illwood.

A real little china doll was Mrs Roth, pink and white and blue-eyed, and her hair was a silvery colour piled up in curls on the top of her head. She wore a dress of cream-coloured silk with the new long, full skirt, and high-platformed shoes of the kind you couldn't buy in England. All Mrs Roth's things came from abroad. Nora looked down at her own low-heeled, government-approved utility shoes and sighed. She would give a month's wages for a pair of shoes like that, but it wouldn't be enough, even if she could find them.

On the other hand, Nora soothed herself, she was glad she wasn't married to Mr Roth. He was quite old, and cross, and had already stopped taking notice of the argument and was picking at all the sandwiches on the tray by his side. The Roths were forever complaining about the food.

Mr Karl, who was tall and dark, with a dimple in his chin, was not as excited as Mr Diener, though he was not smiling the way he usually did. He was saying something to Mr Diener as he handed cake to Mrs Roth. Very nice looking and a really nice gentleman was Mr Karl. Nora had had quite a crush on him before Mr Diener came.

Mr Diener was, well—right now Nora was carrying the sheets off his bed. When she did his room, on Scotchie's day off, she would always change the sheets though it was supposed to be only every other day. She would wait until tea-time, when Madame Braun, the owner's French wife and a real Tartar, was busy in her office and couldn't interfere. It was Nora's pleasure. The sheets smelt faintly of some eau-de-cologne that Mr Diener used. Nora had never known a man to use any sort of scent and it made her feel quite breathless.

She wished that Jim, the butcher's son in the village and her steady boy friend, would do something like that, but he thought it was soft. He got annoyed if she even mentioned Mr Diener. Nora sighed. All Mr Diener's things were so fine. She would peek in the drawers on Friday afternoons. Of course, the Roths had nice things too, but they weren't kind and thoughtful like Mr Diener. Such a gentleman. Mr Karl was very nice and he used to pinch Nora sometimes and make her laugh, but Mr Diener was not that sort at all.

Mr Braun, the owner, was crossing the lounge from the entrance hall to see what was wrong on the terrace. Nora shrank further into the curtain, but Mr Braun did not notice her; he was too concerned with the row. Mr Diener was actually shouting, his face was redder, and a lock of his hair, that was always so smoothly brushed back, had fallen over his forehead.

Mrs Roth had given up talking and was sipping her tea slowly, sitting back in her chair, which was the nicest one on the terrace, a deep basket chair with blue cushions. Mr Diener seemed to be hollering at Miss Rilke, who was standing in the corner where the potted plants were arranged. Miss Rilke was not saying much but then, she never was much of a talker. She looked frightened.

Miss Rilke was not pretty like Mrs Roth, but she was young and tall and thin, with sad, dark eyes and very smart—Miss Rilke was a model and her picture was on that month's *La Belle*. Nora had seen the magazine in lots of rooms, Lady Cecily's, Mrs Roth's, Mr Diener's. Miss Rilke had been wearing a hat with red and gold leaves with more leaves flying all around her. Now she was wearing linen trousers and a soft blouse of the same colours. Nora looked at the clothes with longing, but Miss Rilke was leaning into the shrubs, not caring that the twigs were catching at the gauzy stuff of her sleeves, as if she were trying to shrink and hide like Nora in the curtain.

Mr Braun spoke to Mr Diener and quieted him down. He put an arm on his shoulder and brought him into the lounge. Nora backed her way quietly through the door of the dining room but she continued to watch. Mr Braun poured Mr Diener a drink

and soon Mr Karl joined them at the bar. Madame
Braun walked by as she escorted a visitor out to the
terrace, Captain Fitz-Marley, who came over from
Marley Castle most afternoons to see the Roths.

Before Nora was halfway across the dining room,
Mr Diener was off again. Charles Lawdon, who was
an Honourable, Lord Lawdon's son, came in off the
golf links and stopped and looked interested. Usually
he was bored. The Brandenburg was a quiet place for
a handsome, lively young fellow, but the cook said his
father had sent him there to be quiet and behave himself.

Mrs Roth came and joined the others in the bar,
leading Miss Rilke by the hand as if she were a
naughty little girl who had to say she was sorry, trail-
ing a twig on her sleeve. Nora leaned forward in her
excitement to see what was going on. The linen in her
arms grazed a pile of plates on the serving trolley; the
top one fell and crashed on a table top and the broken
bits jumped to the floor. Madame Braun looked up,
caught sight of Nora and came towards her, looking,
as Nora later told Scotchie, like the Wrath to Come.

Nora said she was told off 'good and proper' and
her wages were docked for the plate, but for once she
didn't mind. The Germans argued away until dinner
time, when Captain Fitz-Marley left, and they sat
down trying to look friendly at dinner. But the waitresses said you could see Mr Diener was still angry
with Miss Rilke, who looked as though she'd been
crying. The staff talked about nothing else all evening.

On the next morning, when poor Miss Rilke's body
was found, dead and battered horribly people said, all
of Illwood was talking about the murder and the row
the night before. The police came and asked a lot of

questions and searched all through the hotel and the grounds, even on the golf course. And after the whole place had been turned upside down, and Mr Braun beside himself, and Madame Braun watching everything with her lips pursed up and a frown as if she had a bad headache, two more detectives came and people said they were from Scotland Yard. There had never been anyone murdered in Illwood as far back as anyone could remember, and people were shocked even if Miss Rilke was a foreigner and the murder most likely was done, the village was sure, by another one of those foreigners up at the Brandenburg.

Nora's mother had never liked her working there. Nora would have done better serving in a shop among decent English people, she always said. She tried to insist that Nora give in her notice; with murderers on the loose it was no place for a young girl. But Nora told her mother she could hardly leave Madame Braun when she was in trouble, and had to wait a while.

The gossip was that Mr Diener would be arrested and Nora could no more have left than she could have walked out of the cinema in the middle of a picture. And it was something that didn't happen every day, having detectives come.

The elder one, Superintendent Snow, was rather sharp and cross but Nora liked the tall young sergeant who came with him and was as good-looking as an actor. Surely they wouldn't take poor Mr Diener to prison again. He couldn't do anything horrible like that. It must have been a loony. It was all so upsetting she could hardly sleep. . . .

English officialdom was also troubled with the Brandenburg affair, from Superintendent Pritchard of Div.

H.Q. in Illwood to the Chief Superintendent at Cl. Pritchard and his men had begun the investigation. The murder weapon, a heavy golf iron that had been found in the ditch by the girl's body, had been immediately checked for fingerprints, and the one set obtained had been immediately identified. The blood on the clothing of the suspect had been sent to the laboratory and proved to be the same type as the victim's. The ditch, which showed signs of a struggle, had been photographed and searched. The staff and guests had been questioned thoroughly. The hotel and the grounds had been subjected to a most intensive search for any traces of blood or signs of violence having taken place elsewhere, but none were found.

Superintendent Pritchard had looked over his assembled evidence. The glory of handling Illwood's only murder case since he had been on the force could be his. Without any further investigation, he could be justified in making an arrest. Only one problem remained: he was extremely reluctant to do so.

Pritchard had sympathized with the misfortunes of the German nationals who had been swept up in 1940 and interned for the duration. Like most of the English, while he felt it had been necessary to protect the country during those very dark days, he also felt it was uncommonly bad luck for the people who had been gaoled so long without having committed any crime. As a policeman who knew that the majority of real criminals are never apprehended at all, he thought that the German internees, who were mostly refugees from Hitler anyway, had come under the influence of a peculiarly malevolent star.

Franz Diener had been one of the worst cases. He denied any interest in the Fascist party or the German Nazis. He had lived in England for ten years before the war, and in the summer of '39—somewhat too late!—he had applied for naturalization. His ownership and direction of a large arms works had brought him to public notice at the beginning of the war, and he had gone before the usual tribunals. Pritchard had not been made free of the M15 files on the Diener case, but he had come to know the agent who still checked on Diener from time to time.

The agent hinted there was little to justify the long imprisonment, as far as he knew. A son in Germany, living with Diener's wife, had belonged to the Hitler Jugend—but so did almost all boys in Germany at that time. His wife's brother, who lived in England, had been a Nazi sympathizer, a member of the Anglo-German fellowship called The Link, and the fact that Diener had allowed this brother-in-law to use his house in the Midlands and his estate in Wales had weighed heavily against him. There were records of arms sales to Germany, but he had sold no more than English firms and there had been no secrecy.

But for whatever reason, the tribunal had voted to imprison Franz Diener, and his works had been run by a committee. Diener had made continuing efforts to get free, drawing on the influence of some English notables, themselves rather suspect at the time. He had been badly advised to do so, the M15 man said, and these manoeuvres had resulted in Diener's being among the last to be released, and then only on a deportation order. By refusing to go back to Germany he had become virtually stateless and his future was obscure.

Pritchard had known Franz Diener since he had been released from prison the previous Christmas and came to live at the Brandenburg Hotel. It was necessary for Diener to report to the local police station every month. Perhaps because Pritchard had been in the army for six years, which seemed like a large hole in his life, perhaps because he had been born in London and was still considered something of an outsider in Illwood, a certain rapport had grown between the two men. They occasionally had a drink together. Pritchard had been aware of Diener's friendship with the young Miss Rilke but, knowing that the man had been separated from his family for seventeen years, he had not seen fit to condemn him.

Pritchard, although he was a good husband and father himself, nevertheless thought Diener had behaved like a gentleman, for instead of keeping the girl at his side, he had sponsored her training as a photographer's model and was proud of her success. And now this. . . . The case seemed disagreeably open and shut. Half the hotel had heard the quarrel the night before the murder. Reluctantly, the other Germans had divulged that the quarrel took place because Miss Rilke had decided to leave the Brandenburg for her own flat in London, and Diener had objected strenuously.

Pritchard sweated all through the warm, late summer night, remembering that as a deportee under restriction, Diener was not allowed to travel more than five miles. He would not have been able to see the girl at all, unless she wanted to spare the time to go down to see him at the Brandenburg, when she wasn't busy, and if she hadn't made too many other friends. Diener was forty-five. Ingeborg Rilke was twenty. It seemed a classic case.

It was Diener's own golf iron, and the only prints on it were his. He had no explanation, other than that he left his bag on the porch of his suite and the iron must have been stolen. But the porch door had a lock and only Diener and the hotel owner had a key. The lock had not been tampered with. The blood on his clothes he had accounted for by finding the body while taking an early morning stroll, he had said. He had telephoned Pritchard himself. If Diener were guilty, he had picked a most stupid way to commit his crime, and Diener wasn't stupid. And yet. . . .

After his sleepless night, Pritchard put through a call to the Chief Constable, who then officially requested the presence of Scotland Yard. After all, Pritchard told himself, the Yard had the men with the experience. There were few major crimes in the Marley-Illwood area. Most police work revolved around petty theft and trespass. Boys stealing apples. The young riders from Illwood stables jumping fences and trampling grass. His own work was light. He might have missed something. He was too close to the people involved. It was possible he was mistaken. The Yard might come to a different conclusion. He found himself hoping strenuously that they would.

The Chief at C1, on getting the request, had problems of a different sort. Finer feelings did not concern him at the moment; he was counting bodies and coming up one short. There had been an outbreak of murder and mayhem around the British Isles, and all available men were already out on jobs of equal importance with the Brandenburg affair.

It seemed a simple enough job and at first he wondered why Illwood didn't get on with it themselves. All foreigners involved, he noticed. MI5 interested. No wonder Pritchard wanted to pass it along. The Chief had been in SIS himself and had the usual opinion of the rival service. Still, that was what the Yard was for, he thought philosophically, to take care of other people's dirty wash.

He would have to send Snow, although Snow had been about to take leave for medical purposes. He needed to go into hospital to have some tests—nothing urgent, but Snow was no youngster; he was already close to retirement age. Not that Snow would raise an objection. He was of the old school, the kind of policeman who worked until he collapsed and then wrote up his notes in the ambulance. The Chief would have preferred not to ask him, but he had no choice.

It shouldn't take long. As far as he could see, the Yard was just wanted to make an embarrassing arrest. The Chief looked through the duty roster for a Sergeant, First Class. Young Capricorn had just finished that job in the north; he would probably come down on the night train. He would send him to Illwood with Snow.

The Chief paused for a moment and smiled. Snow would sniff a bit at that. Not that he could object to Capricorn's work—any Sergeant, First Class had to be good, and the Chief had worked with Capricorn during the war in SIS and had a high opinion of him. But Capricorn had come from a theatrical family and had been brought up to be a magician. Although he had abandoned that career to become a policeman, some of the older men, like Snow, were still suspicious of him. The actor, they called him, and it was not meant as a compliment.

Well, Capricorn was the only sergeant free and Snow would have to put up with him. With luck it would only be for a few days. The Chief hoped fervently no new murders would take place until he got some men back. The criminal class had no consideration for police problems, he thought with a certain grim amusement. If Pritchard had his facts straight and it was just a question of arresting the girl's lover, perhaps Snow could get into the hospital by the beginning of next week. Snow was a good man. He didn't want anything to happen to Snow. Damn Illwood anyway. And damn MI5.

ACT ONE

1

Sergeant Capricorn drove Superintendent Snow down to Illwood village through a green and gold afternoon. The late summer day was warm, the leaves on the trees changing colour, and Illwood was set in gently rolling countryside. Capricorn was glad to leave London, which had looked dusty, shabby and dull, but Superintendent Snow was edgy and pleased with nothing. His junior wondered what was wrong.

Neither man had slept much the night before. Capricorn had travelled on the night train and reported to the Yard as soon as he had returned, but he was young enough to miss his sleep without much discomfort. Superintendent Snow had been awake most of the night with abdominal pain of the sort that had troubled him more and more lately. No one knew of his illness except the Chief. With Snow's fresh pink complexion and clear blue eyes, his upright carriage and well-brushed hair, he looked like a man in perfect health, and his junior resigned himself to Snow's acid humour as a slightly worse manifestation of his usual temper.

Superintendent Snow was known as a terror by all the sergeants in the Murder Squad, and was referred to, out of his hearing, as 'Old Icy-Eyes'—not because of his name, but because of his freezing glance at any error or less than disciplined manner on the part of his subordinates. Capricorn also had been aware, on their first job together, that Snow had not been eager to work with the son of the Great Capricornus. Still, Snow was an experienced detective and Capricorn had learned from him. For that the ambitious young man could endure a little sarcasm.

'Watch out, you fool!' Snow said in great irritation as they swung sharply into the village street, narrowly missing a low red sports car that had come tearing along at great speed round the blind curve. Capricorn had to mount the pavement to avoid a collision. The other driver, a good-looking, very young man, drove on with a wave of his hand indicating, perhaps, regret. It was so obviously his fault that Capricorn glanced at Snow in wonder, and was surprised to see a thin line of sweat on his brow.

Capricorn had never seen the Super agitated. He remembered that in the conference in the Chief's room that morning Snow's manner, though perfectly correct, had betrayed the fact that he did not look forward to this job. Politics were involved and Other Departments.

The Chief had managed to get some information from MI5 and Special Branch on the Brandenburg's German guests. All detainees under Regulation 18b. Except for Ingeborg Rilke, who had been thirteen years old in 1940 and had gone into internment with an aunt, the group had been suspected of Nazi sympathies, or at least there had been rumours, founded or unfounded, to that effect. The girl's uncle, a German lawyer who visited the Brandenburg but lived in London, had been given a clean bill.

'The Roths have applied for a visa from the Argentine and will probably get it,' the Chief had explained.

'That's where they were going in '40. Diener hasn't managed to get a visa for any country—quite a problem for the Home Office.'

'Why?' Snow had asked. 'The war's over. They could all have gone back to Germany.'

The Chief shrugged. 'A lot of internees refused to go back. I suppose the Jews and anti-Fascists might have some rotten memories of the place and any Fascists we picked up might be wary of running afoul of the de-Nazifiers over there. Anyway, this lot wants no part of Germany. Otto Karl can stay here if he wants—he has an English wife and children. But the others have to go.'

Snow had looked as though he thought this an excellent idea. 'Unless we detain one of them at His Majesty's pleasure,' he said drily.

He had given a grim little smile. He disliked foreigners in general, foreign criminals in particular, and for foreigners who came to commit murder on British soil he had a sharp and particular loathing.

'It might be my pleasure,' he'd added.

Illwood station stood unobtrusively between the butcher's shop and the post office that also sold newspapers, oddments and sweets—when it had them. A sign in the post-office window read:

NO chocolate, NO cigarettes, NO tobacco,
NO flints. Please do not ask.

Capricorn wondered for a moment just how long the war-induced shortages would continue. It was two years now since the war had ended. The high tide of patriotism, the sense of pulling together against a common enemy, was ebbing, and the black market, considered disgraceful in wartime and easily checked, was now the breeding ground for a new class of criminal, the 'wide boys.'

But he forgot city problems as he followed Snow into the quiet country station. The front office was empty except for a constable behind the bench. Superintendent Snow sent in his card to Superintendent Pritchard, very formal and correct. Pritchard, a thin, dark, worried-looking man, came out and ushered them into his office with as much courtesy and greater warmth.

He drew up extra chairs at his old wooden desk. A number of exhibits and file folders were already laid out for their inspection. Capricorn glanced round as he took his seat—the usual country station office, worn linoleum, ancient file cabinets, faded paint, and the only ornament the photograph of the King, looking younger and stronger than when he had pinned a decoration on Capricorn at the war's end.

Pritchard's telephone rang almost immediately.

'What, again?' he said. 'Not my pigeon, you know. Superintendent Ross . . . oh, he's not? The orchards? Young fools, they could kill themselves. You're not sure when? Yes, I'll make sure he hears about it. He'll get on to the stables. Yes. . . . Just a moment.'

'We don't get much excitement down here,' Pritchard told them, 'the worst crimes are what young Charles Lawdon does with his car. Lord Lawdon's son. His score in Illwood so far is two sheep and a Morris Minor.'

'A red Aston-Martin,' Capricorn said, remembering the two-seater that had almost crashed into the police car.

'Yes, how did you know?' Pritchard said. 'Anyway, now I'm getting complaints from irate farmers. Boys from the riding stables trampling the orchards. Usually they're trespassing on the golf course taking a short cut. I'll see if I can find Ross, old Peabody won't talk to anyone less than a Superintendent this morning.

'Please use this office,' he added, as he stood, sighing. 'When you've looked through everything we'll have a talk. You've got the results of the post mortem. The inquest was adjourned, of course. The girl's uncle came down—Krause, a German lawyer, lives in London. His statement is there, but he hadn't seen her for months.'

He was thanked and departed, and the two London men settled down to study the files.

'Look at that,' Snow said, in acute disgust.

They examined the photographs taken of the body before it had been moved.

'Dear God,' Capricorn said softly.

He had seen many murder victims, but this was peculiarly sickening. The man who had done this was not just a murderer but a sadist in the true meaning of the word. It was as though he had tried to kill her ten times over. The girl's face, famous all over England, was unrecognizable.

Yet he had seen this kind of death before. It was part of his wartime experience he had tried to forget. Even now he didn't want to remember and he stared out the window as if to keep the pictures from crowding through his mind.

The office was in the rear of the building with green fields and bronze-tipped trees as far as the eye could see. The air from the open window was fresh and sweet. Someone had planted flower beds, white vervain, yellow marigolds, tall blue delphinium and chunky dahlias. A flock of long-tailed tits were working their way through the branches of a birch, with a low, continuous, 'zuz-zuz.'

Peace.

But even in war, Capricorn thought, it was rare to see that kind of mutilation. A soldier's wounds, however ghastly, were most often randomly inflicted by distant guns. This conscious maiming he had seen on victims of the Gestapo; on hated officials, torn apart by mobs, and on the corpses left behind by *partizani:* bodies of their enemies, or assumed enemies, in those days when the combatants were in a state of flux, grouping and regrouping, as the conflict ended, or seemed to end.

It was a grim sort of justice that he, Capricorn, who had spent years in trapping Nazis and German spies abroad, should now in England be charged to deliver to the gallows the killer of a German refugee. Or, more correctly, to help Superintendent Snow deliver that killer.

'The swine,' Snow was saying. 'But according to the p.m. most of those wounds were made after death. Death was caused by severance of the cervical spine. That contusion there on the back of the head—' his long, dry white hand pointed out the spot—'that was made before she died. She could have been unconscious from the first blow.'

'I wonder why . . .' Capricorn said thoughtfully.

Snow shrugged. 'Frantic rage. A sexual pervert. Or a man who wanted to make it seem the work of a maniac. Take your choice. You notice there were traces of wine and brandy, but not nearly enough to knock her out.'

'She was last seen alive on Diener's porch, where she was drinking brandy with Diener, the two Roths and Karl, according to the staff and other hotel guests,' Capricorn remarked as he read.

'Pity there wasn't a bit of blood found on that porch,' Snow said. 'It would have tied the case up like a Christmas present from one of the big shops.'

He looked through another folder.

'Pritchard certainly did a thorough job, according to this. Had men over from High Marley to help. Went through Diener's rooms and the girl's with a fine-tooth comb, and did a job on the grounds.'

'Golf course too,' Capricorn said. 'I suppose it's adjoining. No sign of forcible entry on the hotel grounds.'

'With the amount of blood they found in the ditch,' Snow said, 'it's plain enough she was killed there. But he did right to make the search.'

He pursed his lips and with his usual method, went over each statement and report again, making careful notes, and Capricorn did likewise. They looked at the exhibits, Diener's blood-stained clothes, the heavy iron, the pathetic torn, stained nightgown.

As they were finishing, Pritchard returned.

'Looks bad for Diener,' Snow commented. 'If he'd killed her on the porch, counsel might have got him off the capital charge. But once he dragged her out to that ditch to finish her off, there's premeditation and that's that.'

'If he turns out to be the murderer,' Pritchard said, unhappily.

'We'll make a full investigation,' Snow was brisk. 'But at first glance—the girl would hardly go wandering about the grounds in the dark in her nightgown with a man who was not, shall we say, an intimate? Time of death between one and five.'

Pritchard sighed. 'Yes. That's what makes it almost

certain it was someone in the hotel. The gates are locked at midnight, and have to be opened by the night porter. As you saw, he said no one entered that night. He didn't hear anyone on the road outside. The gates are tall, the hedges high and thick. Anything bigger than a rabbit would have trouble getting through. Otherwise, I would have thought it the work of a maniac.'

'Unfortunately,' Snow said, in his direct manner, 'we haven't had any reports of escaped lunatics. We'll have to work with what we have here.'

Pritchard flushed. 'Yes, well, you notice that we know the iron was with the other clubs while the party were having their drinks on the porch, because Otto Karl had borrowed them and returned the whole set after dinner. He's certain of that.'

Snow nodded. 'The statements of the two Roths and Karl are quite clear about the events after dinner,' he said. 'The stroll about the grounds, the drinks on Diener's porch. No renewal of the hostilities between Diener and Rilke after dinner, in front of the others. Paul Roth went to bed at ten. Otto Karl went to his room to telephone his wife at Cobleigh, and then to bed, at ten-thirty. Lise Roth left to join her husband at eleven. She says she left the girl with Diener. Diener says she left with Lise Roth. And she's not seen again until she turns up dead the next morning. So. All the statements check except Diener's.'

'It was a silly lie,' Pritchard said slowly. 'It didn't help him. Even if she had left with Lise Roth, there was nothing to stop her going back again, or his going to her room. The man was in a panic,' he said, miserably. 'After all, he's already been in prison for more than six years for such little things. If he'd applied for naturalization earlier. If he'd publicly made it clear he disapproved of the Nazi antics of his wife's family. If he hadn't been so much of a gentleman and got a divorce. And I think he had a couple of drinks after he found the body.'

As he talked, Snow's blue gaze turned cold. Capricorn watched with resignation as Pritchard lost the favour he had won with Snow by his good work. Witnesses, Snow might have said, who were drinking could be taken into custody until they were sober. But Pritchard went on, not noticing.

'The poor devil's got into the habit of drinking more than he should. Nothing much he's allowed to do, work, travel, or anything. Just sits up there as if it's another prison, only more comfortable, and soaks. He's a decent sort,' he mourned, his brow wrinkling like a spaniel's. 'I had cocktails with him, a few times, at the hotel. Weird ideas, he has. Hated Hitler, but thinks we were all wrong, helping Russia. Says that Stalin's worse.'

Snow looked down his nose. He had no interest in the suspect's politics. Pritchard had admitted to drinking with a man reporting into the station. He was displaying bias in a suspect's favour. Pritchard, now aware of the drop in temperature, stared across his desk defensively.

Capricorn gave an inward sigh. Hardly an hour had passed since he and Snow had arrived in Illwood, and already there was antagonism between the two superintendents. It often happened. The provincial officer, willing to give up the problem of a difficult case, yet hating to surrender the authority. And a Yard man like Snow, impatient of anything except getting on with the job.

Snow stood decisively. Pritchard offered to accompany them to the hotel, and Snow politely declined. He thanked Pritchard for his cooperation and the Illwood man walked with them to the car, giving them information about the Brandenburg estate and pointing out the direction.

'Heinrich Braun, the owner, is expecting you. You'll find him helpful. He was born in England but was visiting Germany in '39 and he was stuck there. Went into hiding.' He shook his head. 'Plain bad luck—that whole crowd seem a decent lot. In the wrong place at the wrong time, that's all. The Krauses were refugees. The Roths were at sea but they were taken off the ship. Six years. Perhaps it drove Diener crazy, though he seemed all right. Anyway, they've all been very cooperative. Nervous of the police but very straightforward. The girl was one of them, of course.'

Snow used the weapon his juniors found most devastating, which was silence. They left Pritchard standing on the curb, staring after them. Capricorn felt sympathetic. Pritchard, he judged, was both capable and sensitive, but that sensitivity, to Snow, was a fault in a policeman. He was even moved, uncharacteristically, to comment, as they pulled out of the village street.

'Too much respect for the big house. Has to treat them with kid gloves. If it was a village lad took a club to his girl, that Super would've locked him up the next morning. But then,' he added sarcastically, 'the village lad wouldn't have entertained him with cocktails.'

Snow drank beer or whisky and thought but poorly of men who sipped at what he considered to be women's drinks.

Capricorn thought about it, and although Pritchard didn't strike him as either an awed yokel, or effeminate, still there was a certain, uncomfortable truth in what Snow had said. There usually was, he reflected.

They drove through a mile of winding lane. According to Pritchard, from here on all the land belonged to the Brandenburg. An odd name for an English country hotel. Pritchard had said it dated from a Prussian family who bought the estate back in the twenties when their own lands became Polish territory after the postwar dismemberment.

The hedges were unusually high, about five feet, and the lane was shadowed by tall trees. The first yellow leaves were drifting down from the sycamores. From the distance came the sounds of calls and laughter. The golf course was already re-opened. A murder must not spoil the summer pleasures of the guests.

They came to the top of a rise, and had a clear view of the orchard, heavy with fruit, to the north and the smooth golf greens to the south. Diener was an indifferent golfer, according to the reports, and rarely played.

'It seems immensely stupid of Diener,' Capricorn remarked, 'to have used his own No. 1 iron, left his prints, and just to wrap it up, dropped it next to the body after the very public scene that afternoon.'

'Drunk,' Snow said. 'Man's been drinking heavily for months, according to our friend.'

He grimaced slightly at the word 'friend.'

'He and the girl were going to bed. She got undressed. Probably he was still drinking on the porch. It occurs to him this is the last time the girl would stay with him. He worked himself up into a terrific drunken state. When she came out looking for him he struck her with the first thing that came to hand, the golf iron.

'Maybe he meant to kill, then, maybe he didn't. But when he saw her unconscious he got the idea all right. He just carried her out—she only weighed a hundred pounds or so—dumped her in the ditch, and still in that insane rage he finished her off.

'He calls Pritchard at seven, still partly drunk, but not stupid. He had to account for the blood on his clothes. No way he could get rid of them, and even if he could, the maids might notice there was a missing outfit.'

Capricorn was silent. As a hypothesis, it fit the known facts.

'The prints are to be expected on his iron,' Snow continued. 'The other fellow, Karl, said he didn't use it. As defense counsel will certainly point out, it would be suspicious if Diener's prints had been wiped off. The murderer, counsel will intimate, wore gloves, or used a doily, or some such clever thing.'

He snorted. 'Fortunately for us, Sergeant, most crimes are stupid. No finesse. You, I believe, were brought up to diddle the public. Now you see it, now you don't, and all that. But the average man is not. When he gets angry with his woman, he's been known to knife her in a pub full of her friends on a Saturday night, push her off a cliff at Broadstairs on a Bank Holiday Monday, or wring her neck in front of three children, a cat, dog, and a parrot. Compared to that, chummy was a model of restraint. You'll learn,' he said to the younger man, who wished he'd kept his mouth shut. 'You'll learn.'

2

The Brandenburg looked like an ordinary country hotel. A solid, substantial building of brick and stone, the old manor house, with the addition of a glassed-in terrace, shaded from the lane by tall trees. To Capricorn, only the gates looked forbidding and foreign, heavy gates of tall iron bars, surmounted by a pair of black eagles.

They left the car on a grassy verge, while a young porter in smart green uniform opened the gates. The drive led up to the entrance, but Snow struck off immediately across the lawns towards the golf links. Before the boundary hedge four little flags indicated the place of the murder, still guarded by two constables.

The men on duty were standing at ease, looking a little sleepy and bored—the body was long since gone, the excitement all over. Guarding an empty ditch for the Yard to inspect was just one more dull, routine job. On the peaceful late summer afternoon only the buzz of flies around the dark, rusty stains at the bottom of the ditch were a reminder that anything had happened, and the sycamore leaves were blowing gently over the hedge, burying the blood with their brightness.

The Yard men regarded the torn and broken weeds, the churned earth bearing witness to the violence of the deed. Here the crime had taken place. Capricorn recalled the picture of the girl alive, on the cover of *La Belle*, pale, with shadowed eyes, prophetically against a background of dead leaves. Ingeborg Rilke, a refugee child who had become successful, envied, sought after. Now it was over, and all before she was twenty.

Snow was brisk. 'Might as well get our hands dirty.'

Despite the thorough search that Pritchard and his men had made, the Scotland Yard men combed through the ditch inch by inch, looked around it and along the hedges, but they found nothing. Snow dusted his hands off in some disgust, regarding the depth of the steep incline.

'He wasn't so crazy after all,' he said. 'He'd seen this ditch often enough; he knew he could stand in there at night and who could see him? No one on the other side of the hedge in the lane. no one from the house unless they were practically on top of him and carrying a torch. And he wore a dark suit. Now if he were telling the truth, why would a man get up at seven in the morning and put on a dark suit?'

Snow did not expect, or wait for, an answer. Instead he glared at the two constables, particularly the younger, a gangling youth with sleepy cow's eyes.

'You men pack up and report back to Superintendent Pritchard. Nothing left to do here.'

They gathered up their ropes and flags with alacrity and moved with surprising speed towards the gates.

'Going for their tea, look at them,' Snow said. 'I wonder if they've been keeping their eyes open. It's been four days.'

He brooded for a moment. 'Everybody barging about. If the killer had wanted to retrieve anything from that ditch, he could probably have done it while they were yawning. Well,' he shrugged, 'if it was Diener, he didn't have to bother. He was in that ditch as a good Samaritan. Could have carved his initials and laughed at us.'

A young-looking, fresh-faced man, with thick brown hair, a smile professionally pleasing, wearing clothes well-cut enough to disguise a slightly spreading waistline came across the lawn to meet them. He was walking quickly but his contours suggested a more characteristic indolence, an inclination, perhaps, to the life of a bon vivant. He seemed relieved at the disappearance of the flags.

'Gentlemen,' he said. 'I'm Braun, the owner of the hotel.'

Snow introduced himself and Capricorn, and Braun expressed his shock and horror over the affair.

'I hope this matter can be cleared up now,' he ended. 'It has been a terrible strain, you can imagine, particularly for our German guests who have had . . .' he waved his hand in a continental gesture. 'So much difficulty, as you doubtless know.'

His English was fluent but his accent noticeably German. If Capricorn hadn't known that Braun was English born, he would not have guessed it. Apart from that, Braun's manner was that of any hotel owner confronted with a crime on the premises in the middle of his busy season: he wanted the fuss to be over.

Snow cut him short. 'We may ask you for another statement, Mr. Braun, in due time. For the moment, we would like to see Miss Rilke's room, and we want to talk to the people who were in her company the day before she died.'

'Ingeborg's friends?' Braun said, looking harassed. 'Superintendent Pritchard already . . . .'

But as Snow's gaze bore down on him he added quickly, 'Naturally, they will be pleased to assist you. Of course, they are most grieved, as you would expect, most grieved. . . .'

A light laugh sounded as a group of people strolled across the lawn towards an area set up with croquet hoops. Three men accompanied a very pretty woman, all behaving with gallantry, carring her mallet, her bag and scarf as she spoke softly and laughed again. The rays of the late afternoon sun touched the soft, shiny stuff of her dress and she shone bright as a dragonfly against the green lawn. Her silver-coloured hair glistened, and her blue earrings sparkled to dazzle the eye.

Braun, watching her, gave a rather fatuous smile.

'That's Mrs Roth,' he said. 'Mrs Roth was very kind to poor Ingeborg. And her husband, and the dark man is Mr Karl. They had dinner with Ingeborg that night, together with Mr Diener. The man holding her mallet is Captain Fitz-Marley, but he is Mrs Roth's guest and was only here briefly that unfortunate day.'

Capricorn felt startled for a moment. Part of his surprise quickly melted away; friendship was a term loosely used, including acquaintance with little emotional bond. And for that matter, the policeman thought with a mental shrug, even the death of a close friend rarely causes a man or woman to lose his appetite for long, or to spoil the pleasure of flirtation on a fine afternoon.

But 'refugees' the girl's friends had been called. Of course, he knew that there were rich refugees as well as poor ones, and Diener, at least, had been described as a very rich man, but Capricorn had had some kind of composite image in his mind, an amalgam of the survivors of Nazi camps; the Soviet nationals who had fled from their own armies, only to be rounded up and sent back home, crying and howling or in silent despair; the refugees he'd met in England, mostly harried and troubled, trying to put their lives together again. Some of these last had displayed wealth, but very few lightheartedness. And the name 'Fitz-Marley' tugged at his mind.

'You mustn't thing them unfeeling,' Braun explained with a certain embarrassment. 'They are very unhappy, but they have been so used to suffering, they take each day as it comes.'

'We'll start with the girl's room,' Snow said, and with a quick, appraising glance at the lawn party, followed Braun into the hotel. He took them through the front entrance, down a fine hall to a broad, carpeted stairway. The light paint of the walls was fresh and gleaming, the carpets were new and soft and thick. Late summer flowers in every shade of gold graced the vases on hall tables. Waitresses in crisp green dresses were carrying tea-trays laden with delicious-looking sandwiches and cake.

The Brandenburg seemed to be immune to the problems of austerity. Capricorn wondered how Braun performed the trick. Although it was a very English house, its smartness and comfort, in those days, gave it a slightly outlandish look.

On the first floor Braun led them to the rear of the building on the westerly side. A maid in a print dress came from a large sunny room carrying a duster.

'Just finishing the room, sir.'

The girl, very young and blushing slightly, spoke to Braun as if excusing her presence.

'Very well, Nora, run along then.'

She scampered away with a backward glance at Capricorn.

Snow was looking down a narrow flight of stairs at the end of the passage. 'Where does this lead?' he asked.

Braun was glaring after the main. 'Those girls,' he muttered. 'Finishing Lise Roth's room at this time. She wanted an excuse to look at the London policemen, that's all. Oh, the stairs. They go to the passage on the ground floor leading to Mr Diener's suite. It used to be a way to the gardens. A previous owner had that suite arranged for himself and put the door across the passage. A lot of guests complain because to get to the gardens they have to go to the front of the hotel and walk around. When Mr Diener leaves us, we'll open the passageway.'

He stopped at the last door in the row, opposite the staircase. The lock of the door was covered with police tape.

'This is poor Ingeborg's room. It's locked of course.'

Snow removed the tape and Braun went on talking nervously.

'Superintendent Pritchard asked about the key, but there was no point in him taking it, as all the room locks and keys are the same except for Mr Diener's suite.' Taking a key from his ring, he fitted it into the lock. His hand trembled and his face was pale.

Snow was pacing the private corner of the corridor opening on the victim's room and the staircase. 'Very discreet,' he observed.

Braun appeared not to hear him. His lips moved soundlessly. Then he gave a quick, hard push and the door opened.

The corner room was another sunny, pleasant room

with windows to the south and west. It was impeccably neat. The bed had not been slept in.

'We'll take a look around, Mr Braun,' Snow said in dismissal, 'and then we'd like to talk to Mr Diener.'

Braun had recovered his composure, and was once again the solicitous hotel-keeper. 'Mr Diener's in his suite. I expect he'll be there until dinner—in fact, he hasn't been in the dining room at all since—since. He's very upset.'

'And I'd like a key to that passage door,' Snow continued. 'I assume you have one.'

'My wife has one,' Braun said. 'There are only two keys. Mr Diener has a liking for privacy. When he came he had all the locks changed, the passage door, the porch door, the door of his sitting room. He has a set and my wife.'

Snow let him go on, although Pritchard had written a full report on the matter of the doors and the keys.

'What happens if Diener wants anything at night?'

'He rings for the housekeeper or the night porter, and has to let them in, of course.'

Braun was thoughtful. He had realized the importance of the lock to that door leading to the porch where the clubs had been kept.

'Does your wife keep her keys with her at all times?'

'In her handbag, naturally.'

Snow nodded. 'Thank you, Mr Braun.'

Braun still hovered. 'About this room, will it have to be taped up again?'

'No. As soon as we've removed Miss Rilke's things, you can open it up.'

'Good—I'll send you up the key, then,' Braun said, a little happier, and departed.

The room was very quiet. Capricorn glanced through the windows. To the south, Miss Rilke had

had a view of the flower gardens. To the west was the croquet lawn, where her good friends were playing. Further westward, she could have seen the boundary hedge with the ditch below in which she was to meet her death.

At night that ditch would not be seen, except in a bright flood of moonlight. On the murder night the moon had been mainly obscured by cloud. Yet there must have been some light for the murderer to have made those very deliberate blows. And if there was, he had taken a chance of being seen when he carried the girl from the house across the lawns.

Capricorn wondered if he should mention this to Snow. Better not. He was there to take notes and to assist. If he volunteered he might hear more about 'now you see it, now you don't.' He was still young enough to smart at ridicule.

'He took a chance of being seen, sir, didn't he? Carrying the girl from the house to the ditch?' he heard his own voice saying.

'Not really.' Snow was benign. 'He just waited for a nice blanket of cloud. If you checked the meteorological, you would have noticed there was very little wind. He was safe enough. The curtains are all drawn in these bedrooms. And no one could surprise him by coming in with those gates locked.'

'The night porter?' Capricorn suggested.

'The night porter, like all night porters, was probably asleep in his cubbyhole.

'Good Lord, look at this. We're going to need a lorry to get it all out.'

He was gazing into a wardrobe, a large piece of furniture that looked as if it had been designed to an individual order. It was full of dozens of dresses, coats, suits, slacks, and blouses. Capricorn helped to take them out. On the floor, on racks were about twenty-four pairs of shoes. All of the garments looked new and hardly worn.

'Foreigners,' Snow said in disgust. 'They have no trouble with coupons. And Englishwomen walking around with threadbare coats so they can buy school clothes for the children.'

Capricorn, who had heard his aunts complaining that they had to pay two shillings each for black market coupons, could only remain silent. Snow burrowed down and examined each pair of shoes, although Pritchard and his men had reported going all over the room and finding nothing. He turned his attention to the chest of drawers, filled with neat piles of underclothes, handkerchieves, night things, all new and expensive.

'Well, she was just at the head of the stairs,' Snow said cryptically.

Capricorn was packing the clothes. He looked up.

'According to the maids who took care of her cleaning and laundry,' Snow explained, 'all her dressing gowns are here. Also coats. Not a speck of soil on them, or the slippers. Even her shoes are either brand new or else well-cleaned.'

'The murderer could have brushed her things,' Capricorn said, puzzled, 'but. . . .'

'We'll send it all to the lab, but I'll lay odds they won't find anything to help us. She must've slipped up and down in just her nightie. Immodest wench.'

Capricorn nodded slowly. 'She could have done. Yet Diener went to some trouble to keep up appearances. They could have had adjoining rooms, or he could have kept her with him.'

'The girl's technically a minor—was, I should say,' Snow pointed out. 'In a position like his he had to be careful. He could've gone back to prison for crossing Piccadilly against the light.'

He roamed around the room, opening drawers and looking on shelves, clicking his tongue against the back of his teeth. 'Look at this damned desk,' he said at last. 'Nothing. Blotting paper not blotted. Pen not used. Except for a shop window of clothes, there's nothing personal in this room. Yet she kept nothing in Diener's rooms, according to Pritchard.'

He stared all about him with his clear, intelligent gaze, the lines around his mouth deepening in dissatisfaction. 'It's strange,' he said. 'You'd never think it was a young girl's.'

Capricorn was listening with half his attention. As he packed the nightdresses, with the quick, expert movements of a lifelong traveller, noticing the luxury of the silk and some fine, soft stuff—chiffon, was it?—he remembered the tattered, blood-stained garment that was now an exhibit, neatly tagged. There was something about that nightdress, he remembered, something . . . but Snow continued talking and cut off his thought.

'You should see my daughter's room,' he said, with a rare allusion to family life. 'Letters, notes, keepsakes in boxes, photos, stuff cut out from magazines—most girls are squirrels. But not this one. It's as though she had no personal life, just a clothes horse.'

Capricorn had finished with the chest of drawers and turned to the bedside table.

'There's this,' he said.

He had opened the concealed drawer and brought out a large photograph, not a studio portrait but an enlarged snapshot. A tall, blond, powerful man with a commanding air and thoughtful look stood in front of the doorway of a Palladian house. The photographer had taken the picture from a distance to bring in a background of mountain peaks. He, or she, had meant perhaps to make the scene impressive, but it had given the subject an air of desolate loneliness.

'No inscription,' Snow examined it. 'I suppose that's Diener. Given in happier days.'

The photograph was framed but not covered in glass and was smudged as though it had been handled often.

'The only prints they found on it were the girl's,' Snow glanced at his notes. 'Well, Pritchard said there was nothing useful. I wonder how often she slept in this room. She was here for morning tea, according to the staff. If you've finished packing, let's push on and tackle Diener. We can get the heartbroken little chums later on.'

He glanced at the croquet game. 'Look at that.'

Braun had joined the party on the lawn. His arms were around Mrs Roth and he was directing her shot at the ball. She was laughing, her husband looked resigned, Otto Karl was amused, and Fitz-Marley, a lean, wiry man with a military look about him, seemed annoyed.

Snow was not the only one watching the group. A window was up in a room towards the front of the house, and a woman was leaning slightly outward, her gaze following the players, a big, heavy-shouldered woman, with harsh, swarthy features, dressed in black. Her stare was fixed on Braun, his arms still about the little Roth woman. As Braun leaned down, smiling, his cheek brushed Mrs Roth's hair.

'Bees around a honey pot,' Snow said. 'And the spider waiting close by.'

3

The two men made their way down the narrow stair that must have been, in effect, the murdered girl's private staircase. For a moment Capricorn imagined her slipping down, thin, white-clad, barefoot. She must have known that her affair, however clandestine, was public knowledge, like that of a royal mistress.

At the foot of the stair was a door with a sturdy lock. Snow used the key Braun had sent him and they found themselves on a porch. The porch was an extension of the terrace and the wall was solid glass, except where a door had been cut in. This door, too, had a serviceable lock and also an inside bolt. The bag of clubs had been removed but a chalk mark still indicated the spot where it had stood.

The windows to Diener's room were curtained, although the sun still shone bright across the lawns. A record was playing the slow movement of Beethoven's Seventh Symphony. Snow rapped at the door and a rather harsh voice called:

'Come in, come in. The door's unlocked.'

They entered to find themselves in a small room, dusky with the eastern windows shaded by the overhanging branches of a tree. The atmosphere was close and stale with the smell of liquor and dead cigars.

Capricorn blinked, wondering for a moment why the star guest at the Brandenburg had chosen quarters so dismal compared with the bright, airy and spacious rooms elsewhere.

A big, sturdy man, with a tousled, leonine head sat in an armchair at the empty grate, a glass in his hand and a brandy bottle at his side. It was the man in the photograph, deteriorated but recognisable. He didn't move from his slouched position, but glared up at them from red-rimmed eyes.

'Seeing that I can't keep you out if I want to,' he said, 'why lock the door? You're from Scotland Yard.'

He laughed sarcastically, a barking sound. 'You see, I am familiar with the police. Those nice lounge suits, they don't deceive me.'

The record came to an end, and he rose, turned off the gramophone, and resumed his seat. 'Have you come to arrest me? I'm experienced in such matters.'

He scowled at them with a frank animosity, untinged by any respect for the Metropolitan Police. So might a patrician Roman have regarded an assertive slave on the Saturnalia, Capricorn fancied. He understood already why Diener had had ill success with the tribunals that decided his fate.

Snow was not liking it either. 'I'm Superintendent Snow and this is Sergeant Capricorn,' he said. 'We are here to make inquiries about the murder of Ingeborg Rilke.'

He nodded to Capricorn who took his notebook out. 'You are not obliged to say anything unless you wish to do so but what you say may be put into writing and given in evidence.'

'Used as evidence against me, you mean,' Diener said, sneering. 'Don't I know that! For seven years everything has been used against me.'

His voice rose. 'If the Crown Jewels were stolen, you would say, "Diener did it." Now a dangerous killer is loose. Do you look for him? No. Diener did it! You lost Hitler, so hang Diener. The war's over! Hang the arms maker!'

'We are not here to discuss politics,' Snow said, stiffly.

'That's what *you* say,' Diener retorted. 'But that's precisely why you are here.'

His r's were slightly guttural. It was that mostly which gave his voice the harsh, foreign sound.

'Politics! Why else would you be here? Don't pretend you don't know who I am. All England knows of Franz Diener.'

He was wrong there, Capricorn thought. Diener obviously thought his case was famous, but England had had too much to worry about in 1940. Rightly or wrongly, the newspapers had given very little space to the internment of Germans at the time.

'Mr. Diener,' Snow said coldly. 'I must ask you to answer a few questions. We only want to get the truth.'

Diener laughed. 'The tr-ruth! You think you want the truth? What would you do with it if you got it?'

He didn't wait for an answer, but jumped to his feet with surprising agility, strode to the window, and turning his back to them stared out into the branches of the tree.

'Damned if I do,' he growled, 'and damned if I don't.'

Behind the CID's traditional poker-face expression, Snow was betraying his annoyance. His subordinate could see, even in the gloom, an ominous red tide rising about the Super's collar. But Snow persisted, his voice very calm.

'About the night before the murder. I understand from your statement that Miss Rilke had joined you and some other friends for drinks on the porch outside. Exactly what time did she leave?'

'I don't know exactly,' Diener said, rather as though he was thinking of something else. 'Why should I? I didn't look at my watch. It was probably around eleven, because she left with Mrs Roth. Mrs Roth usually goes to bed about that time.'

'And you did what after she left?'

Diener turned a little towards them. 'Oh, I suppose I stayed out there for a while. It was a warm night. I had a few more drinks, I expect. I came in. I played some music.'

'And what time did you go to bed, Mr Diener?'

'I don't know. I was restless. I undressed. I lay down on the bed, but I wasn't sleepy. I may have dropped off, but I remember watching the window until it turned grey and then the morning sun came very bright through the leaves of the branches. The bedroom faces east,' he said. 'The maid had forgotten to draw the curtains. I got up to close them, but it looked fresh there, outside. I put on some clothes and went out for some air.'

'The dark blue suit,' Snow said.

'Yes,' Diener shrugged. 'I had thrown the clothes on the chair by the bed when I lay down. It was the nearest thing. I wasn't dressed to go to breakfast. I wasn't bathed or shaved.'

Checkmate to Snow, Capricorn thought. That would sound reasonable enough in court.

'I see,' Snow said, seemingly unperturbed. 'And how long had you known Miss Rilke?'

'Not long,' Diener said, his voice falling away in a

sound like boredom. 'January, I think. No, Christmas. Lise Roth brought her. She would know.'

'You paid her bills here at the hotel?'

Diener turned and slouched back to his chair. 'Yes. I pay the bills of a lot of people, it seems.'

'Indeed,' Snow said. 'But about Miss Rilke. You paid for her training as a model?'

Diener waved a hand. 'Lise Roth thought something should be done for her. The Roths' money is very tied up just now. It cost very little. And,' the shrugged, 'we thought, for once, we had some small success. Something that could not be used against us. Something the maniacs of the world could not turn to their advantage.'

'Yes,' Snow said, cutting him off. 'And you have lived here all that time, and Miss Rilke lived here also, except for a few nights in London?'

'I don't know how many nights she was in London,' Diener said. 'She had an uncle, but I don't think she stayed at his house. Since she began working, she shared a room with another girl. Sometimes she worked late one day and early the next. I didn't keep a record,' he said broodingly. 'When she was here, she was with us at dinner. When she wasn't, she wasn't. I wouldn't remember.'

'And it was on Friday evening you had a quarrel?'

'Quarrel with Ingeborg! Bah!' Diener said in disgust. 'How could one quarrel with Ingeborg? You didn't know her, so you don't know how stupid that is. Ingeborg was timid. She was afraid. She was easily impressed—too easily. I shouted at her, it's true. She was a very foolish, dull-witted girl. Not her fault,' he said with a shrug. 'She was—*sie war furchtbar erschrocken*—too terrified all her life to be normal. Someone had persuaded her to leave the protection of this hotel. I shouted at her for her own sake. She was any man's prey. She was. . . .'

Capricorn's pencil flew across his notebook, in an effort to keep up. So that was going to be his defense. Another lover, out of a multiplicity of lovers. Well, it was about the only one possible, apart from a peripatetic madman. But he had to blacken the dead girl's reputation. Capricorn noticed the rigidity of Snow's posture. The old man had seen that and did not like it. For all his years on the Force, Snow was still old-fashioned about many things. To commit murder in hot blood was one thing, but coldly to defame the victim after. . . .

'She was thinking of moving on the next day, Saturday?'

'So she said. She asked for my car and chauffeur to move her things. That girl was stupid—'

'And how long had you been on intimate terms?'

Diener jumped up, facing Snow, with a quick anger to meet Snow's cool wrath.

'By God, are you accusing me of being that wretched child's lover? Is that how you think you're going to hang me? Pritchard wouldn't stoop to it so they sent you to do the dirty work, is that it? The local *Polizei* are too delicate, send the SS! I should throw you out,' he stormed.

Capricorn wondered if he were drunk, and looked at Snow.

'Why, I could tell you. . . .'

Diener stopped, abruptly. The colour receded from his face. As the belligerence left, he looked older and tired. Slowly, he went back to his station at the window.

'Damned if I do, and damned if I don't,' he said again.

Snow motioned to Capricorn to close his book, and walked to the door without a word. On the porch he paused.

'There's Pritchard's maniac,' he said in disgust. 'But he's full of drink. I'll go and arrange for a warrant. You'd better stay and watch him. Pritchard's sure he can't fly the coop, but he looks capable of anything.'

'A warrant on the murder charge, sir?' Capricorn asked softly.

'I'd like to,' Snow said. 'But I think we'll hold him on something else. If only for form's sake, I'd like the case shipshape. There's routine inquiry at the London end—I was going to have you do that tomorrow. The girl's aunt and uncle, the Krauses, and the model she stayed with. Don't want any loose ends. But we have to take him in to sober him up and get some answers and a statement that will stick.'

He strode off, exuding displeasure, to consult with the despised Pritchard. His tall, erect figure moved in almost military fashion. Such a capable officer, in so many ways, Capricorn thought. Snow should have been at the head of a large body of men. He could have run a Department. He was almost wasted in the Murder Squad where the work was on a one-to-one basis, and personal relationships, often with doubtful characters, were so important. A fine policeman.

'*Ach Gott,*' a gloomy voice came from behind him.

Franz Diener was leaning against the door jamb, watching Snow's departure. 'How I hate'—his voice lingered on the word 'hate'. 'How I hate policemen.'

4

The next few hours were something outside of Capricorn's previous experience.

'He's left you to see I don't escape,' Diener had said. It wasn't a question. 'You might as well come in and sit down.'

Capricorn followed him back into the gloomy room. 'Policemen, generals, and bureaucrats,' Diener grumbled as they took their seats. Diener's chair was large to fit his frame, but the one that Capricorn sat in had been meant for a woman, and he had some difficulty bestowing his long legs.

Diener noticed. 'Ah, the world isn't meant for tall men,' he said. 'They will try to cut you down to their size. As they did to me!'

'That Superintendent,' he went on, 'he looks like the chairman of the committee who decided I was too great a risk for England. He had a factory not five miles from my works at Cobleigh. He paid his hands a quarter of what I gave my men. So he cut me down.'

'Have a drink,' he added.

'Not on duty,' Capricorn answered.

'But you detectives are nearly always on duty, aren't you?'

It was true, and Capricorn sternly repressed a sigh. He didn't want a drink but he was remembering that

Snow had not wanted to pause for lunch, and that he himself had had no breakfast either.

Diener went over to the gramophone on the opposite side of the room. He pushed the button and another record began, a gloomy song with a German singer. 'Zarah Leander,' Diener said. ' "Gloomy Sunday." Many people in Germany killed themselves after hearing that record.' He spoke as though that was some kind of commendation.

In the half-dark room, filled with the smell of brandy and old cigars, as Capricorn listened to the mournful sound and watched the curiously abstracted glance of the man, virtually his prisoner under suspicion of murder, tapping his foot and humming along with the music, Capricorn wondered if Diener was truly a little mad. As Pritchard had said, a man like that, obviously active and full of life, imprisoned for so long. . . .

'You don't look like a policeman,' Diener said abruptly. He stared at Capricorn, his eyes narrowed. 'You look like a magician that used to perform at Cobleigh Music Hall. What was his name—?'

'He was my father,' Capricorn said, in resignation, hoping that Diener had not seen one of his own performances as a child prodigy. It would really be too much.

'Ah!' Diener threw himself back in his chair. 'And you,' he grinned. 'You did not wish to produce the impossible, hm? You would rather go after what you English call sitting ducks!'

He was amused with his witticism and laughed. 'But your father—he was the great escape artist, I remember. He would be nailed up in a coffin.'

He shrugged his massive shoulders. 'Better I had learned to be an escape artist, than a munitions maker. An independent munitions maker.' He filled his glass. 'Now, if I were Krupp, hand in hand with the government, ah, it would all be different. This is the way of the world.'

'Krupp?' Capricorn asked, surprised. 'But Alfried, at least, is awaiting trial.'

Diener waved his hand. 'Trial or no trial, Alfried will soon be back in business. He will work with the new government as he did with the old. They will need him. It is men like Krupp who rule.'

Capricorn had seen Alfried, Krupp von Bohlen und Halbach in a stockade known to the British as The Dustbin. He hadn't looked much like a ruler there.

'You think, you English, that you have won the war,' Diener continued. 'But you are wrong. All you have done is to make the world safe for dictators worse than it has known before. In this long war, all the men who would have fought them have been killed off. You have left the enemy entrenched. The Hohenzollerns are the victors!'

Certainly he was a little mad, or was he just pretending, Capricorn wondered.

'Yes, you smashed Hitler. But you also smashed all of Europe and ruined yourselves. Was Hitler Germany? Was Krupp Europe? The dictator Roosevelt and your Churchill at their great meeting in Quebec, they wined, they dined, they discussed a peace offer to Germany. And what did he say, your Churchill? "Heavens, no. They might accept." And they laughed. They laughed and Germany died and there will be no one to stop the Russians. And so after you went to war to save Poland from Dictator Hitler you end by handing it to Dictator Stalin. Stalin, a worse dictator than Hitler.'

Suddenly he roared with laughter. 'Yes, you great

freedom lovers, after you kill your best young men in the name of freedom, you use the ones you have left together with the Americans, those naive *Narren,* to round up, like the cowboys with their cattle, yes? all those who had escaped from the Russians and you sent them back in box cars. Under guns! Under Allied guns!'

He looked at Capricorn in alcoholic gloom. 'Our world is finished, you understand? It is the *Götterdämmerung,*' he shouted, 'The *Götterdämmerung!*'

As Capricorn listened, wondering if he ought to be taking notes of this rigmarole, part of his mind noted that a lot of things Diener was saying were perfectly true and had troubled Capricorn himself at the time they happened, and another part warned him of what Snow would think if he came back and found his sergeant apparently engaged in a political discussion.

Then both men were distracted by a light tap of heels outside.

'Franz, Franz *du bist—*'

Diener had left his doors open, and the bright little dragonfly fluttered in, bringing to the musty room what seemed like the scent of a thousand roses.

As her eyes grew accustomed to the gloom, she saw Capricorn sitting there and froze momentarily, her skirts still swinging around her. Then her defense of charm took over and she smiled at Capricorn, tilting her fine-boned face towards him, with the full gaze of her wide, light blue eyes with curious dark flecks until, withdrawing a little, she let the lids tremble down until she was peeping demurely through softly fringing lashes.

'O-oh, you are the policeman,' she said. 'How do you do.'

Her voice was soft, gentle and delightful, her German accent merely a caress and an enticement. A Viennese, perhaps. She had deliberately set out to allure him, Capricorn thought with resignation, and she had succeeded in half a minute. For a determined bachelor, he had a weakness for women of the very feminine and pretty sort, and was at that time just recovering from the loss of such a one. While in the north he had seen his childhood friend Rose Raintree transformed into the wife of Sam Lavender, a prosperous middle-aged business man, a very happy wife, but charming as ever to Capricorn's eye.

Lise Roth turned to Diener. 'Franz, you had no luncheon. You said you would join us this evening. It is not good to be here, like this, alone.'

Diener had risen to his feet. 'Please don't disturb yourself, Lise. I am about to be taken in charge.'

Her eyes widened again, but this time in fear. '*Warum?*' she asked.

She continued speaking quickly in German and Diener answered her in the same language. Capricorn, whose German had been good enough for SIS, listened with as much of an appearance of not understanding as he could.

'But you are a fool, Franz. Why don't you call Mr Upham?'

She made two long syllables of Upham.

'You need a lawyer. You don't realize how serious—'

'I do realize. But I think it no use. Whatever I do— But don't worry, Lisechen. They can arrest me, but we know they cannot convict me for this murder. It is only troublesome.'

She answered quickly. 'I have spoken,' her voice was soft and breathy. 'That is, Paul has spoken to Mr Upham for you. And Otto, also. Mr Upham says, you will need other lawyers. But he will come down if you

want him. I had thought, before these men came, that
it was over.' Her little white hand gestured helplessly.
'The policeman Pritchard seemed satisfied it was none
of us. And Paul was pleased today, so happy, with his
news. We were all playing croquet and Heinrich told
us Scotland Yard was here. Heinrich is a fool, he
should have. . . .'

'It makes no difference,' Diener repeated.

They argued in a disjointed, circular fashion, leaving odd gaps where they understood each other without words. The little light that had come into the
room was fading. The melancholy record that Diener
had put on was set to repeat and it went on and on, a
macabre counterpoint to the half-whispered talk.

'But what could I do, what could I say?' Diener
shrugged at last. 'There is nothing else, after all. But
don't worry, Lise. Perhaps it will work out. I hope it
will. But if not. . . .'

Her hand went to her throat. 'Let us not even
think—I have telephoned Lord Lawdon,' she said.

'That old fool.' Diener was contemptuous.

'We need influence,' she whispered.

'We have had too much influence,' Diener said.

The word *Einfluss* hung in the air.

'Never say that, Franzel,' her voice sank to just a
breath. 'Never.'

The evening seemed to stretch on endlessly. Lise Roth
fluttered off to dinner. Otto Karl, the dark, sensible-
looking man, came in and tried to persuade Diener to
leave his room and join the others, but with no success
either. He took the gloomy record off the machine
and tried to distract him by displaying a copy of
American Marksman, with an article on a new design

for a submachine gun, but after one glance Diener
had no interest.

'New,' he said in disgust, 'What is there that's new?'
He jabbed a finger at the page. 'It's Thompson's gun,
lighter and cheaper. Probably no better. Maybe
worse. *Office boy* designs.'

His voice was heavy with contempt as he empha-
sized the words 'office boy.'

'But who is there to design today? Where are the
new Otto Karls? Those Americans, they used to have
them. All over those States, men who shot and knew
guns.'

He paused long enough to fill his glass. 'So! Roosevelt passes the Firearms Act, and not one in thousands
can pay the tax. So the young designers go where they
are driven, they invent new openers for tins and bottle
stoppers.'

He glared at Capricorn. 'Just as young Englishmen
fiddle with motorcycles. If Hitler had invaded in
1940, what would you have done for marksmen? A
disarmed citizenry, that is the dream of all dictators.
And the people agree to it. They are soft, *verweich-
licht*,' he shouted. English could not do justice to his
indignation and he was off in a flood of German, pro-
phesying again the *Götterdämmerung*.

Karl gave Capricorn a look that suggested amusement and sympathy. Capricorn would like to have
questioned him about the murder, but Snow had left
him as a watchdog for Diener and would be annoyed
if he did anything else. A pity, because Diener wasn't
going anywhere except into a drunken sleep, and Karl
might have provided some needed answers.

But Diener was not drunk enough yet, and noticing
Capricorn's lack of attention, switched back into English, though not, Capricorn was relieved to hear, to

the disarmed Britisher. Diener was quite capable, he thought, of going back to the Saxon bowmen, and expounding on their superiority to the modern football fan.

'We should be producing fine automatic weapons to train our young men for the new wars the politicians have arranged for them. But what do we do? Already the Western allies begin to disarm. If I should start up again, who would I build weapons for, the Russians? Ah, Lenin said'it, when they hang the last capitalist, he will have sold them the rope.'

'We haven't quite come to that, Franz,' Karl said cheerfully.

'You think so,' Diener replied. 'America went to war to protect herself from one Eastern power; she has created another far more deadly in Russia. The East is doomed. Russia has taken Dairen, Port Arthur, South Sakhalin and the Kurile Islands. Who was there to say boo?'

'As long as Chiang Kai-shek—' Karl began.

'Roosevelt gave away the Manchurian railroad, so Chiang Kai-shek will lose the north and then all of China,' Diener interrupted. 'America will help with one hand and betray him with the other. Roosevelt's man Lattimore will deliver China to the Communists, mark me! It is the fall of Western man. China and Russia will dominate the world. Very likely they will go to war over India. Russia has always wanted India.'

By the look on Karl's face, Capricorn gathered that this was part of an argument so familiar that Diener no longer had to begin at the beginning because his usual listeners were so familiar with all the stages.

'Yes, America will lose the East,' Diener was grumbling. 'The British are abdicating from their Empire faster than Windsor abdicated from the throne, without even a pretty lady in exchange. And Europe,' he said, 'what of Europe? Russia takes eastern Poland, part of Finland, Lithuania, Estonia, Latvia—and what do the Western allies say? Nothing. Nothing. The Four Freedoms. No people must live under a foreign dictator's rule—unless it's Russian! Heil Roosevelt! Heil Truman!'

'We agree, Franz,' Karl said soothingly, 'But in the meantime—I will have them send you something. And you too?' he asked Capricorn.

Capricorn wondered what on earth Snow was doing. He must be having a lot of trouble getting that warrant. Possibly he had stopped for dinner somewhere with Pritchard, though it was unlike Snow not to make his arrest first. Perhaps he had to wait for the magistrate.

'Don't trouble for me,' Diener said heavily. 'Don't you know unless these clever policemen find the murderer—' He snapped his fingers with a somewhat sneering grin at Capricorn—'Hey presto! I am going to be taken care of by His Majesty's Government.'

'You're making a fool of yourself,' Karl said.

Diener scowled at him, and went back to German. 'That's your opinion, damn you, and I didn't ask for it.'

'It's always been my opinion,' Karl said shortly, in the same language, and changing to English, added, 'I'll send you some food.' He looked resigned, not angry, and smiled at Capricorn as he left.

Diener went on with his *Götterdämmerung* as if he had not been interrupted. 'Roosevelt led Churchill by the nose,' he wound up. 'By the time Churchill realized what he'd done it was too late. He was out of office. Will Attlee save the world?'

He laughed. 'No, the Hohenzollerns will win.'

Capricorn couldn't help wondering what the devil he was talking about.

It was fully dark in the room now and as Diener showed no inclination to switch on the lamps, Capricorn lit the one by his desk so that he could see his notebook. The light fell on Diener's face, making the shadows more pronounced, the lines more deeply etched.

A knock came at the door and a maid entered carrying a tray. She was a gaunt, bony woman in the green dress of the hotel, but hers was so dark as to seem almost black. Her hair was drawn back in a tight bun and she wore no make-up. Her look was grim and at first she seemed middle-aged; it wasn't until she came quite close and the lamplight disclosed her smooth unlined neck that Capricorn realized she was young, certainly still in her twenties.

'Yurr door out there was open,' she said. 'What are you doin' in the dark, drinking yoursel' silly?' Her Scotch burr was unmistakable, as was her privileged position.

'Eat that.' She banged a tray down on the low table with a plate of sandwiches, a pot of coffee, and two cups.

She looked at Capricorn severely. 'There's some for you, too. Have you come to arrest him?'

'I'm staying with Mr Diener until Superintendent Snow returns,' Capricorn answered, rather wishing he could give a direct answer to a direct question.

'Hmph!' she sniffed. 'You've got the wrong one.'

'Oh?' he asked. 'And do you know who the right one is?'

She gave him a look that carried him back, absurdly, to his childhood, to his rare times of playing with other children. What was it that look reminded him of, in silly children's games? He nearly smiled, remembering. It had meant that taunting childhood phrase: 'That's for me to know and you to find out.'

But in her statement, Mrs Dermott—for this must be she—said she had been off on Friday and spent the night in London. She had had no information to give.

'Shall I shut that outside door?' she asked Diener.

'Why bother?' he answered. 'I am in the protection of the police.'

She gave one more unfavourable look at Capricorn.

'Hmph,' she said again, and departed.

'A war widow,' Diener said. 'The world is full of war widows. And for what? So that the Hohenzollerns of the world will have their way.'

He ignored the food and coffee but Capricorn could not. The coffee smelt delicious and his stomach was rumbling. Snow probably wouldn't care for him eating with the suspect, but Snow wasn't there. He poured the coffee. It tasted almost as good as it smelt. He ate a sandwich. It was smoked Scotch salmon and delicious.

'What do you mean, Hohenzollerns?' he asked, recklessly, thinking of sheep and lambs.

Diener's eyes gleamed. He had been longing, obviously, to be asked the question. 'The Hohenzollerns of the mind,' he said. 'The old Hohenzollerns, those Junkers, they held their lands as feudal lords. They had their peasants under their heels. But once the men of brains and ability began building factories and offering cash wages, the Junkers could not keep their peasants. Except that Lassalle, then Schmoller taught them how it could be done. Socialism! They had to crush the men of free enterprise. Bismarck borrowed the theories that you probably think came from Marx. Marx was not the first, or the only one of the breed.

Landesfürstlicher Wohlfahrtsstaat in the eighteenth century. The *Sozialpolitik* in the nineteenth and the twentieth. State socialism. You see the plan?'

Capricorn was interested in spite of himself. As long as he didn't say anything, he could not be said to be 'talking politics with a suspect.' He drank more coffee. He felt sorry for Diener, thinking he would wake up with a very sore head the next morning in the cell in Illwood station.

'Lassalle stood for proletarian socialism. Bismarck was for state socialism. They were supposed to be opposing parties and their followers were willing to fight each other to the death. Yet these two men met secretly and plotted together. You ask, how can that be?'

Capricorn hadn't asked but he was willing to listen.

'Because their beliefs were the same and Bismarck knew it.'

Diener crashed his hand onto the little table, and smashed a cup. He took no notice whatsoever. Capricorn, watching him ride his hobby horse, wondered if a man who had recently committed a brutal, savage murder could have put it out of his mind so completely, to be totally absorbed in politico-economic history. Reluctantly, and he noted his own reluctance, he had to admit he could. He remembered Arthur Blaikie, who had chopped his girl friend up and left the bits in a pile of firewood. When they caught him he had been out on Dartmoor, innocent and happy, flying a kite. He had been terribly concerned, when he was taken into custody, that they would be careful with his kite—a large box affair—and had only come along peaceably when one of the local men proved himself knowledgeable about kites and promised to take care of it personally.

'The same!' Diener said, in triumph. 'The State is God. It was Lassalle that said it, but it was Bismarck intended it to be true. Bismarck saw what socialism could mean. The only quarrel between Bismarck and the Marxists was which gang would rule. Well, the two wars have decided that. The Hohenzollerns of the blood are finished. But the Hohenzollerns of the mind remain.'

He was quiet for a moment and actually took a sandwich and bit into it. Capricorn felt somewhat relieved. It was more seemly to arrest a man who could walk than one who had collapsed from drink. Fortunately, Diener was dressed. He wore shoes, not slippers. For the first time Capricorn noticed a magazine lying on the empty hearth by Diener's feet. It was old and crumpled and looked as though it had been much handled. Peering down, he was surprised to see it was *The New Yorker*. What in that American magazine, with its rather dry humour, would appeal to the Fury-ridden Franz Diener?

Diener had merely paused, he was by no means finished. 'They tell the former serfs, who the businessmen had set free, "Capitalism is evil and must be destroyed." They promise the workers benefits—for which the workers themselves have to pay; they promise them reforms, which will load a hundred civil servants on their backs where one was before. And at the end the men of power—not merely landowners of the Junker type, but all their spiritual successors, businessmen who don't want the labour of imaginative production, the work of competition, who prefer the restfulness of protection by the State; the heirs to great fortunes, who fear they can't keep what their fathers or grandfathers made—they will learn the trick and they will have power greater than was ever dreamed of by the feudal lords. And they don't have to strike a blow. The foolish people will rush to place their lives and their children's lives in their hands as they did with Lenin and Hitler. See what happens to your Magna Charta when England is a People's State,' he said gloomily. 'What you could not do in the name of the King is child's play when the cry is "The People." The People. But who controls the people? Ah!'

He jumped to his feet and paced up and down, running the fingers of his left hand through his tousled hair, but holding on firmly to his brandy glass, which he refilled, with the other.

'It starts so easy, Mr. Policeman. They will tell you, all men must be fed, but not who must feed them. They say, all men must have jobs, but what jobs, and who is to make the jobs, and who will decide where each man will have to go, they don't talk about that. The independent middle class will be stripped of power. They will tell you the friends of the people, the State, they will keep you all.'

He stared out of the dark window, but he was seeing nothing, Capricorn felt, but pictures in his own mind. Was Diener saying all this, merely because he had a captive audience? He could only suppose so. Snow was being a devil of a long time.

'Oh, yes,' Diener said. 'The State will keep you. Not like Franz Diener who if there is no work will let you go. No, they will keep you. And they will tell you where to work, and how long and how much you must be paid, or if you should be paid. Did you ever hear of a strike in the mines at Novaya Zemlya? You can be sent anywhere your masters will choose, in the name of The People and maybe your family will hear from you again, and maybe they won't. And when you are too old to work perhaps they will help you to die, for the good of the people. Oh, yes, what do they call it here? From the Cradle to the Grave.' He threw back his head and laughed. 'Beware of governments bearing gifts. You may find the grave nearer than you think.'

'Yes,' he said suddenly, stopping at Capricorn's chair and looking down at him intently, as if he were really trying to convey something important, something that was to do with the two men actually in the room, suspect and policeman, and not the ghostly mental heirs of Bismarck and the Junkers.

Or perhaps he was imagining things, Capricorn thought resignedly. From experience he knew that lack of sleep could distort his perceptions. He remembered himself as a child in the care of his aunt Dolly, that indefatigable night owl, how in sheer weariness he would see her, a short, jolly woman, as a giantess, and her bibulous merriment would take on a spurious and mystifying significance.

'Land is no longer power,' Diener was saying, marching about again, throwing a frantic shadow on the wall. 'Money can be taxed away. No, power comes to those who can catch the mind of the masses, and get them to give up their freedoms waving flags and chanting. This war,' he said, and his voice had dropped to its brooding tone, 'this war has taught you British to obey your government. It went on too long. Hitler could have been overthrown years before. But there were those who didn't want it.'

He shot Capricorn a curious look that the policeman could not interpret. 'Some in America,' he went on, 'and some here. Roosevelt, that Hohenzollern, he did not want peace. Churchill—perhaps he was a dupe.' He sighed a large, windy, gusty sigh. 'When Hess came to make peace, Churchill preferred to watch the Marx brothers. The Marx brothers! It was a joke, you see. Hess was mad. Hitler said so. Perfect agreement'—his voice sank to a snarl. 'Perfect agreement.'

For a man who had been imprisoned with no access, officially, to news for so long, it was amazing how he had kept up with everything, Capricorn thought. What was the man getting at? That he, Diener, had been imprisoned although he was innocent, and that others really guilty of heinous crimes remained free? Natural for him to think so, but surely he wasn't trying to imply that Churchill. . . .

And what had happened to Snow? Capricorn felt very much inclined to telephone Illwood station. Superintendent Snow would not like it—to him sergeants were creatures to follow orders and not to originate actions or inquire about their superiors—but it had been a long time.

'These modern Hohenzollerns,' Diener was off again. 'They have seen the power of the Soviet rulers. And the possibilities of UNO! World government—one neck for one yoke! They will find a Bismarck for their time. And you will see.'

But what he was to see Capricorn would have to wait to find out. The telephone rang insistently and, annoyed at the interruption, Diener barked into it.

He looked crossly at Capricorn.

'It's for you.'

The strange, nightmarish quality of the evening was distilled into Pritchard's worried voice.

'Sergeant, I'm sorry you weren't notified sooner. I had left instructions, but somebody failed to follow through. I'm afraid I have bad news. Young Mr. Lawdon found Superintendent Snow in Illwood Lane. The car had gone into the hedge when the Super lost control. Not Lawdon's fault, it happened before he got there. The Super said so and—'

'Is he badly hurt?' Capricorn said sharply.

'No, no, he had been driving slowly. He had been taken ill, he was in great pain—we thought it was appendicitis and we rushed him over to Marley General Hospital. It seemed the best thing to do.'

'It couldn't be appendicitis,' Capricorn said, knowing that Snow had had his appendix removed in a field hospital in France in 1917.

'No, no, so the doctors said. Unfortunately, they don't know what it is. They think they will have to operate. Your Superintendent did manage to say, would you get in touch with the Chief at Central.'

'Yes, of course,' Capricorn said slowly.

'He said, just before we left, that you knew what he wanted done. If there is anything—'

'Yes,' Capricorn said. 'Superintendent Snow wanted me to go to London. But he wanted somebody here to . . .' he glanced over at Diener. Having lost his audience, he had sunk into his chair and seemed to be nodding off. The lion's head was lolling on his chest. 'To keep a watch on Mr Diener. To make sure we don't lose sight of him,' he said carefully.

'He couldn't go anywhere,' Pritchard said. 'But of course, I'll send some men up straight away. You'll see that the Super's family is notified?'

Capricorn promised to take care of it. He wondered why he hadn't mentioned the warrant. Well, certainly, Diener wasn't leaving and Snow wouldn't be able to question him in the morning anyway.

'I suppose Central will send another Super?' Pritchard said. It showed the decency of the man that he didn't sound, in the slightest, relieved. He must have known that his relationship with Snow wasn't going to be smooth.

'That's for the Chief to say, of course,' Capricorn said, rather wondering, in the circumstances, where they could spirit one up. If he didn't say anything about the warrant, Snow would be furious when he came around.

'I'll have to leave for London after I've spoken to the Chief,' he said, 'As soon as your men take over. When I have some more information as to what Central is going to do, I'll keep you informed.'

'Thank you, Sergeant,' Pritchard said. He gave Capricorn the details about Snow's doctor and his room in the hospital and said his anxious goodbye, having taken Diener, as it were, back under the auspices of Illwood.

Now why did I do that, Capricorn wondered, annoyed with himself. He looked at the sleeping man before him, looking rather sad and crumpled in his sleep, with the funny magazine open and flapping against his shoe. 'I don't know,' Capricorn thought, in some irritation. 'I just don't know.'

He lifted the telephone receiver again and dialled the number of the Chief in London.

A Song Between the Acts

Capricorn drove back to London through the warm summer night feeling in turn elated, contrite, apprehensive, puzzled, and thoughtful. The elation was simple: the Chief had had no Superintendent available and for the time had counselled Capricorn to carry along on the lines laid down by Snow. Capricorn felt absurdly like an understudy being given a chance at a star part. He pulled a face as the phrase occurred to him, because he liked to forget his theatrical past when people would allow it.

The contrition was because, after all, he was sorry for Snow's illness, and firmly made himself hope for a quick recovery. The Chief had been very kind; he had notified Snow's wife personally and had sent a car to take her to High Marley. Mrs Snow, no doubt, would want her husband to have a full convalescence. . . . A reproachful screech came from the hedge and made him jump; the car had disturbed a barn owl.

The apprehension came from his failure to get a warrant for Diener. Technically, that had not been part of his own assignment, but he hadn't even discussed it with the Chief. Irritable, Capricorn couldn't think of a good reason why he hadn't wanted to arrest the man. Perhaps Pritchard had worked on his feelings about the previous sufferings of all the internees.

No, it wasn't that. Pritchard had called in the Yard with his mind made up that Diener was the killer. Snow, though officially uncommitted to the idea, had been looking for evidence with that in mind. Capricorn realised, before he was a half mile from Illwood, that he wanted to approach the case another way.

Certainly, Diener could have done it.

But to Capricorn it seemed too pat, like seeing a lady sawn in half before your eyes. That's what had bothered him; the case had a decided odour of sawn lady about it. Yet he could hardly tell that to the Chief.

Snow's point about the man who knifed his girl in a pub on Saturday night and other public displays of murderous passion was well taken, but Capricorn felt rebelliously that those crimes involved a different kind of man. Certainly there were exceptions but a man of Diener's abilities would be expected to commit a more sophisticated murder, if he killed at all. He might be overconfident, too clever, but it seemed unlikely he would be so grossly stupid.

And some parts of Pritchard's case were not watertight. The two locks to Diener's doors and the keys. Diener had said simply that he often forgot to lock the doors. It might seem odd that a man who went to the trouble and expense to install special locks would forget to lock them, but it happened. And as for the distribution of the keys and all the fuss about them, Capricorn guessed that keys were passed around by the staff to ease their work and that Braun's key was not returned to Madame Braun every time it was used, that quite likely some exasperated porter or maid had had an extra one cut—and besides which, as a former magician, he thought very little of most locks anyway.

His mind was racing as he drew closer to London,

his former sleepiness entirely fled. Diener's own atti-
tude was strange. He certainly was in despair, yet he
didn't seem concerned about being suspected of murder. Or if he was concerned he showed it very
strangely. The way he had spoken to the little Lise
Roth. . . . Capricorn frowned. It was as though Diener thought the possible murder charge an awful
nuisance, but not the serious problem. He had actually said, 'They cannot convict me.' What made him
think so?

Capricorn had arrived at the outskirts of town. A
light rain was falling and misted his windshield. The
ditch at the Brandenburg would be washed clean at
last of the blood of Ingeborg Rilke.

He looked about him with disfavour. London was
still dim at night with bomb holes gaping. As he
neared the centre of town there were very few people
about and all the restaurants were closed. The capital
was making a languid recovery. The brilliant metrop-
olis of his childhood, that he had imagined somehow
would be waiting for him after the war, had disappeared. Perhaps that London, that England, would
never be again. Diener and his *Götterdämmerung*
must have affected his spirits, because for a melancholy moment it seemed to him that all the former
combatants were now, in a way, refugees.

But he quickly returned to more practical considerations because he was in fact, as usual, homeless. He
had given up his not very comfortable lodgings when
he went on his last job in the north. A few months
before he had spent a good part of his legacy from
The Great Capricornus on a long lease of a flat in an
old house on a quiet square. It had needed a lot of
work and was promised for early summer by the various firms employed in its renovation, but summer

was ending and the flat was still full of dilatory work-men.

His aunt Dolly, the youngest of the Magic Merli-nos, had paused in her peregrinations long enough to acquire, by dubious means, a large house in Padding-ton, and to this house she had invited her nephew un-til his flat was finished. Capricorn's means were straightened for a time because of the work on the flat and he had agreed, rather reluctantly. He was fond of his aunts but he had lived with them as a child and remembered their travelling households as a constant confusion punctuated by frequent outbursts of revelry and riot, unsuited to the sober needs of a policeman.

If the rest of London was quiet, Paddington was noisy enough. Uniform Branch was busy tonight. From upstairs windows light shone out through cracked and ragged blinds; wireless sets and gramo-phones blared. On a corner not too far from Dolly's house a woman leaned over a sill cursing and throw-ing empty bottles down on a man decamping below. Further along a party of drunks were having a fight in the gutter.

His weariness caught up with him and he longed for his bed, and he wished, without much hope, that his aunts would be asleep. His wish was not granted. When he arrived at the house, battered-looking where part of the gutter had been splintered off by a piece of shrapnel and not mended, there were still lights in the basement and on one of the upper floors. He crept into the front hall that was decorated from floor to ceiling with photographs of the Magic Merlinos: Nelly, dark and clever; Dolly, red-haired and fantas-tic; Milly, fair and pretty; and Tilly the daft smiled youthfully upon him. From the parlour came the tinkling of the piano. Dolly was playing and Milly was singing, 'The boy I love is up in the gallery.'

Milly had a sweet voice, unlike Dolly who sounded like a brass gong. Capricorn paused and smiled as the song carried him back through the years. Quietly, he made for his room and undressed. The bathroom with its noisy plumbing was too much of a risk, he would certainly be overheard and asked to join the fun. Anyway, there wouldn't be any hot water.

There was a note for him on the orange crate that served as his chest of drawers in Dolly's large, childish yet elaborate hand.

A man phoned from the flat. The wires was in wrong and they had to pull the plaster out. Nelly told you not to bother with that old dump, more trouble than its worth. Bad as this but we got it for nothing. The rations are used up so if you want breakfast have it out like a good boy.

He gazed at it despondently. A month ago it had been a leaking pipe that had brought the plasterers, slowly and expensively, back again. The flat would never be finished. It would sit there, eating his income until he grew old. He fell asleep on the gloomy thought, although a quarrel started in the basement and a shouting match took place outside his door.

What seemed to be political argument mixed with the sound of quarrelling lovers, while Milly's voice wove plaintively in the background. He dreamed he was in a Muscovite brothel with Franz Diener's voice saying 'It is the *Götterdämmerung!*' At last the house quieted down and he fell into a deeper sleep at daybreak, pursuing the phantom figure of Ingeborg Rilke, who sang softly, 'The boy I love is up in the

gallery,' came forward, bowed, and disappeared behind a curtain of falling leaves.

Then someone was tolling a passing bell, a strange
new kind of bell, shrill and insistent as the reproachful
owl that had shrieked in the hedge. The bell went on
and on until Detective-Sergeant Capricorn jumped up
and out of bed, barking his shins on the orange crate,
and answered the telephone in the corridor.

The Chief was calling from his home.

'Snow's going to be all right. I thought you'd want
to know. He had such a bad night that they did an
emergency operation on him this morning, but they
say everything is in good order now. Hasn't come
round yet. His wife's with him.'

'What was wrong, sir?' Capricorn asked.

He rubbed his eyes, blinking at the faded, stained
wallpaper that had once depicted, apparently,
bunches of purple grapes. Telephone numbers were
pencilled all over, and someone had amused themselves with a game of x's and o's. There had been
transatlantic guests also, as the ubiquitous Mr Chad
was present bearing the legend, in large round script,
'Kilroy was here.'

'Damned if I understand it,' the Chief said. 'You
know how those medicos talk. I thought you could
only get appendicitis once, but it seems other bits of
tripes can go wrong the same way and have to be
nipped out. Rotten thing to think about. Anyway, the
doctors themselves don't seem to think of it and they'd
been givin' Snow all the wrong sort of slops. He won't
be back on duty for a month now and you'll have to
peg along with Illwood as best you can for a bit. A
bunch of spivs picked last night to razor slash a
bookie to death outside of the Windmill Theatre. No
decent respect for our problems.'

Capricorn hummed cheerfully as he bathed and shaved in the dank old bathroom, the only one in the house. He was not depressed by the mildew on the walls, the continuing absence of hot water, or the rusty trickle of the cold. He was not even dismayed when he glanced in the kitchen in the hope of a cup of tea only to find a sinkful of dirty crockery, a plethora of empty beer bottles, and several broken chairs.

He wondered briefly what the fight had been about, but with little anxiety. The Merlinos doted on rows. As he made his way along the first floor corridor, the bare planks sighing under his tread, he passed the open door of Dolly's parlour. A thin, towheaded man was curled up on the broken-springed sofa, sleeping quietly. Tod Parks, his aunt's newest husband—or supposed husband—had been ejected from the connubial bed again.

Yet surely it had been a girl's voice arguing last night? There were a number of young women staying in the house, who didn't seem much like magicians. Capricorn dismissed the unfortunate thought when a newspaper slid under the door. The front page was unfamiliar—the *Daily Worker*. He remembered his dream of a Muscovite brothel and shuddered.

Tod Parks thrashed in his sleep and cried out protestingly. Capricorn looked back at him and grinned. His aunts were strong-tempered women, sentimental only in song, faithful only to their audiences. The boys they loved were up in the gallery. And Ingeborg Rilke? Whom had she loved?

ACT TWO

1

To Capricorn that morning, even Paddington looked beautiful, shabby as it was in the bright sunlight. A little café by the station was actually open and served breakfast. Feeling much refreshed, he was swiftly on his way to his first stop. Models were likely to go out early.

The address he had was in Bayswater. It looked almost as run down, if not as raffish, as Paddington, and the house where Ingeborg Rilke had stayed with her friend was one of the shabbiest, with the number 19 painted in crude lettering on the pillars of the porch. Capricorn thought of the popular concept of model girls, living a gay life in the West End.

There was nothing very gay about 19 Burlingwood Square. It reminded Capricorn of all the sleazy lodging houses he had ever lived in. The door was open and inside a worn, shabby strip of carpet did not entirely cover or hide the uneven floorboards. He trod carefully, as the milk bottles outside each door suggested that the residents were sleeping.

Most of the light bulbs were out on the upper floors, and he had to peer from door to door looking for the letter J. He found it on the third floor all the way in the back, but it did not look very promising. A row of unopened milk bottles stood by the door proclaiming the tenant's absence, but he rapped anyway. He was heartened at hearing sounds of stirring inside and after a few minutes the door was opened by a large girl in a flannel dressing gown, hair in curlers, with a wide, friendly grin.

Capricorn started to introduce himself, but the girl had caught sight of the milk bottles.

'Oh, for heaven's sake!' She laughed heartily. 'I didn't notice last night, I was just too done for. Would you believe—I mean, you'd think they'd *notice* after a while that no one was taking them in. If I didn't come back, d'you think they'd go on leaving them for ever? I mean, row on row leading to the Eternal Blessedness or something? Oh, well, as least there's milk for this morning. Come on in,' she added, smiling again and giving Capricorn a quick, appreciative glance from bright green eyes.

She picked up the last bottle in the row and, leaving the door open for Capricorn, swung back into the room with a long, easy gait. A kettle was handy to a corner basin, and was soon filled and set on the gas ring. The room was sunny and though the print curtains were scant and the bedspread, showing signs of having been pulled hastily over the bed, was faded, and the few furnishings in keeping with the house, still, occupied by the big, tawny-haired, smiling girl, it had a Bohemian cheerfulness. It did not seem so strange, after all, that the twenty-year-old Ingeborg Rilke might have preferred it to the luxurious but stuffy Brandenburg. And a cheerful English girl of her own age, he reflected, must have been a tonic after so many refugees.

He had addressed her, according to his records, as Miss Clarke, but she urged him to call her Randy.

'Everybody does,' she said, dealing with the tea-caddy and a pot shaped like a cottage. 'My real name's Miranda, can you imagine?' she giggled.

Taking some buns from a paper bag, she settled down at a small table covered with American cloth in front of the empty fireplace on one of a pair of kitchen chairs and motioned him to the other.

'Want some? The buns are yesterday's, I'm afraid. I know you've come to ask about poor old Swanny, but I can't think till I've had my cuppa.'

Capricorn declined refreshment, and asked for assurance that by 'Swanny' Miss Clarke meant Ingeborg Rilke.

'Ingeborg, that was her real name,' Miss Clarke bit into a currant bun with a flash of large healthy-looking white teeth. 'Such a mouthful. One of the photographers called her Swan-Neck one day and it sort of stuck, Swanny for short. She didn't mind. Never minded anything. If you'd called her Spot or Fido it would be all the same.'

Capricorn considered that for a moment. It did not seem to fit in with the mental image of the independent young woman who had dealt so decisively with her lover that in desperation he had killed her. That had been Pritchard's image, and Snow had accepted it. Regarding the sparkling eyes and the cheerful tilt of the head of Randy Clarke, he could hardly imagine her as answering to Spot or Fido. But then, Miss Clarke did not strike him as a likely murder victim either.

'I do have some questions, Miss Clarke—Randy,' he said. 'I hope I won't be keeping you from an appointment?'

She pulled a face. 'Wish you were, Sergeant. But things are a bit slow right now. That's why I took a few days off. A friend of mine took me up to the Lake

District. I'll go down to the agency later on to see what's happening. You see, I'm not the rage like poor old Swanny was. Been in the business four years, but I only just make a living.

Her resignation was cheerful and without rancour.

'Now Swanny went almost straight from model school to being one of the top models in the country. I'm too healthy-looking for magazines like *La Belle*,' she confided. 'I just get jobs for Whitey-White toothpaste, or Family Favourite Porridge Oats. But you're not interested in that,' she said, wielding the pot briskly for her second cup. 'You want to know who did Swanny in. But I haven't a clue, really. It makes no sense at all. No one could want to kill Swanny.'

'Yet someone did kill her,' he reminded her, thinking of the multilated body. 'When did you see her last?'

'Oh, not for a couple of weeks before I went away. I can't remember the day exactly.'

'She hadn't been here then, for almost three weeks?'

'Well,' she was thoughtful, her high and broad pink clear forehead wrinkling childishly. 'I wouldn't say that. She had a key, you see, and could come in and out when she liked. I could've missed her. That's how she came to stay with me, at first she would just come to rest between jobs, you know, modelling's hard on the feet. She gave me something towards the rent. Then if she had to work early the next day she stayed over. I've got the two beds and it's a long way back to the hotel, though that boyfriend of hers down there would always send a chauffeured car if she wanted it.'

She sighed. 'A chauffeured car. You know what my boyfriend got for me in the Lake District? A bike. Biked all over, we did. Good thing for once the weather was fine. Said it would help keep my hips slim, but biking is terrible on the legs.

She grinned. 'As if I'm not developed enough already. Anyway, I heard about Swanny, and I got fed up. Took the train back yesterday though I don't really know what for. Nothing to do, if you see what I mean, and yet it seemed rotten to stay on holiday, somehow.'

Capricorn did know what she meant. It seemed a natural emotion, and he thought for a moment of the gay party on the lawn of the Brandenburg.

'The day before she was killed, Miss Rilke had spoken of leaving the Brandenburg quite soon, perhaps the next day. Had she discussed that with you at all, or written to you?'

'She never wrote,' Randy Clarke said, 'and she hadn't said anything, but of course she didn't have to. As I said, she could come here any time she pleased. She probably was here while I was gone because she worked on Thursday, she had it booked.'

'But the milk bottles,' Capricorn pointed out.

'That doesn't mean anything. Swanny never made herself even a cup of tea, and she wouldn't think about it.'

She avoided his gaze. Capricorn fancied Miss Clarke didn't want to intimate her friend might be stupid. He liked her for it.

'Did she ever mention going anywhere else?'

'No. I had asked her about it because Swanny could do better than this.' She looked around the shabby room stoically. 'But she showed no interest. Very helpless she was.' Randy Clarke shook her head. 'No push of her own. Helpless.'

She chewed another bun thoughtfully.

'Had you known her long?'

'No, just since the end of last winter, though it does seem like an age. The model school she went to asks some of us to go down and talk to the girls that finish the course, give them some tips, some idea of the business, what they should expect. But I tell you the truth,' she said meditatively, 'I hardly thought it worth while to tell Swanny anything. I never thought she'd even get a job.'

She reached for her bag, looked into it, frowning, and searched around the room.

'Damn. I'm out of cigarettes.'

'Allow me,' Capricorn said, smiling, and offered her one.

She found a saucer to use as an ash tray and they smoked companionably.

'You didn't think Miss Rilke the usual model type?'

'God, no. It wasn't even her idea. I think somebody suggested it to that boyfriend of hers, he told her to do it and she did. They had an awful time with her at the school,' she told him. 'They could hardly get her to stand up. She's tall—was I should say.' Her sunny faced clouded for a moment. 'And she had very good long legs, but she always wanted to shrink. A real violet if you ever saw one. And she looked like a starved cat and was terrifed to say a word.'

She blew a long column of smoke. 'If we'd had to choose I would have picked her as the girl least likely to have any sort of a career. And I still think she might not, except that Kenyon saw her and. . . . That droopy long neck of hers fascinated him, and that terrified look she had, staring at nothing.'

Robert Kenyon was *the* fashion photographer, Capricorn remembered. More than that, he was also considered to be one of the real artists of the camera, and a lasting subject of debate between those who judged

photography merely a craft and those who did not.
Old Blarney of the *Morning Voice*, who had once referred to photographers contemptuously as 'chemists',
had entirely reversed himself with the arrival of Kenyon, and wrote articles bitterly deploring modern artists who had remained in the tradition of pictorial art.

Kenyon was employed by *La Belle*, which liked to
be somewhat avant-garde, to the bewilderment of
some of its readers. Rose Lavender, Capricorn's friend
in the north, was quite a fashion plate herself but she
had been puzzled by Kenyon's work, dark and full of
motion, as though his models stood in a high wind.

'The girls look so—desperate,' she said plaintively,
and Capricorn had had to laugh because it was true.
Their bony looks were very different from Rose's pink
and white soft prettiness, as they were different from
the healthy, attractive Randy Clarke. If Kenyon was
the leader in fashion photography, it was obvious why
Randy was left with Whitey-White.

'You see?'

Randy displayed the *La Belle* cover that Capricorn
had already seen. He examined it more carefully. The
pale face was shadowed by an autumn hat crowned
with the red and gold leaves that seemed to flutter up
and around to form the background of the page. Her
eyes were partly veiled by drooping lids and the expression at first glance had been indefinable.

But 'terrified'?

'Terrified?' he repeated.

'She was the most terrified creature I ever met—I
had a pet mouse with more spunk than Swanny. It
was all that being in prison, I suppose. She'd gone
from one to another, since she was a little kid, in Germany.'

Randy looked thoughtful. 'Not that she talked about

it much. She hardly ever talked anyway. Her English wasn't all that good. Some people thought she was, well, sort of dense, a bit backward, but I think she just didn't understand. Kenyon would be nasty as hell, he's a sarcastic swine, and she would just take it. I think'—she gave Capricorn a troubled glance—'she'd only ever learned one way to get on with a man, and of course, that wouldn't work with Kenyon. She never complained. Never heard her complain about anything. You couldn't even get her to say what she liked,' she went on, puzzled. 'Sometimes I got the idea that girl was so—so sort of squashed that she didn't know what she liked. Look,' she said, jumping up.

She pulled at the bottom drawer of a painted wooden chest. It stuck, although she jerked hard, and Capricorn helped to get it open.

'Is this all she kept here?' he asked.

Randy nodded. 'That's it.'

The drawer held a small case containing the usual model's paraphernalia: make-up, hairbrush, curlers. There was a toothbrush, and two nightdresses, neatly folded, similar to the ones he had seen at the Brandenburg.

'Look here,' Randy said, reaching into a corner. She brought out a coil of black stuff, looking rather soft, that smeared her hand. Capricorn recognized it from his own childhood—licorice whip-sticks they had called them.

'We were in the grocer's one day, and they had these for the kids. And Swanny picked one up, she had the funniest look on her face. *"Lakritz"* she came out with, or something like that. She paid for it and bit into it, and she actually smiled. You see'—she looked at Capricorn earnestly—'she'd remembered something she'd liked, once. Strange, come to think of it, that was the last time I ever saw her. I was so surprised, her having a fancy and saying so. We brought it home and what she left I put in the drawer for when she came back.'

Suddenly Randy's green eyes were filled with tears, and she hurriedly went back to her chair and sniffed into her handkerchief.

'You took her in because you were sorry for her,' Capricorn said gently.

The big girl fidgeted, embarrassed at being caught in a good deed.

'Oh, well, I don't mind a bit of company. My Mum and Dad live in Crossley—that's way out past Chipping Ongar so I only get home Sundays. I have to go for my Sunday School class and my girls—my mother's Band of Hope, Mother's Union, Temperance Society, Guides, Sunbeams, anything you can think of, so I have to do my bit.'

She grinned, arranged her facial features in an expression idiotically demure, and sang: 'A sunbeam, a sunbeam, Jesus wants me for a sunbeam.'

'Oh, you should see me after a big Saturday night, horribly hung over, with thirty screaming kids. Well, nobody was more quiet than Swanny. And she wasn't here that much. Weekends she was always down with that funny lot of friends she had.'

'You mean the refugees at the Brandenburg? Did you know them?'

'I went down there a couple of times with Swanny for parties. Her boyfriend Franz was great for giving parties. He seemed all right.'

She stared at Capricorn. 'She was killed with his golf club, wasn't she? Do you think . . . ?'

'I don't know what to think,' Capricorn said honestly. 'We are just making inquiries. But there is evidence they had a quarrel the day before the murder. About her getting a flat of her own in London.'

'Really?' She looked surprised. 'He never seemed to mind her staying here. We had talked about her getting a place of her own but as I said, she didn't want to. But I don't remember Franz saying anything against it.'

'You were only down there a couple of times,' he reminded her.

Her cheeks grew a little pinker. 'To tell the truth, the first time I went, they had asked me down to be a dinner partner for Otto—have you met Otto?'

'I know who he is,' he said, recalling the humorous, intelligent-looking man. He had been one of the porch party on the night of the murder, someone who should be questioned again before Diener was charged with murder. Snow had probably intended to do that himself.

'We sort of took to each other. I mean,' she tapped the ash off the end of her cigarette into her saucer, 'of course, he has this wife, but she doesn't come down with him when he comes to London or the Brandenburg, and he's fun. We get together quite often. He's well off so it's a nice change from my friend with the bike. Otto never said anything about Franz not liking Swanny to stay in town.'

'But you know Diener's not allowed to travel to London,' Capricorn reminded her.

She looked at him thoughtfully. 'Are you anything to do with that? I mean getting people into trouble for going beyond the five miles and all that?'

'Not my department,' he assured her.

'Well, then, he wasn't supposed to but he did. He didn't drive himself, you know he can't get a licence, but he had this car and chauffeur and sometimes he would come to town after dark and we'd all go to the Blue Dahlia.'

'All? With Miss Rilke?'

'And the Roths.'

'Still, it wouldn't be as convenient for him to see Miss Rilke.'

'No. I didn't think he worried about it that much, seeing Swanny, I mean. He looked after her all right, she could buy anything on his account, and he made her order every outfit she modelled. But he never struck me as being so mad about her. Of course, I didn't see them together often. I suppose you can't always tell.'

She rubbed her head in puzzlement and noticed her curlers. 'Lord, I must look a fright,' she grinned.

At that moment the alarm clock that was sitting on a tin plate went off with an enormous racket.

'You see what it takes to wake me up, as a rule,' she shouted over the din. 'I'm going to have to get dressed now, Sergeant, or I'll miss anything that's going.'

'I won't detain you more than a minute, for now anyway,' Capricorn said. 'But I must ask you, do you know of anyone who had any animosity towards Miss Rilke, anyone who was angry with her in any way, or could possibly have had any motive or any wish for her death?'

She shook her head decidedly. 'I'd love to be able to tell you' she said. 'God knows I'd like to get whoever did it. But I can't imagine. Swanny couldn't get anybody angry, she was just the most inoffensive creature you ever met. I don't know much about her life before I met her, because of her not being a talker. She didn't even tell me about the prisons and the camps, I got that from Otto. Swanny could sit here with me all evening in front of the gas fire and she wouldn't say a word. Wherever you put her, there she'd sit, quiet, doing nothing. You can't imagine anyone wanting to do her in.'

She paused, deep in thought, her thumb going to her mouth as if she were a little girl at her lessons. 'I can't help thinking it must have been a mistake. Perhaps in the dark she was taken for somebody else. Or maybe it was a loony.'

That convenient lunatic again, Capricorn thought. If Miss Rilke hadn't been so physically unusual, thin and tall, the idea that she was killed in error might have been interesting. He could imagine a man getting in a passion of jealousy over Lise Roth.

Randy was taking the curlers out of her hair, and Capricorn rose to go.

'That Mrs Roth,' she added, as if half-divining his thought. 'You should ask her. She knew Swanny from the camps, and she knew everyone that Swanny did, outside of the modelling lark.'

'That Mrs Roth?' Capricorn repeated, catching the slight derogatory emphasis. Of course, Lise Roth had the kind of looks and charm that other women often resented, but Randy Clarke didn't seem the resenting sort.

'Um.' One of the curlers caught in her hair and Randy pulled a face.

'Well, she was supposed to be her friend, and all that, but she would make fun of her in a way you could hardly put your finger on, sneaky-spiteful. She soon stopped asking me there, I can tell you. It was Diener who paid for the parties but Mrs Roth was the hostess. I think she liked Diener herself and was jealous of Swanny.'

'But she introduced them, didn't she?'

'Yes, but that was before Swanny was a model and had good clothes and was smart and was getting to be well-known. Swanny's young—I have an idea that Roth was frightened she would get over all that prison stuff, forget about it and really blossom out.'

Randy sighed. 'Swanny could have been really smashing if she were more—well, more at home. And that Roth, she's no spring chicken,' she added scornfully from the vantage point of her twenty-one or twenty-two years. Mrs Roth had looked youthful enough to Capricorn; she was closer to thirty than forty.

'They won't tell you down *there*'—Capricorn again caught the slight emphasis; Randy Clarke didn't like the Brandenburgians, except for Otto Karl and perhaps Diener—'But I got it from Otto. Diener didn't only pay Swanny's bills but he takes care of most of the Roths' as well. They were supposed to have lost everything when they ran away from France. They lived in France, you know, not Germany. You'd think Lise Roth had been the Queen of Paris to hear them talk. Old Roth is in business here now, but he still lets Diener help them out.'

'You didn't like the Roths,' Capricorn observed.

Randy paused for a moment in her hair twisting. 'Hadn't thought much about it,' she said, 'But I s'pose I didn't, much. Or the Brauns. Mrs Braun—damned if I'll call her Madame—always gave me the fish-eye. There's a nasty one if you ask me. Like one of the witches in *Macbeth*. And that Fitz-Marley is a stinker. He was a friend of Hitler's, did you know? Just a funny lot,' she shrugged her shoulders. 'Couldn't tell you any more but they struck me as a funny lot.'

Capricorn paused with his hand on the door.

'But there isn't any one of them, that you can remember, or anyone else, that Miss Rilke ever mentioned being nervous or emotional about?'

Unthinkingly, Randy threw off her dressing gown as she stood by the sink and stood revealed in a long, school-girlish white nightgown. With her hair in its uncombed stiff little curls she looked like a child who'd bitten the magic mushroom and shot up to nearly six feet.

'Well, she worshipped Franz Diener, you know,' she said. 'Whenever she spoke she would say how "*fabelhaft*" he was.' The German word sounded comic with her very English intonation.

'He was the only person, I would say, that she *wasn't* afraid of. She was like a little dog with him, a spaniel if you know what I mean. But she was nervous of almost everybody else. Nervous, really,' she shook her head. 'It doesn't describe it. Like I said before, she was terrified. That girl was terrified and I don't know if it was of any one person or any special thing but I know she just lived in terror. All the time.'

With that she turned to run the water in the basin and tugged at her nightgown. Tactfully, Capricorn left, more puzzled than when he had first found her. Why had Miss Rilke been so determined to leave the only man she wasn't afraid of?

Dutifully he checked the other tenants, who, with only one exception, were at home, getting ready to go to work and impatient of intrusive policemen. None of them had ever seen Ingeborg Rilke. He found the landlady, who owned two houses and lived next door, a plump woman with her grey hair in a large bun, and a motherly look that proved deceptive. She had never seen Miss Rilke and had been unaware of her existence, and was extremely annoyed when she learned of it.

'I rent to singles only,' she said. 'Business people out all day, nine to five. I only let to Clarke because I thought she was all right, her father being a clergyman, but I've had doubts. Like that nurse,' she added. 'Out all night and she says night duty, but who's to know? And if Clarke's been having somebody stay, she owes extra rent and if she doesn't pay she can be put out with two minutes' notice and you can tell her so.'

Capricorn escaped, to meet the nurse, still in uniform, on the steps of Number 19. He accompanied her upstairs as she wearily made her way to the top floor. Her eyes were dark-ringed, her feet were sore, and Capricorn learned that the landlady was wrong in suspecting her of a life of merriment, but that was all. Unlike the other tenants, she had from time to time had a glimpse of Ingeborg Rilke coming and going during the day, and believed that she had passed her on the stairs about three o'clock the previous Thursday, but she had never seen her accompanied that she recalled.

Score nothing, Capricorn thought moodily, as he took his leave. As he ran down the steps, he noticed the row of milk bottles still outside Randy Clarke's door. You're as good a detective, he told himself, as the milkman who had not deduced after five days the possible absence of the tenant. A whole morning gone, and all he had learned was that Ingeborg Rilke was terrified. But terrified of what, or of whom?

2

'Terrified?' Ingeborg's aunt by marriage said later
that day. 'I don't know about that. Nervous? I suppose
she was. We all are. It would be amazing if we weren't,
after everything.'

It had taken him some time to get to see the
Krauses. They lived in a flat in another old house near
the Brompton Road, a better house than the one
Randy Clarke inhabited and in fairly good condition.
A brass plate by the door said simply 'Martin Krause.'
Mr Krause, a German lawyer, of course could not
practice his profession in England, and Capricorn had
information that he earned his living by providing ad-
vice for refugees on matters to do with immigration
and naturalisation.

The first room he had entered was a waiting room,
fairly crowded with refugees, varying from the
shabby and indigent-looking, who waited patiently, to
the well-dressed and demanding. A harried, untidy
servant had taken his card and brought the message
back that Herr Krause was busy with a client and
would the sergeant be good enough to wait. Frau
Krause, when inquired for, was busy with a child who
had the measles.

Capricorn had waited as patiently as he could wondering if he should really be getting a warrant for Dien-

er. After all, he could have done that first, and attended to this after, and kept himself in his Superintendent's good graces. Fortunately Herr Krause, perhaps mindful of the wisdom of cooperating with the police, saw him as soon as his client departed, leaving the rest in the waiting room to eye the tall figure with resentment as a late comer being given a preference.

On first seeing Herr Krause, Capricorn thought him the fattest man he had ever met. Then he realized that although the man rising from his seat at the desk was indeed very heavily larded, he was not as gross as some fat men. It was the way the fat was distributed that gave him a look so grotesque, falling fold on fold on his face, his chins hanging pendulously one upon the other, a pale, yellow-white fat that glistened with copious beads of sweat from his pudgy hands to the top of his bald head, although the day was just mildly warm, and a breeze came through the open window behind him rustling through the green-gold leaves of a tall birch.

'Sergeant Capricorn,' he said, with a gasping breath, 'So sorry to have kept you waiting. You have come about my niece. Poor Ingeborg! Tragedy, always tragedy. The poor child.'

His eyes, set in circles of fat, had seemed pig-like, but as he approached Capricorn could see that the eyes themselves were blue and mild in expression with the slight stare of a man who sees badly without his spectacles. He fumbled for a pair on his desk among a pile of papers, and then shook Capricorn's hand agitatedly with his own hot wet one. The sensation would have been disagreeable except for the concern in those blue eyes. Someone, apart from the ebullient Miss Clarke, had feeling for the dead girl.

They sat down at the large mahogany desk, the principal piece of furniture in the room. It was a pleasant room overlooking the garden, airy and high-ceilinged. The framed certificates on the walls were all in German relating to his profession as a lawyer, *Rechtsanwalt*. He had apparently practiced in Vienna. There were also photographs, somewhat faded, of Herr Krause with various dignitaries at banquets and other functions—churchmen and what were probably political figures and several of a man robed as a judge. One of the churchmen looked familiar to Capricorn and he recognised him after a moment as Cardinal Gewiller, the famous anti-Nazi who had been murdered by the Nazis at the time of the *Anschluss*.

'Ah, you see my past, the tragedy of us all,' the emotional Krause said. 'You come to me to know what happened to my poor niece, but I cannot tell you. Except that her tragedy started here.'

He gestured towards the photographs on the wall. Capricorn reflected it was difficult to get the facts in this case, as the people concerned, except for Randy Clarke, only wanted to talk about politics, and their misfortunes caused by politics. However, it was useless to try to rush Krause. He would tell what he knew in his own way.

It was probably his habit with his clients to talk and mourn over the old days, as they assessed their chances for entering this country or that or of staying in England, and this was the reason they went to him, instead of some German-speaking English lawyer, who could have handled their problems with a tenth of the time they spent here, but without the shared sorrow, and their strange homesickness for a land to which they refused to return.

'That was Ingeborg's father,' Krause said, pointing

to the judge. 'How proud I was when my sister married Johann Rilke of Munich, one of the finest, most upright, of judges. *Gerechtigkeit* was his passion. A true *Rechtsgelehrter*—jurist, you would say. Before 1933 he had put many Brown Shirts where they belonged, behind bars, and as soon as they came to power, he and my poor sister Gerda, they were sent to one of the first camps. Before we even knew what the camps were.'

He shrugged his fat round shoulders. 'That camp was not like Dachau, but they both died there, after two, three years. The terrible thing was when the Nazis took them they took also Ingeborg, a little girl, seven years old. She had been the only child, her father's joy. Eventually we got her released to my wife's custody. But we could see the way the wind was blowing. My friend the Cardinal'—he nodded at the photograph—'he warned me to go, though he would not save himself. Vienna was not safe for Catholics, those of us who had been known as anti-Nazi. So, just a year before *Anschluss* we went on our travels. It was hard on my wife,' he confided.

On his desk stood a portrait in a heavy, ornate silver frame adorned with cupids. He turned it for Capricorn to see, a younger, thinner but still gross Herr Krause, and a very pretty, dark young girl who looked about twenty years his junior.

'When we married,' he said in explanation, 'my Willi and I, she was a poor girl, very poor, the daughter of my housekeeper. With my law practice, the land and buildings I had inherited from my father, funds I had in Kreditanstalt, I was a substantial man, you could say, to her I was a very rich man. And then. . . .'

He shrugged again. 'Perhaps you know what happened to Kreditanstalt, although you are young. That was the first blow. Then, as life became more difficult in Wien, my law practice went down and down. When we rushed to leave at last I sold the land and buildings for almost nothing. And so we were almost penniless refugees, with three children of our own and Ingeborg, a terrified child with her nerves gone, screaming all night every night. In France we went from one town to another. I tried to establish myself, but the French were not anxious for Austrian professional refugees. Life was hard, my wife had much to do with her own children.' He looked sadly at Capricorn. 'She cannot be blamed that to have Ingeborg as well, a sick child, sometimes was too much.'

He looked abashed, as though he felt he had been disloyal to his wife. 'My wife has been faithful, as good a mother as she could be,' he said simply. 'In France, she was still young, still pretty. Many young women in her position—ach, you can imagine.'

Capricorn could imagine.

'I was, in any case, worried about France. I was proved to be right. We came to England in 1939. In 1940,' he sighed. 'I, for myself, can't blame the English. How could they know who among us were spies, traitors? They did not, for a certainty, know their own. But for young persons like my wife, they could not understand. And we were separated. She had the children with her in the women's camp, and Ingeborg. Ingeborg never had a chance to forget, you see. She grew up in the camp and was the first of us to be released.'

'She was eighteen, I believe.' Capricorn said.

Krause nodded.

'Where did she go, do you know?'

Krause looked down at his hands. 'You must understand, Sergeant, that in the camps there were difficulties. You would expect it. We older ones, we realise that life was hard for the English themselves during the war. No doubt they did the best for us that they could. But among the younger women, with children, you can see. . . .'

Two thrushes lit on a branch of the birch outside and as if to point up what the refugee lawyer did not wish to say, quarrelled away energetically in the noonday sun. Capricorn felt a sympathy with the fat man who was trying to excuse his niece's break with her family without criticizing the wife who had driven her away.

'We did not hear from Ingeborg after she left the camp. She was released at the same time as Mrs Roth, and it was from Mrs Roth that we got news of her from time to time. I don't know what she did. She was trained for nothing. My wife tells me she always spoke German in the camps and did not bother to learn English well, although my wife advised her to study.'

Capricorn was interested in this time in the girl's life, about which there was almost no information in the files.

'You and your wife came to this address when you were released?'

'Yes. I had started this kind of work when I was in the camp, and somehow Willi and I have made a life.'

'But your niece never came to live with you?'

'No,' he said unhappily. 'She had made friends, she stayed with them. She never told us who they were.'

Miss Rilke had been required to register her address as an enemy alien after leaving the camp. The first she had given had been a cheap lodging house, where no one remembered her, and after her uncle and aunt had taken the house in Kensington she had given that address as her own.

'You had no idea at all?'

'When my wife saw Mrs Roth—we have worked on the Roths' emigration papers for the Argentine—Mrs Roth would sometimes say she had seen her and she was well. But until this year when she went to stay with Mrs Roth at the Brandenburg, we did not know where she was. She did not visit. I had thought she might want to see the children,' his blue eyes were mournful, 'but, you see, everything here must have reminded her of camps and prisons.

'Have you seen anything of her this last year?' Capricorn asked.

'At the Brandenburg. I visited the Roths at the Brandenburg. Also, I have been working on a visa for Franz Diener. The United States, I believe, will grant him an immigration number any day now. He is eligible as he was a legal resident of Great Britain when the war began. If the war had come six months later, he would have been a British citizen. But you are not interested. . . .'

Capricorn was extremely interested. A man with an opportunity to go to the United States was not the hopeless, stateless man that had been portrayed by the files he had read.

'Did he know about that?' he asked.

The blue eyes stared. 'But of course. Naturally. He was delighted. We don't have it yet, you understand, but I believe it is almost certain. He has been aware of the negotiation for months.'

'When you saw your niece at the Brandenburg, did she discuss her life with you, her friends, her plans?'

He shook his head. 'No. No. You would not know but Ingeborg was very quiet, a very silent girl. And I hardly saw her, only a few minutes here and there. Franz Diener had this idea, from one of the American

ladies at the hotel I believe, that she should be independent, and he had her trained as a model. You have
heard about that, no doubt. She did well, poor little
Ingeborg. Her parents would have been proud.'

His face was shadowed with grief. Capricorn understood that to the older man who dreamed so much of
the past, the fact that his brother had not lived to
know of his daughter's success was as painful as the
sudden death of the girl who had become a stranger.

He seemed to know nothing of his niece's life, but
the question had to be asked.

'Before she became a model, Mr. Krause, have you
any idea how your niece supported herself?'

The lawyer did not meet his eyes. 'I don't know,
Sergeant. I like to think that Mrs Roth helped her. We
could not, at that time. She didn't, as far as I know,
have any job. She was untrained, uneducated, and
not,' he struggled to find the English words, 'not what
you would say capable, enterprising. And it was two
years. The Roths have their own troubles. As a man, I
can only guess. I would rather not know.'

Capricorn remembered some of Randy Clarke's
comments and felt mortified. England had not been a
haven for that sad child. True, it had kept her safe
and fed through those years of danger but. . . . And
at the last it could not protect even her life.

'And you have no idea of anyone who might have
some animosity towards your niece, anyone who
might be involved in her death?'

'Oh, no,' the lawyer said energetically. 'How could
it be? Ingeborg could have no enemies, that timid
girl.'

In another minute he would be presented again
with the madman, Capricorn thought.

'Ingeborg was beaten to death with a golf iron,' he

said deliberately. 'In the hotel grounds, with the gates locked. Someone had reason, or thought he had reason, to commit this crime, and it is the job of the police to discover who it was. The local police,' he went on, 'have questioned Franz Diener. He was apparently your niece's—sponsor. He paid all her bills. They quarrelled about her having a flat of her own in London. Do you know anything about that?'

The fat man sagged in his chair. He looked old and tired. 'Mrs Roth told me he had paid for Ingeborg's training. I did not know about the hotel and other bills. Perhaps as her uncle I should not have allowed it, but it was all arranged before I heard. . . .' His eyes went to the photograph of his brother, the judge, and swept back, shamed, to Capricorn. 'But there is no point to lie. Mr Diener is rich, he helps many people, and my wife and I—our means are very small. Most of my clients cannot pay. To suggest to my wife that we take bread from the mouths of our children to send Ingeborg to school—' He raised his hands palms upwards to the ceiling.

'Apart from that I know nothing of Ingeborg's relations with Diener. He is a fine man. I cannot believe he murdered anyone. Of course, as we all know, between men and women—who knows?'

And he stared at Capricorn, a tired, defeated old man who had bought himself a young wife, and had had to live through more than a decade of her dissatisfaction and reproach.

Added to the discomfort Capricorn had experienced about the fate of Ingeborg, he now felt the odd compunction—out of place in a policeman, he thought—that came upon him in an investigation when people were forced to expose the pitiful shabbinesses of their lives that normally were kept decently hidden, even from themselves.

Both men rose, with a common impulse to end the interview.

'By the way,' Capricorn asked suddenly. 'Did Miss Rilke like licorice? When she was a child?'

'Licorice?' Krause looked at him in bewilderment.

'Black sweet stuff,' Capricorn explained. 'Some children are fond of it.'

'*Lakritz*,' Krause said, wondering. '*Lakritz*—so many years—' He stared at Capricorn. 'I do think I remember, but so long ago, before—before everything. Before everything,' he repeated, slowly. His voice was soft as he searched his memory.

'I visited them once in München. We went to the park. The band was playing. Her father carried Ingeborg. A man was selling *Lakritz* on a—what do you say? A stall. Long loops. And Ingeborg asked, and her father bought her some and my sister was cross, she did not like her to eat trash, and Ingeborg laughed. She was a *fröhlich*, a merry child. Had she remembered that? Dear God,' he said heavily. 'Dear God.'

Herr Krause had turned away, his heavy shoulders shaken by sobs. Capricorn waited until he recovered and then asked gently, 'I know your wife is busy with the children, but if I could have just a few minutes . . . ?'

'She couldn't tell you any more than I have,' the lawyer said.

'Just to complete our records,' Capricorn replied.

Herr Krause nodded. He appreciated the necessity of complete records. 'I will go and see myself if she is free,' he said.

Perhaps he had intended Capricorn to wait, but instead he walked with Krause to the stairs and followed him to the second floor. A thin, nervous, sharp-featured woman in a cheap print dress and worn slippers, carrying a basin with water and a towel, emerged from a front room onto the landing as they came up. She frowned at her husband and spoke quickly, with a rather shrill voice, in German. She was scolding her husband for bringing a client to the private part of the house. Her expression did not soften when he, in a placating tone, introduced the tall sergeant and stated his business.

Frau Krause looked up at Capricorn with an impatient, hostile glance. 'I really have no time—obviously, I am busy. We have a child with measles.'

She turned to her husband and resumed speaking in German. 'The doctor has not come yet today. He should be here. You know how it will end. Hans and Viktor will catch it also. I am wearing myself out, trying to keep them apart. Why did you bring this man here? We know nothing of Ingeborg.'

'I am sorry to disturb you at this time,' Capricorn said. 'I can see how terribly inconvenient it is, and how distressed you must be. If you could just give me a moment, I promise you I won't delay you more than is necessary.'

Capricorn's voice was soothing. Frau Krause looked up at him, noticing for the first time that he was a very attractive young man. Her expression of taut crossness lifted and for a moment he could see a resemblance to the pretty young girl of the photograph.

'Let me get rid of this—' she disappeared for a moment into another room with the basin, and then returned and showed him into what was obviously the family sitting room, above Herr Krause's office. The size of the room and the view were similar, but the walls were bare and needed repainting, and the furniture was old and shabby without the distinction of having been handsome when it was new. The boys, about twelve and thirteen and already resembling Herr Krause by almost bursting from their clothes, were fighting on the sofa, their heavily shod feet tearing into the faded cover.

Frau Krause shrieked distractedly, and Herr Krause quietly separated them and with a hand on each of their collars, prepared to march them downstairs.

'I'll see they stay in the garden, *Liebchen*,' he said. 'Bad boys, you know you mustn't come up here while your brother is ill—I will leave you two to talk.'

He descended the stairs quietly for a man of his bulk and left his wife fingering her apron and staring at Capricorn in the room that was suddenly and blessedly quiet.

It felt stuffy. Frau Krause was sweating a little. The windows were shut tight.

'Would you like me to open the window for you?'

She nodded, and Capricorn went to the windows and flung them up. A wave of cooler air came in, freshened by the leaves of the birch. The garden, he noticed, had been planted with chrysanthemums, and a few of them had been put into a glass vase on the table by the sofa, and had been knocked over by the boys. The flowers lay in a pool of water, the petals soaked, giving the room a forlorn, slovenly look.

Frau Krause noticed the vase at the same moment as Capricorn, and her lips twitched. He felt that she was about to burst into tears or hysteria.

'Allow me,' he said, and picked the flowers up, shook them, and put them to rights in the vase, while Mrs Krause mopped the spilled water up with her apron. The tension seemed to ebb, and Capricorn quietly took her hand and helped her to seat herself on the sofa. He sat beside her and offered her a cigarette, which she accepted and he lit for her. After a minute or two, she smiled.

It would have been a pretty smile, but her teeth had been neglected and a gap at the side of her mouth gave her a look of being older than she was. Capricorn asked a few routine questions to begin with, to which he already knew the answers, about her arrival in England with her family and her husband's niece, and their experiences in the camp.

When she seemed to be answering steadily, and he could feel sure she wasn't about to plunge into hysterics, he went on to inquire if she knew anything about Ingeborg's life after she left the camp, and if she knew of any reasons, beyond her childhood experiences, why Ingeborg should be constantly nervous or terrified as Randy Clarke had said.

It was then she had answered that they were all nervous. 'It would be amazing if we weren't, after everything.'

It was certainly true that she herself was a very nervous woman. But on the other hand, Capricorn reflected, no one would have called her 'terrified'. Tired, worn, hysterical, but not terrified. Not even afraid. Resentful would be the adjective for Frau Krause. Life had turned out to be very different from her expectations, but she faced the world with anger, not fear.

'I asked your husband if he had any idea what Miss Rilke was doing, where she lived, how she supported herself, who her friends were, in the time after she left the camp until she went to the Brandenburg to stay with Mrs Roth.'

'She never went to stay with Lise Roth,' Frau Krause said scornfully. 'If my husband likes to pretend, he needn't expect me to make up fairy tales. I've known Lise Roth since she was first interned and I had heard about her long before. I can tell you that Lise does nothing for anyone unless there is something she will get from it for herself.'

She drew quickly on her cigarette.

'Lise was old Roth's mistress in Paris,' she spat the words out as if she were glad to have the opportunity to say them. 'And not only his, people said. He used her in his business. Some men you bribe with money; some with women. His wife in Berlin became disgusted. She divorced him and went to live with her grown sons in the Argentine. Lise married him only for money,' she said. 'Roth was a banker, you can be sure *they* got their money out in time. Lise is lucky. That kind of woman always is. The sons were angry because of her; at first they would not help when old Roth came out of the camp. But the mother died, and just this week they cabled; they had arranged papers. Lise will never want for anything. Even in the camps *she* always managed to get the little luxuries. But they tell Diener they are ruined because a woman like Lise Roth would always rather spend some man's money rather than her own. You know the type.'

Capricorn murmured something affirmative.

'But your niece. . . .'

'My husband's niece.' She flicked the ash from her cigarette with a quick, angry movement.

'On top of everything else I've been saddled with Ingeborg since she was a child. Well, everyone is sorry for a child who loses her parents, but I can tell you, Sergeant, that Ingeborg was always a silent, sly girl. I did my best when we were running all over Europe with no money and my husband having no work, but always my husband thought I was not kind to Ingeborg. How could he have got such an idea if the child did not put it in his head?'

How indeed, Capricorn thought, but remained quiet.

'Then I had her as well as my own children in the camp here. And Ingeborg was growing up. You ask how she supported herself. I should think it was obvious. She was a girl without morals. My husband refuses to know about it, but I tell you that when we left Vienna she was only ten years old and already I had reason to suspect. . . . When she left the camp she must have gone from one man to another, that's all. She couldn't work, there was nothing she could do. At the camp, there were classes started for the young ones, but Ingeborg was not interested. She preferred to sit and listen to the tales of someone like Lise Roth, nothing better than a prostitute in my opinion, who liked to talk of her days of grandeur in Paris, the little darling of the bankers, who would leave their wives at home when they went to visit Roth and his mistress, how she was the first woman to have a driving licence of her own, and how she drove her own little car, and how the couturiers all vied to dress the darling Lise Roth.'

Capricorn let her grumble on.

'You've heard that Ingeborg was a model,' Frau Krause continued, 'So you might think she was pretty but she was not. She was a very plain, awkward girl, and Lise Roth never helped her. Ingeborg was young, Lise would not want her to be pretty as well. So I can't tell you what Ingeborg did. She never bothered with us from the time she left the camp. But whatever she did, I know she had no success at anything until she met this Diener.'

Shouts and cries came from the boys in the garden below. Frau Krause jumped to the window and yelled, *'Seid ruhig!'*

'Ah, those boys! You wouldn't find Lise Roth tying herself down with a family. One child she had—and she would not have had her except she was in the camp when she knew she was pregnant and could do nothing. So, there were no men around, she let Ingeborg fetch and carry for her—Ingeborg who would not lift a hand for me and my family, after all we had done. When she was a child, at least, she helped, but when she got to be thirteen, fourteen, she was good for nothing, always in a corner dreaming, or listening to such as Lise Roth, no wonder she became what she did. Girls of that age, so ungrateful, thinking only of their pleasures. . . .'

She railed on, while the sun, already climbing down from its noon height, shone into the shabby room unkindly, showing up pockets of dust and patches of wear.

'You had not seen your husband's niece at all, then, since she left the camp?'

'Never. Nor did I expect to. I heard only, from my husband, that Lise Roth came across her, I don't know where, at Christmas or New Year, something like that. She was not well. Lise took her to the Brandenburg, he told me, and introduced her to Diener and they took up with each other. It makes no sense,' she said angrily. She brushed a lank curl from her cheek, leaving a smudge of cigarette ash. 'Lise Roth doesn't do favours, and a man like Franz Diener could have had anyone. What could he have seen in Ingeborg?'

Her eyes turned restlessly to a heap of old maga-

zines in the corner. The boys must have been playing
with them, they looked worn and ripped, but conspicuous on the top of the heap was the *La Belle* with
Ingeborg's thin face floating in the dead leaves.

He was wasting time, Capricorn thought. Frau
Krause had no facts to give him, only the anger of
prettiness faded and, she felt, slighted. It was amazing
that a girl could live in England for nearly two years
and so little be known about her by anyone. The photographers and models would only know of the last
few months, the school not long before. Yet she could
not have disappeared into a void. Only Lise Roth had
known her in that time, yet from her statement, she
claimed only to have seen her at about last Christmas.
He would have to inquire more about that meeting.

He thanked Frau Krause and bade her goodbye,
letting himself out, leaving her to a few moments of
rest on the faded sofa, her eyes following him with a
sudden look of a faded Cinderella who knows that
Prince Charming will never search for her and that
the clock has struck twelve on her glory for the last
time.

3

Capricorn came out into the dusty Brompton Road in a chastened mood. The London inquiries authorised by Snow had been fruitless. No fresh suspect had appeared. It was time to inform the Chief that Snow had intended to arrest Diener. If he did not, he was failing to carry out instructions. The Chief would learn of this failure as soon as Snow was well enough to talk. Capricorn knew that sergeants derelict in their duty had a short career in the Murder Squad. Certainly he should drive back now to the Yard.

Further down the street was an eating house of sorts. Leaving his car parked where it was, he went in and asked for lunch. The lunch, he was informed, was over. Teas would start in five minutes. If he would wait, the kitchen would see what it could do. While he waited, he made for a telephone booth in the corner and put through a call for his friend Manning, of the Special Branch. Manning might be able to dig up some more information on the Brandenburg crew. But Manning was out.

What the kitchen could do turned out to be a mixture of something trying to look like ham that wasn't, with an egg that had fallen into a factory and had something horrid happen to it, and chips. The chips weren't very crisp but at least they were real potatoes. He ate a piece of National bread and forgot the stuff cooling on his plate as he thought over what he had learned.

Something unexplained in the relationship between Ingeborg Rilke and Lise Roth. Frau Krause believed that Lise Roth was jealous of the younger woman's success. Capricorn dismissed the idea of Lise Roth as a suspect. Physically, she could not have committed that crime. It could have been a woman, but only a big, powerful woman, like Madame Braun. Madame Braun who ran the hotel and even butchered her own meat, according to report, to provide her continental guests with the cuts they were used to. No, Lise Roth would not take to violence. If necessary she might instigate someone else to do it. But the motive was too weak. Only in the fairy tale was 'mirror, mirror on the wall,' a cause for murder.

And there were the missing two years. Ingeborg's aunt and uncle assumed she had been a prostitute. But even a prostitute lives somewhere. And besides, England has laws against soliciting. If a girl as naive as Ingeborg Rilke had gone on the streets, surely in all that time she would have been arrested at least once. But she had no such police record.

He pushed his plate away, frowning. Unless she had been taken under the wing of a 'protector'. If that were the case, and if she had escaped from his clutches there might be a motive for murder. It had happened before. Even the sadism of the killing might be explained. But how could the man have entered the locked-up Brandenburg?

He lit a cigarette and gazed through the smoke, his gaze registering the scene outside the window without his conscious thought, a group of children with a

teacher, lady shoppers with parcels, a postman walking briskly, and a fairly steady stream of traffic. Lorries, vans, bicycles, big family cars and a light, open
sports car, blue, with a familiar figure at the wheel,
bright silver curls flashing in the sun, blue-striped
scarf flying briskly. For a moment he thought his imagination had conjured her up with her male companion, but then he realised that she must be going to see
Krause. She parked her car, and leaving her companion to read a newspaper, disappeared into the lawyer's
house.

Capricorn forgot about reporting to the Chief at the
Yard. He found himself curious about Lise Roth and
her doings and had a strong desire to ask her some
questions before the day was done. As long as he was
here, he might as well wait. He could watch her car
from the telephone booth.

He paid his bill and ensconced himself in the booth,
slipping in just ahead of an indignant matron with her
pennies in her palm. Keeping an eye on the blue car,
he called in turn each of the West End police stations.
A prostitute who was careful could avoid arrest, but
she was nearly always known to the local police. They
might not know her real name but they would know
her description and have an idea of the man who was
running the show.

He described her carefully, her timid manner, her
poor command of English. He explained that the girl
would not then have resembled the now famous *La
Belle* cover portrait. Uniform Branch was as helpful as
could be, but when Capricorn neared the end of his
list, he had had no luck at all. He tried a few areas
outside the West End, without much hope, and unsuc-
cessfully, while the man in the blue car turned the

pages of his newspaper fretfully, and outside the telephone booth a queue of women formed, orderly but resentful.

Each station had supported his belief that it was aware of the traffic in women in its vicinity; women of many nationalities, convicted and unconvicted, were known to them, but the name and description of Ingeborg Rilke drew a blank.

'The only ones we might *not* know,' he was told by one of the West End stations, 'are the telephone tarts. They work by appointment, and we only hear about it if something goes wrong and there's a ruckus. But they have to have money behind them. Expensive flats, nice clothes. Doesn't sound likely for your girl.'

Capricorn agreed. As he put the receiver down he became aware at the same time of the low hum of agitated women waiting for the telephone, and the figure of Lise Roth, blue earrings glinting in the sun, approaching her car.

He left as hastily as he could, but his way was obstructed by the members of the queue, who were nothing loath to detain him a few seconds with gently reproach.

'Not fair shares . . .'

'Or considerate of other people.'

Heads, hatted and unhatted, nodded towards him.

'Too late now for Jane to get the fish.'

He apologised and ran, but the blue car was already moving and he jumped in his own and followed. She went north to Knightsbridge, passed the Wellington Arch, bowled along Green Park down Piccadilly and drew up outside the Ritz. Capricorn, taking longer to find a place for his larger car, saw her chatting with her companion and disappearing inside. He recognised the man, lean, not too tall, with grizzled hair, as her visitor at the Brandenburg. Captain Fitz-Marley.

When Capricorn followed, he found them sitting by the fountain, ordering tea. He certainly had not found Mrs Roth in a clandestine meeting. She was very much at her ease, as pretty and as unselfconscious as a flower in a garden. Or was she?

Capricorn took a seat some distance away, thinking he would let the lady drink her tea before he asked her to answer his questions. Apparently she was listening to her companion who was very voluble, her head slightly bowed. But when the tea came, she leaned back in her chair, lifted her cup and behind that protection allowed her glance to meet his own.

She was not only aware of his presence, she seemed intrigued by it. Her round blue eyes flashed a message that said demurely her companion was a frightful bore, and wasn't she being kind? And how amusing it all was, not only to herself but to a kindred soul like Capricorn?

Her escort went on talking, gesticulating, pointing out various spots on his skull that seemed to have no particular interest—certainly not, Capricorn thought, to Lise Roth. After a few minutes the Captain rose. He said something to the lady and she shook her head, smiling, and gave him her hand. Before Fitz-Marley was out of sight, a waiter was at Capricorn's side.

'Sergeant Capricorn? Mrs Roth asks if you would like to join her at her table for tea.'

There was nothing at the moment that he would like better. He joined her at the table by the fountain observing how she commanded her surroundings. She was not only the prettiest woman in sight but with her beautifully cut coat of some fine, lightweight stuff and its matching skirt, rather long with graceful folds, she made other women with their skimpy dresses just covering their knees look awkward and old-fashioned.

'Have you been following me, Sergeant?' she asked demurely.

Her glance suggested that she thought the idea great fun. She was so frankly flirtatious that for a moment he was almost thrown off balance, not quite sure if he were being addressed as a man or a policeman.

'Not long,' he said. 'But I did want to ask you some questions, and it really must be today.'

'Oh!' She pouted prettily. 'And I had thought. . . . I am so tired of questions, Sergeant. Already I have answered over and over again and signed statements. And I must tell you that all this—' she waved her small, ringed hand, as if to wave away the death of her young friend, 'All this has made the Brandenburg so *düster*, all day, every day. Franz plays his gloomy records, my husband is unwell, the Brauns I think wish now we would all go away. Thérèse looks more and more like a gaoler.' She pulled a face. 'Even Otto only laughs a little, it is very bad for him, what happens to Franz.'

'He worked for Mr Diener before the war,' Capricorn recalled.

'Oh, but more than that. He was one of his chief designers, he designed a rocket—a very clever man. I think he would have become a partner.'

Surely, Capricorn thought, entranced for a moment, no one had ever said the word 'partner' more charmingly, with a soft exhalation on the 'r'.

'And Franz had offered him a partnership in the United States, because if Franz goes there the Custodian of Enemy Property will allow him to take his capital and he could start again. He talks of a new Diener works in a place called Gary, Indiana. Indiana!' she said, her eyes wide, as though contemplating redskins galloping over the plains.

Her attention went to the teapot. She regarded it thoughtfully, and shook her head. She nodded to the waiter to pour the tea. 'Too heavy,' she murmured. 'After everything, I have no strength.' She sighed deeply over the horrors of war.

'So, I was glad to have an excuse,' she resumed, 'to come to London. A little business about our visas, I saw Herr Krause for a few moments, and I brought the Captain, his car has broken down and he has a meeting tonight at the Phrenological—' she giggled. 'Is that right? The Phrenological Group. You know—' her hand twirled about her head, 'these bumps, they show he is a fine character. He shows me, every day. But I think, Sergeant, it is because he was in the cavalry. I think the bumps are where he fell off his horse.'

Her eyes shone in delight. Fitz-Marley must really bore her, he thought, for her to enjoy her little revenge so much. She accepted his company at the Brandenburg, most probably for lack of very much choice.

'He is an old friend of yours?' he asked, knowing better.

'Oh, no.' She looked shocked. 'You must understand, Sergeant, that Paul and I were always against the Nazis. Not that the poor Captain was a Nazi, but he was a Fascist, an English Fascist, you know?'

Capricorn knew.

'It is only, I think,' she said earnestly, 'that he is an eccentric. Like the head bumps. He has ideas.' She shook her head as though the world of ideas were a dangerous jungle.

'He says her family was once powerful, important, rich, descended from Normans. He thinks this very important, to be from *Normandie*. They owned much land, all of Illwood as well as Marley and other villages, houses.' She shrugged. 'And now, none of these things. Perhaps he thought to be a Fascist would make him rich again. And he would have people to work for him.'

Her lips dimpled at the corners and she looked mischievous again. 'Oh, it is funny—that castle. He uses a few rooms only and it is very *schäbig*, broken down, with only two very old people to look after everything. They were from his father or his grandfather, and one is deaf and one half-blind, they cannot go out and he has to get his own shopping in the village. He says it is too expensive to have the tradesmen come.'

She leaned forward and lowered her voice. 'I had this German friend from the camp, Olga de Lange, who is a great snob, she claims her husband was a French nobleman, a marquis, who was killed in the war. She met the Captain last year and thought it would be very chic to live with this great aristocrat in his castle.'

Giggling, she allowed the waiter to give her another eclair, which she attacked with dainty greed.

'What a disappointment! He took her nowhere, he only goes to meetings for men, you understand, and he gave her no money, not even for stockings, and she was shut up in the castle and he expected her to cook the dinner and help the servants.'

Her laughter shook her for a moment. 'Oh, how she complained when she left. How mean she said he was.'

'He might be really poor,' Capricorn remarked.

'Perhaps,' she agreed, pausing for another mouthful. 'He drives only a very old wagon—what do you say?—

an estate van? Always breaking down. The day before Ingeborg was—was—' she gave it up, 'his car broke down entirely outside the hotel and he had to have a taxi to take him home. But he still has horses, very fine, and a man for the horses. Not Lippizaner, but . . .' her free hand fluttered, in a gesture that denied comprehension of the economics of life for the English landed gentry.

'He is *not*,' she shook her head, 'the sort of man we would know. But it is you British made him a friend,' she complained. 'He was in the men's camp with poor Paul. In the same house. Franz and Otto were there also, this was in the beginning. Later they were not together. The Captain was very kind to Paul. One day Paul fell down, he had a heart attack and it was Captain Fitz-Marley who recognised it, and insisted a doctor come at once, and he saved Paul's life. So,' she said. 'What can one do? His ideas are foolish, this Norman business, what is it? But he was kind. And the Germans, the Nazis and the Fascists, they are *kaput*. They will not trouble us any more.'

'Your friend Franz doesn't think so,' Capricorn observed. 'He seems to believe, if I understand him, that they will join forces, or have joined forces with the Communists to rule the world.'

'Ah, poor Franz,' she said regretfully. 'He has had too much time alone, to think. He is a man born to be doing. He upsets himself, brooding, brooding. Before the war, I think, he did not get on with the old Junker generals. In England he felt free, until the Regulation. He was shocked. He had never believed it could be. Now it is over, but for Franz, he cannot forget. It is better to forget,' she said, and for that one moment, Capricorn believed, she spoke from the heart.

'I'm sorry to have to remind you of unpleasant

things,' he said gently. 'But what I principally wished to ask you, Mrs Roth, is what you know of Miss Rilke between the time she left the camp and the time you took her to the Brandenburg.'

She looked at him with wide eyes, blue and clear. 'But I know nothing. I have already told Superintendent Pritchard. Nothing at all.'

He realized when she answered, in spite of the stab of disappointment, that it was what he expected her to say. The tinkle of the fountain, the chatter of the female voices around him, seemed suddenly unfitting to the matter being discussed. The very comfort and elegance of the place, the natural milieu of Lise Roth, made his mental image of the ruined body of Ingeborg Rilke in its crust of blood darker and more terrible. It made no sense, he knew. Squalour bred more crime than luxury, yet it was here today the taste of evil was bitter on his tongue.

Imagination run wild could only carry him away from his job. He looked at the very lovely woman before him, so charming that he was mildly surprised to find himself not charmed. It was perhaps because he felt she lied. He had no reason for the feeling; he did not give much credence to the envious Frau Krause, but something about Lise Roth rang false. He was also very frustrated. A door had slammed across the last corridor that might have led to . . . what? A killer other than Diener. That was what he was looking for.

When frustrated, ask more questions. Capricorn kept his face expressionless as Snow would have done and went on with hardly a second's pause. 'You must have met her somewhere in order to take her to the hotel.'

'Oh, yes,' she said. She took out a cigarette case, a

very dainty affair of gold set with sapphires, tapped a cigarette and waited while Capricorn lit it for her.

'It was just before Christmas. I remember, it was chilly and wet and I had come to town in Franz's car. I was looking for presents and I went to Fortnum to look for a gingerbread house for my little daughter— she is away at school but they send her to me for Christmas. And I saw Ingeborg. Not in the shop, somewhere on the pavement, and I stopped the car. She looked very thin and pale and she told me she had been ill. So,' Lise Roth smiled at Capricorn, 'I asked her—after all it was Christmas—I invited her to come for the holidays.'

'Did you take her somewhere to pick up her things?'

'No,' she gazed into the smoke curling up from her cigarette. 'No, I don't think—no, I know that I did not. I left her in the motor where it was warm while I got my shopping and took her back with me. She didn't say she had to tell anyone, or collect her things. Ingeborg didn't say much at all. I gave her all things necessary—my nightgowns were too short but she didn't care. Madame Braun, I can tell you, she raised her eyebrows at her coming with no luggage. She didn't like to have her there. Thérèse Braun,' she confided, 'you know, she is much older than Braun and very jealous. Who can blame her? So big, so ugly. A Marseillaise. Did you know that at the beginning of the war Braun escaped as far as Marseilles? Thérèse had a hotel there and she took him in. So when the war ended,' she shrugged. 'Braun had nothing. His father had lost the little he had while he was interned. Thérèse's hotel made a good *dot*. Braun sold it and came here and bought the Brandenburg. Thérèse hates to have a young girl. Always she is suspicious of him.'

Capricorn remembered the dark woman who had watched from an upper window while her husband flirted with Lise Roth on the croquet lawn. 'Did she have cause,' he asked, 'as far as her husband and Miss Rilke were concerned?'

Lise Roth looked at him gravely. 'Well,' she dropped her voice, 'you know men. Poor Ingeborg, you must have found out, she was not a bad girl by nature, I don't think, but she had a strange life. It was her way. I believe she was afraid to refuse if she were asked. Naughty, it would have been very naughty of Heinrich Braun but of course, men are like that.' She put her head on one side, as if reviewing the historic depravity of the male, more in contemplation than anger.

'I don't believe you mentioned that to Superintendent Pritchard.'

'He did not ask,' she replied.

'But I believe you told Superintendent Pritchard that Miss Rilke was the mistress of Mr Diener.'

'He knew that already. He visited the hotel. Superintendent Pritchard and Franz were quite friends,' she said.

'Did Mr Diener know of Miss Rilke's association—'

'I don't know. In many ways, he is a great innocent. He had a mistress for, oh, many years, in that place, Cobleigh. His Lucy. He loved his Lucy. And he was amazed when, after he was interned, within two weeks she married another man. A Mr Weeks, of Cobleigh. Franz could not believe it. But Otto's wife, she has told me that in the town everyone but Franz knew that this girl was . . .' she waved her little hand again.

'During the time after Miss Rilke left the camp, which was about a month before you did, I believe, and the time you met her—on Piccadilly, was it?—you had not seen or heard from her at all.'

Herr Krause had said she did. Perhaps she thought of that possibility.

'Well, I believe I may have seen her, once or perhaps twice. Yes, I belive twice. Once when I was in my own car, it was new then and I was getting used to driving in your traffic, on the other side of the street, in town, near Oxford Circus, I think. I saw her on the pavement and stopped to talk, but I could not stop long, of course. She said hello, she was well. That is all. And once when I was coming towards Marble Arch, she was just standing there, on the corner. And I spoke, and I asked if she saw her family, because Herr Krause was worried about her. And she told me to tell him she was well. I think she was fond of him but she and her aunt did not . . .' her hand waved helplessly again.

'And that was the extent of the conversation? She gave you no address or any idea of what she was doing?'

'No,' Lise Roth shook her head. 'You would not know, but that was like Ingeborg. She was very silent and very—secretive, if that is the word I mean.'

'I see. The rest, I believe, is very well covered in your statement,' Capricorn said. 'There are just one or two more points and then I won't detain you. She became Mr Diener's mistress almost immediately?'

She sighed. 'You must remember, poor Franz, he had been in the men's camp and the prison so long. No women at all for more than six years. It might seem a strange choice, but she was alone and he was lonely.'

He had not thought Ingeborg Rilke a strange choice, though he remembered that her aunt had, and

Diener had denied indignantly that he was the girl's lover at all. Lise Roth seemed to think it needed more explanation because she continued.

'You never know what a man will like,' she said, meditatively. 'In Paris, I remember a young man of good family, rich, handsome, a real *parti*, but the only woman he could love was like an ape, hideous, covered all over with hair.'

'But Miss Rilke was an attractive girl,' Capricorn protested.

She gave him an odd little look that he couldn't understand.

'Franz was so kind to her, he made her into something one could not believe. But I will show you what she was.'

Still wearing that strange expression, she opened her handbag. It was a large affair for a small woman, made for travelling and holding documents, and as she searched he noticed she was carrying a copy of *The New Yorker* magazine. The cover caught his eye, as it was identical to the cover of *The New Yorker* Diener had been reading, although this was a fresher copy. It was an old issue and he wondered what it contained that had caught the interest of both Diener and Lise Roth. Then she produced a photograph from a little leather folder and he forgot about her literary tastes.

'This was taken of us all by Franz on New Year's Day.'

It was an ordinary holiday snapshot with a large Christmas tree in the background, Braun, overtopped by his dark wife, Lise and Paul Roth, like Beauty and the Beast, the inevitable Captain and a tall, stoop-shouldered maiden aunt in spectacles that even Capricorn didn't recognize for a moment as Ingeborg Rilke.

'It surprises you, yes?' she giggled. 'We women, we are very cunning. As you say in England, "A little bit of powder, a little bit of paint." '

Miss Rilke was not the only surprise. The photograph was an enlargement, but Capricorn knew the type of camera with which it had been taken. It was a very carefully made miniature widely used by spies and saboteurs during the war. Certainly, ordinary citizens might have come across one since, but what had the just released Diener been doing with it? Pritchard had made a search of his rooms, but no camera had been listed among the articles there.

'That was taken with Mr Diener's camera?' he asked casually.

Lise Roth looked at it and frowned, a sharp little frown that for a few seconds made her look to Capricorn as she did to Randy Clarke, a woman past her youth. Then her brow smoothed and the magic returned.

'I suppose so,' she said. 'I don't know anyone else who had one. Of course, all the Americans have cameras, he may have borrowed it.'

'I see. Now you've given a very full, very complete statement of what happened on the day and the evening before the murder. At tea-time a quarrel broke out between Miss Rilke and Mr Diener, when she told him she planned to leave the hotel, almost immediately, to live in London.'

She nodded.

'Miss Rilke did not change her mind. Your party, except for Captain Fitz-Marley who left for home, had dinner, went for a walk, and then had drinks on Mr Diener's porch. Nothing more was said about the sub-

ject of the quarrel that evening, the guests left one by
one, and you were the last to go, except for Miss
Rilke, whom you left sitting with Mr Diener.'

'Yes, that is true.'

'And Superintendent Pritchard asked you how Mr
Diener seemed that evening, and you said, if I remember rightly, rather silent and gloomy, except when he
was talking politics.'

'Yes,' she said. 'He is always excited when he talks
about the *Götterdämmerung*. But otherwise he was
quiet.'

'And he had quite a lot to drink.'

She hesitated. 'Well—he does often. He has little to
do.'

'Tell me quite frankly, Mrs Roth,' Capricorn asked.
'This is not evidence, and I am not going to write it
down and have you sign it, but I would like to know,
do you believe Mr Diener killed Ingeborg Rilke? Or
do you know of anyone else who might have committed the crime?'

She looked at him plaintively. 'Sergeant, this is not
fair. Franz is my friend. No,' she said warmly. 'I cannot, will not say such a thing.'

Thereby saying it, he thought, rather neatly.

'Is there anyone else you could think of that would
have a motive for killing Miss Rilke?'

'Someone else? But who could that be? Unless perhaps,' she said helpfully, 'it was some maniac, someone who just seized upon poor Ingeborg—she may
have gone for a walk—these things happen.'

'Yes. She might have gone for a walk in the hotel
grounds in her nightgown and no slippers,' Capricorn
said. 'But we can find no evidence of anyone breaking
into the hotel grounds that night.'

She gave another pretty sigh. 'It is all so dreadful,

Sergeant. It makes my head ache to think of it. And after all,' she said slowly, 'we can never bring Ingeborg back. If Franz did it, he must have been mad. Perhaps it is all the suffering has made him mad. He does not, really, these days seem quite. . . .'

She looked about her plaintively. Most of the tea-drinkers had gone or were preparing to go. Without a movement she managed to convey the impression that she was being brutally restrained.

'I'm so sorry, can I get you something for your headache?' Capricorn asked. 'I won't trouble you with any more questions now.'

She had begun to smile and shook her head in a gentle negative, but paused at the word 'now'.

'Oh, Sergeant, there is something I have to ask you.'

This time the little hand fluttered as far as his sleeve. Such a delicate hand, with its rosy, polished tips, one would hardly believe it had just tightened a noose around a man's neck, Capricorn thought, and that man her 'good friend'.

'What is it, Mrs Roth?'

'Well, my business today, I told you, about our visas, all is now complete. We can leave within a week, we could get passage on the *Paloma*, that is to say unless—Sergeant Capricorn,' never had his name been pronounced so prettily, except by his special friend, Rose, 'if you arrest—someone—we have been kept here so long, so many weary years, you wouldn't require us to stay for the trial, to be witnesses, would you?'

She looked up at him, her lovely blue eyes soft and moist, the dark flecks gleaming with earnest sincerity. So this was the reason she had been pleased to see him, the policeman noted with detachment. This was what her blandishing had been about. He thought for a moment of the granite-faced Snow with reluctant admiration; she wouldn't have tried it there. Mrs Roth, the very good friend of Mr Diener who had paid her bills and trusted her, did not want to be bothered with the annoyance of his trial. His good friend wished him to face it alone.

'I'm afraid I'm not the only one involved in that decision,' he said.

'Perhaps you will see if you can . . .' she gave him a smile that would have melted the determination of almost any man. 'Thank you for joining me. And now I must meet some friends.'

He escorted her to her car and watched her drive away, with a gay wave of her hand, perfectly composed. Swinging around, she made a U-turn. A constable on traffic duty looked admonishing, she smiled, he let her go. The life and way of Lise Roth, Capricorn thought. It certainly looked like death for Diener.

A Song Between the Acts

After Lise Roth was out of sight, Capricorn's feeling of disappointment slowly lifted. Good sense asserted itself. It was true he had discovered nothing but that in itself had meaning.

When The Great Capricornus had puzzled and astonished his audiences with meaningless flourishes, it had been done to conceal his quite ordinary, mundane and systematic actions. If his son now ran into blank walls it was because those walls were being erected for his benefit.

Randy Clarke had told the truth, but the Germans, he felt sure, were misleading him. Only Frau Krause had been willing to be frank, but she had known too little. The rest, together with Madame Braun, were hiding something. Lise Roth, who knew the most, was lying outrageously. But why?

He tried again to reach his friend Manning on the telephone, and this time was lucky and caught him at his desk, a place where he spent very little of his time. The Special Branch man was another wartime friend and like a lot of the men who had served together were often very helpful without going through official channels.

The perfect detective, Manning was called. Invisi-

ble Manning, not tall or short, fat or thin, his brown-
ish hair already turning grey, he had the gift of fading
into any background. Capricorn could picture him
now, at his desk, looking like a city clerk while Capricorn explained his problem. It was not so long, he recalled, since he had seen Manning in a prison cell
with a group of captured German SS men, indistin-
guishable from the rest, to their eventual undoing.

'So I would be glad,' he finished up, 'if you would
have an unofficial look-see and let me know what you
find out. I don't think MI5 is telling us all they know.'

'Do they ever?' Manning murmured in heartfelt
concurrence. 'I'll see what I can dig up. Like to know
where and when your playmate got that camera. But
about the murder, are you sure you're not looking for
a mystery where there isn't one?' He chuckled. 'Brilliant young sergeant solves case that baffled his superior? Having the war all over again?'

Capricorn's success as a very young man in SIS had
been notable. But war service made no difference to
promotion policies in the Metropolitan Police, and
Capricorn had had to resume his lowly rank, and accept some teasing at the hands of wartime colleagues.

'Seriously,' Manning urged, 'your Germans could be
close-mouthed from habit. Prisoners' dislike of authority, you've seen it often enough. If Diener is guilty,
they might not want to convict him. And yet the girl
was a friend. Rotten business. No wonder your pretty
lady wants to skip. And as far as the Rilke girl vanish-
ing for that time, it doesn't have to be a facer. You
said she was timid, if she was on the game she was
probably careful. Or she could have found a cosy bil-
let with a gentlemen friend. She might have left him
because Diener was cosier. Then when he has her

trained for a good job she leaves him. Seems an obvious type.'

Impossible, Capricorn thought, to convey the image of the girl that had built up, slowly, in his own mind. A waif tossed on the winds of war with terror in her eyes. Outwardly a woman, beautiful and gorgeously dressed, inwardly a child, frozen and numb. And the warmth of friendship and the glow of success building up at last to a moment where she dared remember that in a lost world long ago she had once liked—licorice.

Hardly a type. Yet to be fair, Manning could well be right. Nothing even to hint he wasn't except Capricorn's own conviction.

'You're obstinate, Merle,' his aunts said.

He thanked Manning, who promised to do what he could. Now the only thing left was to collect his things, go back to the Brandenburg and ask a lot more questions. By the next day, he promised himself, if nothing new developed, he would have to ask for the warrant for Diener.

On the way to Paddington he passed the square with the house that was to be his home. The windows of his flat were filthy and splashed with paint. There was no visible sign of work in progress.

Gloomy, he continued to Dolly's house. Someone had been about. The dustbin had been moved to the front with its load of gin and beer bottles. A tabby cat prowled around it with perfunctory interest.

When he entered, another row was in progress. The three remaining Merlino sisters were up, if not dressed. Nelly and Milly stood beneath their own photographs in the front hall while Dolly was at the top of the stairs. Nelly the sharp-featured was bundled in flannel, Milly the sweet-faced was draped in lace, but their expressions were identical. They stared up with amused contempt at Dolly's husband, the thin, dejected, tow-headed Tod who clutched his ukulele while Dolly shook him like a feather duster.

Dolly was short and squat but strong. Still, Capricorn had always known her to be kind, and wondered what enormity Tod could have committed to have aroused not only the quick-tempered Dolly, but also to have lost the sympathy of Nelly and Milly, who by no means always took their sister's part.

Dolly was also the most strong spoken of the three. 'You silly twit,' she hollered, or something like that.

Nelly and Milly made assenting sounds.

Capricorn's mind went to murder and mayhem, but that alone would not cause family disapproval—when his Aunt Tilly had actually sawn her husband in half in full view of a packed house on a Saturday night, it had been the unprofessional aspect that troubled her sisters, and poor Tilly had been forgiven when they found the incident increased their audiences rather than otherwise and they missed her when she had gone to live in the Home.

Tod was not protecting his person but was holding onto his ukulele as though it were a child in peril. Dolly caught sight of her nephew and released Tod suddenly so that he stumbled, and trod hard on Dolly's foot.

'Idiot,' she yelled as she hopped, and then gave Tod a sharp kick upon which he dropped his instrument, lost his footing entirely, and lurched down the stairs.

Capricorn rushed forward and broke his fall, catching him in his strong young arms. Thank heavens, Tod didn't seem much hurt, no bones were broken. He stood upright but sad and blinked his white-lashed eyes as he peered about.

'Where's my uke?' he muttered.

Dolly threw it down with a resounding clatter, and he snatched it up and made for the basement.

'Aunt Dolly,' Capricorn expostulated.

'It's no good, Merle,' Nelly, the calmest one, shook her head. 'It's hopeless.'

'Hopeless,' Milly agreed. 'He'll never be a Merlino.'

Their professional judgement was final. Tod, though he didn't know it, was not the first to be judged wanting. Other husbands and lovers of the Merlinos had had to be ejected on the grounds of lack of competence. There had been a charming man who forgot to code in the psychic act and got himself booed in Birmingham, and Samson the Strong, a fancy of Milly's, who proved to be allergic to rabbits.

Dolly was still muttering on the top step. 'Hopeless is right.'

'You might try a more gentle treatment,' Capricorn suggested.

'Do you know what he did?' she asked, her eyes flashing.

He grinned as she trundled beside him along the passage to his room, because certainly she would tell him. Milly was already tinkling at the piano, the mocking strains of 'you are my honey, honeysuckle, I am the bee,' wafting up the stairs. Nelly would forget the incident and go back to thinking of a new trick. But Dolly was his talkative aunt and he would have to hear her grievance. She kept up with his long stride, compact and inexorable as a tank.

Usually she was a warm and jolly woman, the most motherly of the Merlinos, certainly a peculiar-looking woman, though she had the ebullient self-confidence that turned her oddity to triumph. Her large face normally resembled a pink ham under her fringe of henna'd curls but today it was more the colour of well-done beef, a sign of great stress.

'After I went to all the trouble to get him an audition at the BBC. It took months,' she said passionately. 'And what does the silly sod do?'

'Tell me while I get my things together,' he suggested.

She flopped disconsolately on his bed.

'And he has the gall to come back and tell me, in front of Milly and Nelly, he got half way through his first song and he messes it up. So instead of going on and making the best of it, the stupid bugger stops dead and asks if he can have another chance. Of course, they got rid of him fast. I tell you, it's too much. I'll never make a professional of 'im. Never.' She cursed roundly, from her rich store of epithets, in slowly descending volume.

'Off again, Merle?' she asked when she had exhausted herself.

'Just a night or two.'

'Worse than being on tour,' she said absently. She pulled the garment she was wearing, something blue with stars and feathers, close around her. Even on a warm day the house was chill inside. 'Awfully sick of being on tour lately. No money in it anymore. Your father died at the right time; he would've been miserable now. I had this idea for settling the act in London. That television could be good for us. Nelly thinks so. Not much doing now, but when it gets going.'

Capricorn hadn't thought about it, but Dolly was a shrewd businesswoman. Home entertainment should have a future.

'So I thought to start I'd get Tod in on the wireless end. No good for the act, the wireless, but with a uke you don't need a picture. With that Tod,' she said malevolently. 'Better without. Would you believe. . . .'

'But did it warrant being kicked downstairs?' Capricorn asked, with the freedom of a grown nephew and a first class sergeant from C1.

Dolly shrugged. 'He made me look a fool. Milly and Nelly were right. All he's good for is a few tunes at get-togethers for the Party.'

'I meant to ask you about that,' Capricorn said, wondering if he should ask Dolly to try to get some washing done for him and dismissing the thought. 'It's a new interest for you, isn't it? Politics?'

'Oh, I'm not interested,' Dolly said, her attention wandering to the curls on her forehead. She fingered them lovingly. 'Between you and me, I think all that's terrible boring, really and they do go on. But Tod is very keen. And he says it's bound to come, it's historically inevitable.' She brought it out with a flourish.

'I see,' Capricorn said hastily. He didn't want Paddington's version of the *Götterdämmerung*.

'Well, if it's got to come, I s'pose we might as well be on the right side,' Dolly shrugged again and forgot Marxian dogma, her brow darkening with the remembrance of Tod's blunder.

Anger turned to melancholy. Capricorn was familiar with her changes of mood, but the subduing of her vital, fiery self to something like wistfulness was new to him.

'You haven't been in the business for a long time, Merle. Even before the war you were at that college. It's going downhill all the time. If the Merlinos don't get into television once it really catches on, I don't know how long the act can keep going. One hall after another closing. The Brit gone. They loved your father there. The London Music Hall.'

'Thought you'd gone into another business with all that racket last night,' Capricorn observed.

He took his pyjamas out of the orange crate. There was dust in the folds and he shook them thoroughly and thought of his own flat with a mixture of longing and despair.

'Oh, thanks for your note.'

'They called again today,' Dolly said absently. 'The painter had to be brought back to go over where they'd pulled out. Something about the plaster but I forget what. And the floor man back as well.'

He shuddered, and decided not to think about it.

'What was all the noise?'

'Oh, nothing,' Dolly said. 'There was a dust-up at Tod's meeting downstairs. One of them called another a deevy something.'

'Deevy?'

'Deviationist,' Dolly said. 'It don't mean anything dirty, but he was put out. Some furniture got knocked over.'

'I thought I heard a girl's voice.'

'That was just one of the girls brought a friend home. They had a few words. Soppy twit, that girl. Little blond Sylvie. Engaged to a nice American, she is, who went back to the States. No youngster, he was a major or something. And the mayor of some town in California. Promised her a brass band and everything when she gets there. But she forgets herself, Sylvie does, now and again and brings someone in. Tod don't like it,' she said, thoughtfully. 'Very straight-laced, the Party chairman. And the BBC is particular. It's not like the halls.'

'And what about the BBC and the Party?'

'Oh, that's all right. Lots of them like Tod there. Sympathizers,' she explained.

Capricorn wondered briefly if Diener would consider the young men of the BBC to be Hohenzollerns, or in fief to Hohenzollerns.

'But why was Sylvie shrieking?'

Another nasty thought struck him. Was Dolly's house 'known' to Paddington Uniform Branch? Perhaps he'd better find other temporary quarters. Scotland Yard was 'particular' too.

'Oh, the swine!' Dolly said, energetically. 'Her feller got up to nasty business.'

'Nasty business?'

'Chains and stuff. Oo, if I'd known it,' Dolly said, her red face shining with indignation, 'I would have had his guts for garters. Don't like that sort of thing. You see,' she went on, 'Tod was tenant of this house before I met him. No one wanted it during the war, and he got the lease for almost nothing. Naturally, we don't want a big old place like this all to ourselves, and so many girls about, doing war-work, had no homes. So I took a few in, and it was handy, they paid rent good as gold. And you know me, Merle,' she said briskly, 'I'm not one to tell people what to do. But nastiness I won't stand.'

Capricorn thought of Ingeborg Rilke.

'You're quite right,' he said, 'but if I were you I think I'd get a different sort of tenant. If you want to work for the BBC,' he added tactfully.

'By the way,' he said, as he started out, 'if I asked you to guess, what would a young girl have done to keep herself if she were thrown on her own resources, no money, no friends, at the end of the war? No training, poor command of English.'

'Well, Merle,' his aunt said her eyes wide. 'What do you think?'

He nodded. 'Yes, but there's no record of prostitution.'

'Prostitution!' Dolly said indignantly. She accompanied him to the stairs in her usual high spirits, her melancholy forgotten. 'Just like a man and a policeman. If a woman has anything to do with a man and her not married, right away it's prostitution. Merle, ever since the world began, if a woman is on her uppers, it's natural she'll move in with some man who'll give her a bit of a home for a while.'

Manning's theory again.

'Come to that, when ENSA was finished and the act had no bookings, Tod took me in. Milly and Nelly went with Mystico that season. Of course, it's not the same, me being a professional woman, but still. Tod turned the house over to me to do what I liked with and you know,' she said with a toss of her curls, 'we're not really married, me and Tod. I never did get a divorce from the Incredible Ivan. Don't even know what happened to him after he went to Australia.'

They both looked at the staircase down which the generous, if foolish, Tod had been so summarily thrown. Capricorn took himself off, thinking at such a moment domestic peace might be restored. As he walked by the area railings, he saw through the basement window Dolly and Tod sharing an afternoon tankard of ale. Dolly's voice of brass rose briskly upward.

'You are my honey, honeysuckle, I am the bee.'

ACT THREE

1

On his way back to the Brandenburg, Capricorn thought about Dolly's answer to his question. She had agreed with Manning, that astute policeman. Dolly was a vagabond by nature, and because of that she would probably understand the girl forced into a drifter's life. What was it Randy Clarke had said? Wherever you put Swanny, there she'd stay. But who had put her where?

He arrived at the hotel to find Braun not pleased to see him and Madame frankly hostile. Lise Roth had said she looked like a gaoler, he remembered, but Madame Braun was more ogreish than any woman he had met in the British prison system. Except for her finery—pearl necklace, gold brooch, well-cut black silk dress and high-heeled slippers—Thérèse could have been a guard in a concentration camp. Her thick make-up could not hide her pitted, swarthy complexion, but it gave her an odd, mask-like look.

The hotel was fully booked, she told him, except for the room that had been occupied by Miss Rilke. Capricorn, who had arranged to send the dead girl's things to the lab, took the room with rather ghoulish feelings. But already it was merely a hotel room like the rest, pleasant but impersonal, and only warmed by the smile of Nora, the young freckle-faced chambermaid, who brought in extra towels and another blanket with a conspiratorial air.

'Getting cool at night now, sir,' she said. 'It's really autumn already. Having a shoot over at Marley, they are, tomorrow. Just like before the war.'

Capricorn remembered that Nora was the postman's daughter and probably well informed on local affairs.

'At Marley Castle?' he asked.

'On the Captain's land, yes, sir. Very pleased the gentlemen are, to have a shoot again, my Dad says. A change from shooting Germans,' she giggled.

'There's no bad feeling over at Marley, then, about the Captain? His having been a supporter of Hitler?'

Nora's young face looked rather puzzled. 'The Fitz-Marley's have always been thought well of, sir, hereabouts. The old colonel was a magistrate and his son the Major what was killed at Dunkirk, he was a very nice gentleman. Mrs Fitz-Marley gave the prizes at Illwood school every year, I got a lovely hymn book once for being in the school play.' She was pensive at the thought of glory past, and sighed.

'And the Captain was only one of them Fascists before the war, sir. He resigned from the Army when it started, very proper, my Dad said. But they put him in prison just the same. His father was terrible upset and he died soon after. The whole school got the day off to go to the funeral, and we girls made up wreaths.'

Nora had removed the counterpane from his bed while she was talking, and tucked in the extra blanket neatly.

'There, that's done. And my Dad says it's a shame,' she added, 'because it's not like the Captain done anything wrong, not like that Lord Haw-Haw. People feel sorry for the family getting so poor and everything.

And Dad thinks the Nazis were no good, but he don't think much of the lot we've got now either. Says he hardly thinks it was worth while having the war at all, with what things have come to.'

Capricorn was interested in this expression of opinion from rural England. Fair enough, he supposed, not to blame a man for what he might have done in other circumstances. The war was over and Fitz-Marley had done no harm. And the postman was as dissatisfied as Diener with the postwar world.

The constable on duty watching Diener was seated on the porch outside his door. It was the same young fellow that Snow had suspected of dozing on his feet. He looked sleepy as Capricorn approached but sprang to his feet quickly.

'No, sir, he hasn't tried to go anywhere. He has two lawyer gentlemen inside with him.' He consulted his notebook. 'A Mr Upham and a foreign party, a Mr Krause. But he was talking to me before they came and carrying on very strange, sir.' He looked at Capricorn worriedly. 'I tried to get it all down, but he went too fast, sir. I did my best, see.'

He showed Capricorn his book, rather shamefaced, as he had broken three of the six cardinal rules for proper notebook keeping, perpetrating the sins of Erasure, Overwriting, and Writing Between Lines, and the handwriting, starting out as fairly neat, had soon broken down to total illegibility.

'He was going on terrible about Sir Stafford Cripps, sir. Couldn't make half of it out. Said the Fabe something had conspired against the middle classes, sir, and they had won. We were all going to be wiped out, he said, sir, but he mixed up a lot of German in it and it didn't make sense.'

Capricorn thought fleetingly that he was lucky to

have missed the lecture on the Fabian Society, its or-
ganizers the Webbs, and Mrs Webb's nephew, Sir
Stafford Cripps. He reassured the constable as best
he could, leaving the matter of the notebook to Pritchard, and told him to stay at his post.

At the reception desk he learned that Mrs Roth was
still in town and Mr Roth was not feeling well and
had ordered dinner sent up to his room. Capricorn
thought of his own dinner and made for the dining
room and asked for a table. The flurried waitress disappeared and came back with a grim Madame Braun
who looked as though she would have liked to say:
'Sergeants are not served in the dining room of the
Brandenburg.'

However, she contented herself with saying, 'There
is no table free.' Feeling some explanation was necessary, she added, 'Miss Rilke sat at Mr Diener's table.'

She paused. As Capricorn did not fade away she
went on reluctantly, 'You'll have to set up a single table, Carry. I'll send one in. You can put it there.' She
indicated a spot by the serving pantry.

'Perhaps Sergeant Capricorn will take pity on me
and join me at our table, Madame.'

Otto Karl, smiling and gracious, had entered and
stood behind her.

'All that dazzle of white, so depressing.' He regarded ruefully the largest table in the room, apparently the principal one, set in an alcove facing the garden. The flower arrangement was taller and more
striking than elsewhere, the wine glasses made a more
dazzling display and there was no clutter of napkin
rings on the fresh linen. A special serving cart stood
beside it with an array of wine and brandy bottles, an
ice bucket and a syphon of soda water. Diener's table,
of course.

'I hate to eat here alone,' Karl confided, pulling a chair out for Capricorn. 'If nobody else is eating, I'm almost driven to a tray in my room.'

Madame Braun had retreated with an air about her suggesting she would return to fight another day.

'I'm much too frightened of Thérèse to demand a different place.' He grinned at his companion.

For the moment, it was a civilized interlude. The dining room was spacious and pleasant, the lamps were lit with the curtains left undrawn to a vista of lawns and trees coolly green in the soft evening light. The two men ate companionably. The food was good, extremely good for the times, and Capricorn's policeman's mind noted that Braun must have dealings with the black market. Well, he wasn't here for that. Karl told stories of his early days with Diener and how and why they had come to England.

As he chatted, Capricorn's mind ticked over what he had learned of Otto Karl. A man with much leisure since he had been released, many prolonged stays at the Brandenburg with Diener in the absence of his wife, a man fond of women and not above having an affair with Randy Clarke. Had he been attracted, Capricorn wondered, to Ingeborg Rilke, a girl afraid to refuse the attentions of a predatory male? Could such a situation have become embarrassing?

Capricorn regarded the man before him, darkly handsome, intelligent, humorous. The thought of Karl as a sadistic murderer seemed a sick fantasy, yet there had been more unlikely cases. Otto Karl came and went in Diener's rooms. Even if he had had no key to the porch, assuming it had been locked, a lock of that sort would hardly be a barrier to a man who was a mechanical-design genius. True, he had left the group on the porch to telephone his wife and the telephone call had been verified by Pritchard. But there was only his word that he had stayed in his room after that.

Karl insisted on filling his glass with an exceedingly good hock from the private supply. The man was doing his best to entertain him, Capricorn thought wryly, with a twinge of distaste for himself and his profession.

'Franz's ideas were totally different from anything that had been done before,' Karl was explaining. 'He revolutionized weapon-making. He took the American method of assembly lines, that Ford had developed for cars, and adapted it for our use. It seemed impossible at first. I was one of Franz's first designers and I thought he was crazy.'

He smiled at the lack of vision of his younger self, and Capricorn admired his detachment. Yet while Karl went on elucidating the technical principles behind the Diener works, Capricorn had to consider that Karl had been released over a year before Diener, about the same time as the Roths and Ingeborg Rilke. In his statement, he had mentioned visiting the Roths at the Brandenburg long before Diener was free. If Lise Roth had been in touch with the girl then, she might well have introduced her to the amorous Karl. And if he had been keeping the girl, with his wife in England, it would not be anywhere conspicuous.

Karl was not a rich man. Capricorn knew from Pritchard's investigation that Karl's earnings before the war had been large but his family's expenses during his imprisonment had eaten away his acquisitions. Possibly he would have been glad to let Lise Roth dispose of a passive and not too attractive mistress to their rich friend. Could her sudden metamorphosis have reawakened a passion?

'But you're not eating.' Karl's lazy, amused voice cut across his thoughts. 'You look as gloomy as Franz. Are you searching for suspects, Sergeant?'

Capricorn cursed himself silently but roundly. His face was too expressive; he had not yet acquired the perfect poker face of a good CID man. Superintendent Snow had commented on this deficiency. If a man like Karl had done murder, Capricorn thought grimly, he would have the sense to cover up extremely well. He would not be caught by a detective who let his thoughts be open to any onlooker.

'It's a puzzling case,' he answered frankly.

Karl, with a tact that Capricorn appreciated, went back to his tales of the Diener works in Germany. 'You should have seen Franz with the old Junker generals. You've heard his theory about the Hohenzollerns, I'm sure. No one escapes. I think that's when his aversion to Prussians started. He talked to them about his new designs and methods. They stared through their monocles, clung to their beautiful white gloves, and their lovely black and silver sabre knots. Their duelling scars showed up livid and they decided he was worse than the *verdammt* Reds.

'They felt much safer with Krupp. The Krupps understood them. What did it matter that in the war to come the war would be lost on the Eastern Front because of Krupp's fancy monsters? *"Der Elefant,"* ' he said in disgust, crushing a roll and scowling at it. 'Supertanks, 180 tons. The land monitor, 1,000 tons—they never got that into combat. The Russians outmanoeuvred them while they were stuck in the mud. Perhaps Krupp was surprised by mud in a Russian spring. Franz sounds crazy but he is right. Krupp by then was practically a branch of the government. Government money supports bad design. It almost never fails.'

Capricorn, in spite of himself, was interested in tank battles. 'It wasn't only the mud,' he suggested. 'The German tanks were outfought at Kursk in July. Yet the Russian tanks, certainly, were "government money."'

Karl looked at him with a wry expression. 'The Russians had good fighting tanks,' he admitted, 'But they were based on the American Christie—the Americans kindly sold them models. And American engineers built the plants that produced them. The entire Stalingrad plant was built in the United States, dismantled, shipped and re-erected at Stalingrad under the supervision of American engineers. The Soviets tried to duplicate it themselves at Chelyabinsk, failed and had to call in John Calder and other American engineers.' He sighed. 'We've been very clever. Germany lost to the Russians, but you'll see, all of Europe will pay.'

'So,' he said, with a change of mood, taking a pudding plate from the waitress and smiling at her, 'That is how Franz and I, two young men, came to England. Those were lively days, when we started in the Midlands. We made a success, and Franz perfected his art of making enemies. You can imagine what the local gentry thought of him with his high wages for his men, his flashy American cars, his flashier mistress— oh, that Lucy! And the parties, how we loved those parties, then.'

He laughed. 'The noiser, the wilder, the drunker, the better. What it was to be young!' He helped himself to hock and soda water. 'And this is all I'm good for now. The next stage is domestic fidelity, I suppose.'

His frankness amused Capricorn.

'His workmen were fond of Franz,' Karl went on. 'He was the kind of rich man they would like to have been, not stuffy like the solid burghers of the Midlands. But of course, his men were not on the boards and tribunals that judged us.'

He shrugged. 'But who lost the most? Franz almost went mad with imprisonment, but I settled down on the Isle of Man. We had concerts; there was time to read. Do you know,' he said idly, in his off-hand manner, 'that I was working on rockets when I was arrested? There was no one close to what I was doing. In Germany they were years behind me. Just think, the launching ground for rockets might have been Lowestoft instead of Peenemünde. '42 instead of '45. The war over, perhaps before England had ruined herself. Who can say? Now the Americans want me to go over and work with Von Braun. Life is amusing.'

'Do you plan to go?' Capricorn asked.

'My wife is English. She wants to stay here. Franz wants me to go to Indiana. He is getting his visa. I think this consultation with Krause tonight means it has arrived. He will go, unless you keep him here, Sergeant.'

He did not phrase it as a question, but there was a query in his voice.

'The inquiry is still in an early stage,' Capricorn said. 'For instance, we've found out nothing as yet about Miss Rilke's life from the time she left the camp until she came here. It's important to clear this up.'

Otto Karl's expression was still genial, yet once again Capricorn felt as if a door had closed tight.

'You should ask Franz about that,' Karl said. 'He should be able to tell you. Ingeborg talked to him.'

'I had hoped you would tell me,' Capricorn said deliberately.

Karl looked unhappy and uncomfortable. 'I *know* nothing,' he said. 'But I repeat, you should talk to Franz about it.'

Capricorn began to lose his temper. 'I have talked to him. So has Superintendent Snow. Superintendent Pritchard questioned him extensively and took his signed statement on everything that Mr Diener said. Mr Diener apparently would rather be hanged than tell us what he knows.'

'But you surely cant—' Karl broke off, frowning. He threw his napkin down on the table. 'Franz is a fool,' he said.

'You've said that before,' Capricorn pointed out, remembering the conversation in Diener's rooms. 'But it doesn't help the inquiry.'

Karl looked up slowly. For a moment Capricorn thought he was about to speak and then Madame Braun came to their table. Irritated as Capricorn was at the interruption, he could not help observing her cat-like tread, unusual for such a big woman, and think of Lise Roth's scandal about Ingeborg Rilke and Braun. Madame Braun, jealous enough of her husband to spy on Lise Roth, what had she thought of the Rilke affair, if the scandal were true, or believed to be true? She was another one with access to Diener's porch; she kept the key.

'Captain Fitz-Marley is here,' she said in her low, controlled voice. 'Shall I show him in?'

She needn't have troubled to ask as Fitz-Marley was on her heels. He walked into the room as if he owned it and flung himself into an empty chair without waiting for an invitation.

'Where's Diener?' he said. 'And Roth? You've finished dinner? I was going to join you.'

He looked at the table disconsolately. 'Is dinner over?' he demanded of Madame Braun.

She nodded. 'I can have them make you an omelette.'

'Never mind, never mind,' he said fretfully. 'Send me a sandwich. I'll have it in the bar.'

'Let us take our coffee there also,' Karl suggested to Capricorn, with his usual pleasant manner. 'I thought it was your meeting tonight, Captain.'

'And so it was,' Fitz-Marley said, furious. In the lamplight his entire person, neat and trim, appeared to have been polished. Physically he was certainly a shining character, Capricorn observed, everything about him shone, glistened or gleamed, from his well-brushed hair to his boots.

'I left Mrs Roth halfway through tea because it was scheduled so early, and when I arrived I found they had cancelled it and not let me know. The secretary said she had telephoned everyone she could. Acted as though I was supposed to install a telephone at Marley expressly for her benefit. Used to have a man in that post and it was handled properly. I shall get that woman removed if it's the last thing I do. Scandalous.'

He paused but he was by no means finished. 'Mrs Roth had gone on and I had to find my own way back by train. Impossible these days. The service is a disgrace. Nothing to High Marley until eight o'clock so I caught the six o'clock Illwood local. Thought I'd find Diener and dine with him.'

'He's with Upham and Krause. They've a lot to talk about, and they're having a bite in his rooms,' Karl explained.

'Damned lawyers. Think they run the whole show,' Fitz-Marley muttered, to no particular point, but expressing his general sense of grievance.

They settled down in the bar and food arrived for the Captain while Karl had brandy and Capricorn coffee.

'You're the policeman, aren't you?' Fitz-Marley suddenly swung his head and took notice of him. 'You were here about the murder. Still at it?'

'Yes, sir,' Capricorn replied.

'Huh!' Fitz-Marley was silent after the ejaculation' but his expression suggested that he thought poorly of Capricorn's efforts.

After he had eaten half a sandwich he expressed himself further. 'Should think you'd get on with it. Bad business, a thing like that, and no arrest. Upsets people. Braun was telling me. Guests nervous. Lady Cecily talks of moving to the Dorchester. After all, the war's over. People don't need to stay in these country hotels any more.'

'We'll certainly make the arrest,' Capricorn said silkily, 'as soon as we're sure we have the right man.'

Fitz-Marley glared like a senior officer at a subordinate who ventured a jocular remark. His father had been a colonel, his brother a major. Capricorn wondered how far Fitz-Marley would have risen in the Army had it not been for his unfortunate political choice. Fascism, phrenology—surely a nineteenth-century fad? Perhaps he had been too eccentric for the army in any event. Dotty like Aunt Tilly.

'I was going to ask Diener to send me home,' Fitz-Marley had simmered down to a grumble. 'My motor's still in the garage down in the village. Needs a new transmission and they've got the impudence to tell me that model isn't made any more. Want to sell me another car.'

'I'm sure Franz would be happy to do it,' Karl said, rising. 'He certainly won't be going anywhere this evening. He'll probably want to send Upham and Krause back to London later on, though, so suppose I have a word with his driver now.'

'Oh, all right,' Fitz-Marley grumbled. 'I suppose these lawyer-Johnnies' convenience has to come before everybody's. Braun,' he hollered to the owner who was mixing drinks behind the bar. 'A brandy.'

He gave Capricorn a look, apparently decided a policeman wasn't worth conversation and finished his meal in silence.

'I had wanted to ask you a few questions,' Capricorn said pleasantly. 'Perhaps you would rather I came over to Marley tomorrow?'

'Questions? What questions?' Fitz-Marley said, bristling. 'I've answered all the questions. That Pritchard fellow. Signed a paper for him. Don't know anything about the business. Stupid girl. Bad type. Told Diener not to get mixed up with her. Just the kind to get herself in trouble. Told Lise Roth, too. Agrees with me, but doesn't like to say so. Sensible woman as a rule, Lise Roth, but too soft-hearted.'

To that Capricorn could find nothing to say, but repeated; 'Perhaps I might call tomorrow and take another statement?'

'Shoot tomorrow,' Fitz-Marley said. 'Small affair, just seven or eight guns. You're coming, aren't you, Karl?'

Karl had just returned followed by a ginger-haired young man in chauffeur's uniform.

'Why not?' Karl shrugged. 'But I'm hopelessly out of practice. I can still build you any weapon from mace and chain on, but for using them—I ought to work at a range for a while. Franz should be there, but I suppose if he picked up a gun, the whole Home Office would be down on our necks.'

He smiled at Capricorn as if to take any sting out of his words. He was not the sort of man to brood over his wrongs, Capricorn thought, and that made him a bad candidate for murder. Unlike Diener.

'Luncheon at one in the house. Come then if you must,' he turned to Capricorn, 'you, whatever your name is. You'll have to be quick about it. Can't give you much time.'

Capricorn wondered for a moment how Snow would react to this somewhat cavalier treatment of Scotland Yard. Snow in his way was quite as conscious of his position as Fitz-Marley. But as Capricorn wasn't in charge of the case, and actually had no authority to question Fitz-Marley at all had he but known it, Capricorn agreed quietly to be at the castle shortly after one.

The chauffeur announced himself ready to drive the Captain home.

'Saw your van down in the garage today,' he added. 'You're in luck, sir. Bill told me they've found you a pretty good transmission they took off a wreck.'

'You can wait,' Fitz-Marley said, and signalled Braun to fill his glass. His eyebrows shot up as the chauffeur took a seat, and his face was a picture of disgust when Karl asked the man what he would like to drink, and brought him a glass of ale.

Capricorn watched him, remembering what he had said in his statement. Thomas Price, of Illwood. Right now Price seemed quite willing to make an extra journey even for the ungracious Fitz-Marley. Probably the driver to a man as restricted as Diener found himself rather bored and glad to spend a little time with the mechanics in the local garage.

Before her death he had done a good bit of driving for Ingeborg Rilke, but all the journeys he had listed

had been to places the police already knew. Randy
Clarke's, the hairdresser, the shops, the model agency,
Kenyon's studio. Quite a good-looking young fellow
for a woman that liked ginger hair. Could he perhaps. . . . No. Ingeborg Rilke had been murdered on
his night off and Pritchard had placed him carefully
in the house of a Price uncle on Clapham Common,
where young Thomas had driven his mother and two
sisters in Diener's car for an overnight visit after he
had taken Fitz-Marley home.

'The old van runs like new,' Price went on with en-
thusiasm, not at all put out by the Captain's snubs.
'Save you a packet, that will.'

Nora had said, 'The Fitz-Marleys have always been
thought well of, hereabouts.' Local loyalty apparently
went deep. Maybe they thought of the peppery Captain as merely an odd cull from a fine stock.

'What nonsense are you babbling?' Fitz-Marley said,
and with the briefest of goodnights to Otto Karl, departed.

Karl pulled a face. 'He's a man you can't like,' he
said resignedly. 'But one can't help feeling sorry for
him. Franz, especially. They became quite close on
the Isle of Man. I expect he does a lot of economizing
now, but he hates anyone to know. Virtually no servants and tries to keep up that great barracks of a
place. Probably has to clean those boots himself, but
he's still going to give a shoot tomorrow. Been hard
up for a long time, the Fitz-Marleys and of course
now—I suppose when the Captain dies the place will
have to be sold.'

Capricorn, so long homeless, could find sympathy
for a man desperately trying to keep his home. 'Any
children?' he asked.

'No,' Karl replied. 'From what I gather from our

Lise, who is the fount of all knowledge about such things, I believe the Captain's loves are tempestuous and temporary rather than domestic.'

As the evening wore on and Karl mellowed with brandy, Capricorn managed to steer the conversation back to Diener, but without much enlightenment. Karl had known Mrs Diener, a very proper German *Hausfrau*, who had loathed Great Britain and refused to live in Cobleigh or the country estate that her young and newly rich husband had bought for her. She had continued to live in Germany, and young Franz had been duly enrolled in the Hitler Youth and had later been killed on the Russian front. She and her husband still corresponded but she had no desire to leave Germany. The subject of divorce had never been mentioned and Karl did not believe it would be.

Karl was more forthright than Mrs Roth and told Capricorn that he could not believe his friend would kill anyone, much less a creature like Ingeborg Rilke. He would be willing, eager in fact, to swear to that in court. But as to who might have been the killer, or what the motive could be, he offered nothing.

The two men went for a stroll before bedtime along the green paths of the Brandenburg in the last of the twilight. Capricorn stopped by the ditch in which the victim's body had lain, but he could draw no response from Karl except regret and sorrow. Instead he began to speak of his experiences as an internee—merely to change the subject, Capricorn believed, as Karl was not given to self-pity.

He asked why, as the husband of a British subject, Karl had not sought naturalization. Karl shrugged.

'One did, of course, once it was obvious that war was coming. Before that, simply carelessness, I suppose. You are a young man,' he smiled at Capricorn.

'You will never know our world. It is not so long since one could travel around Europe without a passport. Papers did not have the importance they do now. One should have thought about it, even in the first war there was trouble for Germans in England, but I applied, like Franz, too late.'

He fell silent, and soon afterwards went to his room. Capricorn walked for a long time in the cool, autumnal air. He had often found that problems resolved themselves if he let his mind idle while his body was occupied, but at the end of his walk he knew that too many pieces were still missing.

He passed the entrance on the sun porch that led to Diener's rooms and noticed it was open. There was no constable on duty; Diener must have gone to speed his parting guests and the policeman with him. On an impulse he tried the inner door and it was unlocked.

The room looked much the same as when he had last seen it. The lamps were lit and the fumes of brandy, mingled with cigarette smoke, filled the room. Only the magazine was gone from the hearth. It had been neatly placed in a rack, possibly by the chambermaid, but although it was an old issue, it was still on top of the pile.

Capricorn remembered that this issue had interested Lise Roth enough for her to take a copy on her visit to Herr Krause. Curious, he picked it up and flipped through the pages, wondering what the common denominator of their attention was. An article on affairs interesting only to the inhabitants of New York and its environs, a lot of rather dry, subtle jokes whose import seemed a world away from war-weary England. What. . . .

And then he saw it. As was the way of *The New*

Yorker, it had no splashy headline; it was sandwiched in among advertisements of goods that seemed improbably luxurious, and the very distinguished author's name was only at the end of the article far back in the book. The knowledge of what interested all the Germans, and the import of why they were interested, hit him simultaneously, though the evidence of one by no means established the second, or even explained it.

Yet if ever he felt sure of something, he felt sure of this. Behind the seemingly absurd behaviour of all these people in the face of a capital charge was a threat that to them was greater. How or why he didn't know.

He went to his room and went to bed but before he fell asleep he picked the magazine up again. Lord Haw-Haw. William Joyce. The trial, Joyce's story, the weighing of the evidence, the verdict. The verdict of guilty. Joyce was a traitor within the meaning of the treason statues. Joyce was hanged.

But why should the Germans be concerned? Capricorn puzzled over it after he switched off his lamp. They had been imprisoned during the war. There was no way the prisoners could have committed hostile acts, as even young Nora had pointed out referring to Captain Fitz-Marley. And in the case of the Germans, whatever they could have done had they been free would not have been treachery; they were not British. But neither was Joyce, he remembered, just as sleep closed in. Joyce had been born in Brooklyn. That had been the great question at his trial. Neither was Joyce.

2

Young Nora had been right. Capricorn awoke to a crisp, clear day. Autumn had arrived. His night had not been as restful as it might have been. He had managed to clear his mind, with an effort, from his new crop of puzzles but the Brandenburg had proved almost as noisy as Dolly's.

At about one in the morning he had been startled by the hooting of a car in the road, calls and laughter. At last the gates clanked as they were opened; grumbles floated up from the night porter, also woken from a sound sleep. Terrible Thérèse would be after him in the morning.

Then the hubbub had reached Capricorn's floor. Bottles chinked, a girl giggled, a young man loudly told her to hush. Finally a thud as a door closed down the corridor. The Hon. Charles Lawdon had retired for the night, not unaccompanied. Capricorn had smiled into his pillow, for a moment a young man in sympathy with another, and then the policeman noted the closeness of Lawdon's room to Ingeborg Rilke's. Lawdon had claimed in his statement to be hardly aware of her, yet she was attractive, and he was a bored, idle and reckless young man.

Capricorn was getting into his dressing gown and slippers when his tea and toast were brought in by

Mrs Dermott herself. In her own way she was quite as formidable as Thérèse Braun, without the height and bulk, the mask-like face, the pearls and gold. The housekeeper was gaunt and starched, innocent of make-up and in complete disregard of modern fashions in hairdressing. Yet her dignity was impressive and there was something in her cool grey gaze warning that she would give nothing away.

He tried the smile that had once charmed female audiences, but saw no softening of her expression as he bade her good morning, thanked her for his tea, and asked whether she had brought early morning tea to Miss Rilke.

'Sometimes ah did,' she said shortly. 'Sometimes young Nora.'

'And was it always . . . up here?' he asked.

'Always.'

'And was she always alone?'

'She was. And so she was when young Nora came up,' she added. 'Because if she had not it would have been all over the hotel in an hour. Jibber jabbering,' she said in great disapproval. 'All that girl is good for.'

'And Mr Diener, you bring his tea as well.'

'Ah do. Every day.'

'And Nora does on your day off?'

'I take it on my day off. It's no trouble. I live in the hotel and don't go out until after breakfast.'

'And is Mr Diener usually alone?'

'Always,' she said firmly.

Capricorn had two more questions to ask. They had to be asked, although he never liked this part of an investigation.

'Mrs Dermott,' he said, going straight to the point. 'You are in charge of the linens. You take care of Mr Diener's room personally six days a week, and I believe you said in your statement that you often took care of Miss Rilke's.'

She nodded.

'You are in a position to know whether, although no one but the proper persons were in their beds in the mornings, they had had—shall we say visitors?—during the night.'

'Whether it would be day or night I'd have no way of knowing,' she said coldly, deciding to take his words literally.

'But both Miss Rilke and Mr Diener at various times, obviously had had—visitors?'

'Ah don't have to answer such things,' she said angrily. 'I wouldn't know.'

'I believe you do know,' Capricorn said gently. 'And I'm afraid you must answer. We could be more formal, of course, and go down to Illwood station and you could sign another statement there.' He had an idea that Mrs Dermott would feel it rather disgraceful to go to the police station.

She stood motionless for about a minute and then nodded, frowning.

'And can you tell me how often, and when?'

'With Miss Rilke, not often. About once a month.'

'Could you say when?'

'Ah could.' She looked at him with great disfavour. 'Do I have to be talking about such?'

'It might not be necessary to put it in a formal statement. Even if we do, we will only use it if its absolutely necessary. We don't try to make scandal for its own sake. But the young woman was murdered and we must make the inquiries.'

'It was every fourth Monday,' Mrs Dermott brought out. 'When Madame goes up to London to get her hair dyed.'

She regarded Capricorn with a certain grim amusement as he took this in. So Lise Roth's gossip was true. Did Madame know, he wondered.

'And Mr Diener? When was he visited?'

She frowned. She was not as willing to discuss this. He fancied she would not bring his tea again. Although perhaps she had only done it this time to avoid his talking to the 'jibber-jabbering' Nora.

He waited patiently.

Mrs Dermott gave him a black look but his silent waiting had its effect.

'Almost every day,' she said reluctantly. 'Until—oh, about a month ago. Since then not so often.'

'And the last time?'

'I can't tell you,' she said, her cheeks red. 'I don't go looking for such things.'

'I'm sure you don't,' Capricorn said. 'Just as I'm sure you wouldn't make a point of remembering. But sometimes you couldn't help noticing, of course. Was it recently?'

'Ah suppose.'

Nora had been on duty the night of the murder, but Mrs Dermott was back on duty the next day.

'And the day after Miss Rilke was killed?'

'Ah'll no be answering any more of such stuff,' she burst out, her face red from neck to chin. 'You can take me into the court but there's no law can make me say I noticed any such thing or not. I've been a decent woman all my days and working now because my man was killed at Alamein.' Her sharp gaze was suddenly blurred with moisture.

Capricorn felt like a clumsy fool. Her indignation alone answered the question. Diener had not spent that night alone. It seemed that he had lied after all.

'I'm sorry to have put you through this,' he said

slowly. 'It doesn't mean that Mr Diener wasn't a decent sort of man. Only a natural one.'

And very likely an unnatural murderer, he thought. He began to feel as angry with Diener as if he had worked hard to be deceptive, but in truth, Capricorn knew ruefully, he himself had jumped to the conclusion of Diener's innocence. The truth made him angrier still.

'He's a natural man all right,' she said grimly. 'And a fule, like most men. *He* would always be careful not to embarrass a lady, even if she wasn't a lady.'

And with that obscure remark she left with a decided slam of the door.

Now, what was all that about, Capricorn wondered, gloomily drinking his tea, now quite cold. She spoke as though Diener's chivalry was a disadvantage to him. Yet she was not stupid. She must know that the proof that Ingeborg Rilke had been his mistress would injure his cause. The fact that the affair had seemed to cool off in the last month certainly bolstered the case that Pritchard had already built against him. The girl was tiring of Diener and had decided to leave. They had spent one last night together and then. . . .

What was Mrs Dermott thinking of? A lady that wasn't a lady, certainly that's what she would consider that poor, morally broken girl. The wretched Braun, he thought tangentially, with a disgusted twist of his lips. He stared out of the window without seeing, the bright day holding no promise, left with a disquieting, perhaps unreasonable notion that the loyal housekeeper was still withholding something.

He was about to leave the room, with his towel over his arm, when the telephone rang. His spirits lifted; it was Manning.

'Overnight service,' Manning said, cordially. 'We do

our best for Murder Squad. Ask and it shall be given. . . .'

'All right,' Capricorn said. 'Our policemen are wonderful. What have you got?'

'I wasn't *given* anything by our friends, you understand,' Manning went on cheerfully, not to be hurried. 'But I did run into someone I know who owed me a favour. He's going to dig some more. But he did tell me, right off the bat, that not all your little flock are as innocent as they claim.'

'Diener?' Capricorn asked, gloomy again.

'Nothing about him as yet. But my friend knew of Paul Roth, for one. He had been quite a name in banking circles and on the Bourse in the thirties. And he was very helpful to the Fascist and Nazi movements at home and abroad. Done a lot of business, put a lot of credit their way. But apparently, as the Germans came physically closer, he got cold feet for some reason we don't know. Or perhaps he just felt the Argentine would be more healthy during the war. Took his girl friend and ran. Married her aboard ship. The navy took them off, but only as German nationals. Nothing was known then about Roth's activities. By the way, my friend knows an interesting story about the patronne of your inn, Madame Braun. Her parents and Mademoiselle Thérèse were known collaborators.'

'Not so interesting,' Capricorn said with a shrug. 'So were millions of others.'

'Don't be so quick,' Manning chided. 'They'd also been sheltering young Braun since the beginning of the war. He worked in the hotel. Nobody had bothered him, he was unfit for the army in any case. But in the spring of '45 when the Germans were desperate for men two Gestapo agents came around inquiring

for Braun. They found Thérèse at home, and told her
Braun was British born, which she knew already, but
made her very nervous. That was their mistake because she shot them where they stood, chopped up the
bodies and buried them in the courtyard, all while
Braun was hiding in the town.'

'And she got away with it?' Capricorn asked.

'Oh, no. She was arrested and would have gone to
the guillotine, but by that time the war was over. Instead she was released from gaol and General De
Gaulle presented her with a *medaille de la résistance*.'
Manning was amused.

'Did she by any chance have a grudge against your
girl? A dangerous enemy, Thérèse Braun.'

'She might have had,' Capricorn said slowly.

There was cause for a grudge. And Madame could
have killed the girl. She had her key to Diener's
porch: access to the murder weapon. It would be easy
for her to lure the girl from her room on some pretext.
Yet he would have thought that as a jealous wife,
Madame would be more incensed against Lise Roth,
who certainly dazzled her husband, than Ingeborg
Rilke, that pathetic prey, who was herself trying to
escape from the whole sorry mess.

As for Roth's activities before the war, they made
no difference to Capricorn's case. That was the business of Other Departments who had obviously lost interest: the Roths were going to the Argentine. Was
that why the group was so interested in the Joyce
case? He couldn't see why it would cause them much
concern, let alone lead them to lie about a murder.
Whatever Roth had done, it could not be considered
treachery, even under the broad concept which had
convicted Joyce. Roth had never lived in Great Britain
or a British possession voluntarily; he had never

applied for a British passport. He owed no loyalty to the King. And he could not be considered to have endangered the realm; he had done nothing in wartime except be an unwilling prisoner.

Still, Lise Roth was extremely nervous. Surely she was not so fond of her aging husband as to be concerned for him, and she could not be held responsible for his activities. But perhaps she thought she could. After all there had been at least one notable case, now he thought of it, where a wife had been imprisoned along with her husband under Regulation 18b that Lise Roth knew so well. And of course, without Roth there would be no comfortable home in the Argentine for her, arranged by the sons of his first marriage. It was not certain that her marriage, to the divorced Roth, would even be recognized.

'Einfluss,' Diener had said. 'We have had too much influence.'

'Never say that,' Lise Roth had answered.

What could they have meant?

'Keep digging, won't you?' Capricorn asked, after he thanked Manning for his trouble.

'You wouldn't care to say—for what? About who?' Manning asked cheerfully.

'No,' Capricorn said. 'Just see if there is anything else—interesting.'

It sounded as lame as it was. In the clear light of morning it seemed to Capricorn that he had been suffering from too much imagination, just as Snow would have said. At the thought of Snow he winced. He must, in decency, go and visit Snow today. And he could conjecture the questions Snow would ask if he was well enough. Capricorn had a feeling Snow would be well enough.

'Nothing is too much trouble for our heroes of the

war,' Manning said and hung up quickly, before Capricorn could reply.

The telephone rang again almost immediately, with a far less welcome caller, the plastering firm who had done the work on his flat. The electricians had made a complete shambles, it seemed, when they pulled the plaster to adjust the wiring they'd put in wrong in the first place. The painter and the floor finisher were in and waiting. Would Capricorn authorize the plasterers' overtime? It might save him expense in the long run.

Capricorn agreed recklessly. He would have no money for furniture this year or even next, but what did it mater? The flat would never be finished. He would be at Dolly's forever.

As he bathed, his mind went back to the forthcoming visit to Snow. Yes, Snow was right. Too much imagination. Last night he had been wondering about the jovial Otto Karl. Then Charles Lawdon. This morning, Thérèse Braun. Running off in all directions, Snow would call it, instead of substantiating the case against the obvious suspect. Diener.

Capricorn sighed. At least the Brandenburg was well supplied with hot water, thick bath towels and a decent sort of soap. A world away from his last lodging. He wondered how it had seemed to Ingeborg Rilke when she had arrived . . . from where?

After a quick breakfast in the almost empty dining room, Capricorn inquired for Diener's chauffeur. He learned that Price slept at his family's house down in the village and brought Diener's Rolls up when he was called. It was kept in Illwood's garage and petrol station, and there he was usually to be found.

Capricorn drove his car to the garage to be filled with petrol. It was a pleasant place, with flower beds laid out neatly, golden chrysanthemums nodding against the pumps. Young Price was there, polishing the Rolls. Already it shone with a flawless brilliance and Price, obviously bored, was very willing to stop and talk. Capricorn took him through the matters in the statement Pritchard had taken, and there was nothing that Price wished to change or add.

'By the way,' Capricorn said, 'Mr Diener told me that Miss Rilke had asked for your help in moving her things. Of course, she didn't move, but had she spoken to you about it?'

'Yes, sir,' Price said, 'but not to move all her things. It was the afternoon before she was killed, sir. I was just going down to my tea. She said, would I take a suitcase over to Miss Clarke's in Burlinwood Square. Miss Clarke didn't have much room,' he explained. 'She said she'd send for her other things later on.'

'Take a suitcase?' Capricorn asked. 'She didn't say, drive her with a suitcase?'

'No, sir.' Price was quite definite. 'In fact, she said she'd leave it in her room, sir. It sounded to me like she thought she'd be somewhere else, but she didn't say.'

It struck Capricorn as important enough for them to go down to Pritchard's office and make another statement. Before Price signed, Capricorn tried his memory again, to be sure the young man had driven Miss Rilke nowhere except the places he had already listed. He obviously made an honest try, but he could be of no further help. If Ingeborg Rilke had had any secret rendezvous, she had not let Diener's chauffeur know about it.

The two men chatted as they came out into the bright cool sunlight.

'The Captain was that put out missing Mr Diener

last night,' Price said. 'Carried on all the way over to High Marley, he did. Gets lonely, if you ask me, stuck up in that great pile of old stones. Nothing to listen to except the wind off the river.'

'He seemed a bit terse,' Capricorn observed.

'Oh, his bark's worse than his bite,' Price said tolerantly. 'Always snap, snap, snap. Nobody takes any notice. His father and his brother now, fine set-up gentlemen they were, and quiet as you please. And the Captain like a little monkey next to them, fussing away. Now he doesn't like to let on he's poor. Hates anyone to know he doesn't have a houseful of servants, but there's only old Mr and Mrs Herne up there that can hardly totter about any more. Mrs Terne in bed most of the time, they say, and poor old Herne, he's blind as a bat. Most of the farm's had to be let for years now,' he added thoughtfully.

Capricorn, mindful that he had to get over to High Marley, bade the fortunately loquacious Price goodbye. Mrs Dermott's tight-lipped quality, so admirable in a household, made for a poor witness. Though if he himself ever had a housekeeper, he thought, remembering his flat with a sigh, he would like to have one with such discretion.

Ingeborg Rilke had intended to be somewhere other than the Brandenburg on the morning after the conspicuous quarrel. Or she had intended it as least until four o'clock when she had spoken to Price. But where? She had no modelling assignment that day: Pritchard had made certain of that. Her known friends were at the Brandenburg except for Randy Clarke, who had been travelling. That silent, secretive girl, had she intended to slip away, quietly, on foot to meet some unknown person in the lane?

No enlightenment had come to him by the time he

drove into High Marley. The hospital was in what was called the 'new town': row after row of small, cheaply built houses and a parade of shops, thrown up for the workers at the Marley Cannery. No longer did the orchards in the valley of the Dea have to send their fruit to London; it was tinned on the spot, adding to the wealth of the town, which was displayed in the clean, modern hospital where Superintendent Snow was recovering.

The sister graciously waived the visiting regulations in favour of Scotland Yard, and Capricorn was allowed to stand at his chief's bedside. Snow was sleeping when he entered, and Capricorn's first thought was that the Super looked better than usual, although it was only twenty-four hours, or thereabouts, since he had undergone surgery. His face was still pink but the usually taut line had relaxed. Probably this had been the most rest, if it could be called rest, that Snow had had in years.

His nurse explained that he was still under the influence of a strong drug, but that he might wake up. He did indeed awaken, his blue gaze somewhat dimmed but uncomfortable enough for all that.

'Did you arrest Diener?' he asked, not wasting time or breath in answer to Capricorn's commiserations over his health.

'Not yet, sir,' Capricorn replied feeling as guilty as the boy who had stolen an afternoon, when he should have been practicing his escape from a coffin, to read ancient history with the vicar of Chuffield while hoping to catch a glimpse of his daughter Rose. 'Diener's under surveillance, as I've been clearing up the London end of the inquiry.'

'Then get on with it,' Snow said coldly, and closed his eyes again.

'I expect he'll sleep a little more now,' the nurse said tactfully and led him away.

There were times, Capricorn thought grimly, when you might as well admit you've run into a blind alley. Either he went ahead and made the arrest, or very likely forfeited his rank and his place in the Murder Squad. He had found no other likely suspect, unless he considered the terrible Thérèse, and there was nothing to mitigate the case against Diener. The sum total of Capricorn's efforts so far had only made that case more damning.

The wind was sharp outside the hospital. Lorries thundered along the main road from the cannery to London; housewives bustled in and out of the shops: the new town was busy, clean and ugly. He had come here not only to visit Snow, he remembered, but for his appointment with Fitz-Marley. He might as well get that over and there would be time enough for the warrant. The thought of arresting the man that even now he could not believe guilty gave him a sick feeling, which he tried angrily to ignore. Emotion in a policeman was out of place.

As he came to the old town his eyes, at least, were refreshed. It was really no more than a village, smaller than Illwood, lying at the foot of the incline which rose to a high bluff crowned by Marley Castle. The wheat had been cut and to the east there were fields of stubble as far as the eye could see. To the west the bronze woods sloped down gently towards Illwood village.

The Captain and his guests had a good day for their shoot. The sky was blue and clear except for a few small white clouds bobbing along in a light wind. The narrow road up to the castle was full of ruts and Capricorn left his car in a meadow just beyond a fine old church and walked.

The sheer animal pleasure in the air and exercise on such a day lifted Capricorn's spirits and dulled his forebodings about the outcome of his case. Beyond a hedgerow a few fields had been left fallow. Pale blue succory, scarlet pimpernel and poppy had sprung up gaily. An English scene and English weather at their best. For a moment Capricorn envied the Captain his possessions and the leisure to enjoy them.

Of the castle itself, there was nothing left but the square Norman keep. Built originally, no doubt, to guard the bluff over the river Dea when Marley was a port, and remarkably little done to it since. This was no crenellated manor; not here the grace of Herstmonceux, the confident airiness of Oxburgh Hall. Marley had a hostile air as though marksmen still stood behind the apertures prepared to fight off enemies by land or water.

Capricorn thought for a moment of the wonder of the builders of Marley Castle could they be confronted with modern weapons of war. Rockets, for instance, and his mind slid back to Otto Karl, that would-be builder of rockets. Otto Karl, a guest on today's shoot. Otto Karl, who had been the last person, apart from the murderer, to use that bag of clubs, from which the murder weapon had been taken. Otto Karl, unfaithful husband. Otto Karl, who, Capricorn would swear, *knew* that Diener had not killed Ingeborg Rilke.

If Diener believed Karl to be guilty, Capricorn mused as he strode along, that might account for his silence. And that of the other Germans. But what of the Englishman? What did he know? Pritchard had learned nothing from him. Was it possible to do better with the eccentric, excitable little man?

As Capricorn arrived at the castle, his moment's envy of Fitz-Marley's possessions faded. He could find no entrance except for a door locked, bolted and barred, which looked so old and disused it was doubtful whether the hinges would have worked. There was no bell or knocker of any kind. The walls showed whitish signs of damp; the footpaths were overgrown with weeds. The only structure in sight that looked at all cared for was the stabling.

Capricorn looked at his watch. It was well past one; the shooting party would be at lunch. It was safe enough to make his way around the castle to the cliff side, although his vision would be partly obscured by the stables and the woods. No one would be out with a gun for almost another hour.

Despite the briskness of the day, the heavy oak door on the northerly side stood open, perhaps to save work for the feeble old servant. There was no bell here either, so Capricorn entered to find himself in a long hall, hung about with weapons, that also served as a dining room. Two fireplaces sent out moderate amounts of warmth. Fitz-Marley and his guests, fresh-faced men who looked as though they might be neighbouring landowners, together with the urbane Otto Karl, were helping themselves to cold food and drink from a sideboard.

Otto Karl gave Capricorn a friendly smile and greeting. Fitz-Marley looked up, stared, and looked away again as though he hadn't seen him—quite a feat, Capricorn considered, being six feet four and broad to match. A small, white-haired old man wearing spectacles with lenses about an eighth of an inch thick, tottered over to Capricorn, peered upward hopelessly, and asked his business. Capricorn pre-

sented his card and said he was there to see Captain
Fitz-Marley by appointment.

His card was duly presented to the Captain who,
without looking up, barked, 'We're at luncheon, dam-
mit! I don't have time for the fellow now.'

The manservant stood waiting meekly.

'Oh, well, take him into the library. Let him cool his
heels there.'

Capricorn, realizing he was supposed to be deaf as
well as invisible, allowed himself to be led past the
luncheon party through the length of the hall, into a
small slice of a room to one side. It appeared to have
been partitioned off with no particular rhyme or reason, the great height of the room bearing no relation
to the few feet of floor space, the only window just
below the ceiling and to one side giving little light. To
make up for this the room was whitewashed, which
added to the feeling of damp chill. An oil stove stood
in the corner but had not been lit.

The manservant, who must be the Herne that Price
had talked of, indicated a wooden bench and disappeared. Capricorn, who foresaw a long wait, ignored
the bench and looked around his prison. More weapons. Museum pieces, pikes and swords, continental
guns with decorated stocks, modern shotguns, rifles.
The old Colonel had been a collector, Capricorn remembered. He evidently had not parted with his
treasures, as most people had done, in '39 and '40.

The room was hardly a library. A large wooden
desk, a straight chair, a few shelves of books. The
heaps of papers and forms on the desk indicated its
use as an estate room. The Captain was certainly obli-
vious to comfort. Capricorn wondered if there was
any heat in the castle apart from fires and decided

there probably wasn't. The unused rooms were falling into damp and decay.

He looked at the few books on the shelves. Catalogues from agricultural fairs. Stud books. Hawker's *Instructions to Young Sportsmen in the Art of Shooting*, old, worn and falling to pieces. Some new books on phrenology. Where had that interest come from, Capricorn wondered. Had the Captain so little left to be proud of he had to admire the shape of his head, as Lise Roth had suggested?

The most elaborate volume, calf bound with gold tooling, was titled *L'Histoire de la Famille Fitzmallaux*. Capricorn examined it. The print was grotesque; the pages were illuminated, but the book was obviously of modern manufacture. Included was a portrait of a Norman knight, presumably the Fitzmallaux who had fought at Hastings, carrying a shield of arms, though no such shield was ever borne by the Conqueror and his companions.

Capricorn felt an odd stab of something like pity for the Captain, a man who was of historic lineage, and yet obsessed enough to cherish this spurious relic. But the sense of pathos soon vanished as he looked at the rest of the collection. Translations of the works of German National Socialists, *Mein Kampf*, of course, Rosenberg, Streicher.

No English Fascists were represented. There was Gobineau, but not Houston Stewart Chamberlain. Had Fitz-Marley quarrelled with them, he wondered. Or had his allegiance been personal to Hitler? Certainly, a man of the Captain's vanity would wish to be second to no one in England. Yet he was not of a calibre to lead. An odd man out.

But not a harmless one. Finished with the book

shelves, Capricorn's attention had gone to the desk. Not all the piles of papers were forms dealing with the estate. There were stacks of leaflets of which Streicher himself would have been proud, together with a printing bill from a Dublin firm. The Captain had not retired from his activities now that the war was over; he had not changed his vision since Dachau was exposed.

After about half an hour, the Captain appeared, gleaming and glistening as usual, his colour rather higher, whether from the exercise or the refreshment Capricorn couldn't guess.

'Well, what is it, what is it?' he said irritably.

Capricorn was reminded irresistibly of Arthur Lloyd, an old actor friend of his father's, who specialized in portraying irascible country gentlemen. The Captain's performance outdid Lloyd's. Could this peevish crank ever have been dangerous?

'I won't detain you long, sir,' he murmured. 'Just a few questions in addition to the statement you have already made. You gave Superintendent Pritchard an account of your visit to Mrs Roth at the Brandenburg at tea-time, on the day before Miss Rilke was killed. You arrived at about 4:15, after having trouble with the motor of your estate van.'

'Broke down entirely in the drive,' the Captain scowled. 'Had to be towed to the garage. Just came out three weeks before. Believe that fellow in Illwood uses defective parts. Told him so.'

'And you told Superintendent Pritchard that you had tea on the terrace with Mr and Mrs Roth, Mr Karl, Mr Diener and Miss Rilke.'

'Had tea with the Roths. The Rilke girl was there, hanging about as usual. Karl and Diener were there, they always hang about the women, both of them.

Karl has a wife but he never brings her.' He sounded disgusted, whether at Karl's married state, or his travelling without his wife, was not clear.

'And you described the quarrel that took place between Mr Diener and Miss Rilke.'

'Rotten scene. Very embarrassing for Mrs Roth. Diener's a fool. Flauntin' his affairs like that in front of a decent woman. Should've been glad to get rid of the girl. Sly. A thief, too, in my opinion.'

'A thief?' Capricorn said, startled.

Fitz-Marley snorted. 'Almost as soon as Mrs Roth took her to the Brandenburg, her mink coat was stolen. No signs of any break in. Don't believe it was any of Braun's people. Braun's very careful of who he has on the place. Never turned up. My opinion was, the girl stole it and sold it.'

'What did the police investigation show?'

'Mrs Roth wouldn't report it. No insurance either. But I can't say I blame her. Police not what they were. The Roths have seen enough of them. But Diener knew the girl did it. Bought Mrs Roth another coat himself. Roth told me he would never have let her accept it but as long as the Rilke girl was Diener's mistress it seemed fair enough.'

'Capricorn was surprised that he had heard none of this before, but he persisted in the line of questions he had come to ask. 'And you left before dinner. Do you know the exact time?'

'Of course not,' Fitz-Marley said. 'Why should I? But I know it was early. Had expected Diener to ask me to stay for drinks and to dine, but I had to have his car to take me home and it didn't suit the convenience of his man to leave later. His evening off, or some such nonsense, so I had to be driven back before we'd had a damned whiskey and soda. Wouldn't have a man like that Price work for me. Does almost nothing, and talks. Attend to your driving, I told him. My housekeeper was in bed that day, too.' He glowered over his grievances.

'The only other question I wanted to ask you,' Capricorn said, 'was whether you had ever met or known anything about Miss Rilke before Mrs Roth brought her to the Brandenburg at some time near Christmas last?'

'Of course I hadn't. Why would I have known about her? Stupid girl. Don't know why Mrs Roth had to bring her down at all. Thief. Trouble maker. Women too sentimental.'

'And Mrs Roth never mentioned where she brought her from in London?'

'Don't know where she picked her up. Or care.'

Fitz-Marley took his half-hunter from his pocket. 'Got to get back to my guests. Can't be here all day.'

'There doesn't seem to be anything to add to the statement you've already given,' Capricorn said. 'Unless something develops on this matter of the fur coat. If it does, I may ask you to make a written statement as to what you know about that.'

'Me? Statement? *I* don't know anything about it,' Fitz-Marley said, turning purple. 'Ask Mrs Roth. *She* won't tell you. Had enough of our British police and British justice. A fine woman, never committed any crime, put in gaol with half the rubbish of Europe, and poor old Roth, sent out to exercise with a heart ready to go at any minute, a totally innocent man. . . .'

Exasperated, Capricorn was moved to rejoin, 'Mr Roth was certainly involved in supporting the Nazi movement in Germany from his bank in Paris.'

Fitz-Marley's colour grew deeper. 'How do you

know what he did in Paris? Are you a policeman or a bloody spy?'

He's got you there, Capricorn thought uncomfortably. He had just broken a rule of procedure of the CID: never give a witness information. And worse, he had compromised Manning.

Fitz-Marley's small eyes looked for a moment uncommonly sharp. The trouble with eccentrics, Capricorn thought ruefully, is that they seem quite mad, but the madness is often confined to one area and they are sane enough elsewhere.

'Didn't let you in here to discuss your view on politics and banking on the continent before the war,' Fitz-Marley went on acidly. 'I'll have a word with the Chief Constable about this.'

Fitz-Marley had him on the run, and Capricorn knew it. Neither the Chief Constable nor the Yard would appreciate his blunder. As for Superintendent Snow . . . Capricorn suppressed a shudder. As politely as he could he thanked Fitz-Marley for the information he had given, and said he hoped he wouldn't have to trouble him again. That at least, he reflected, was sincere.

He passed the luncheon guests, now rather somnolent in chairs around the fires. One of the guests, a little flushed with liquor, was telling a dirty story. Otto Karl rose and walked with him to the door.

'I hope that Scotland Yard isn't interested in my shooting,' he said, in mock alarm. 'I assure you, Sergeant, I'm not dangerous these days even to partridges. The Captain despairs of me.'

The storyteller had come to the point, and there was a gust of laughter from the fireplace. As Capricorn was leaving, the old manservant came over hurriedly.

'The Captain said to go by way of the woods, sir. I don't know if the gentlemen will be going out again, but they've been walking up the fields on the village side and if they do go they'll be shooting the north fields towards the river, so you'll be safe on the woods path.'

There was another burst of laughter; the previous story had been capped. Capricorn thanked Herne. The party didn't appear eager for more vigorous exercise but it was better to take no chance. The Captain had looked ready to take a pot shot himself, but Capricorn remembered, with a sinking feeling, that Fitz-Marley had better methods of taking revenge. And he would take them. He was not a man to forgive or forget; he would prosecute the matter to the end.

The visit had been worse than useless. Capricorn had made an enemy without learning anything of significance. The only new piece of information was the theft of the coat. Odd that that had never come up; surely it was nothing to do with Ingeborg Rilke. The Roths wanted no contact with the British police and Diener was generous enough to buy his friend a coat. Old Roth probably used the story that Diener was making amends to save face.

As Capricorn passed the stables, well-cared-for structures with neatly mown strips of grass, he thought they had the look of fancy toys set down next to a ruin. Glancing back at the castle in all its chill, disrepair, and general gloom, he speculated for a moment on how much the place explained Fitz-Marley. Previous owners of Marley had been lords in their own domain, their allegiance sometimes given to the reigning king and sometimes withheld. Taking money from foreign princes was not unknown. A Fitz-Marley

had befriended the Young Pretender. Had some an-
cestor supported the usurping Henry Tudor? Capricorn's knowledge of the family was scant, but he rather
fancied that was so.

This Fitz-Marley could not have given aid or comfort to a foreign power in time of war; he had been
interned and cut off from any means of communicat-
ing. But with this history Capricorn could see that he,
the heir of a landowning family who had lived on
their own land for centuries, could look upon the wartime Cabinet as newcomers; the man whose descent
from the breed of the Conqueror was more direct than
His Majesty's might well feel, however mistaken he
might be, that he himself represented England more
than Crown or Parliament.

Capricorn shook himself from his disconsolate
thoughts and walked on. Fitz-Marley was quite capable of bringing action against him for trespass if he
found him lingering on the castle land. A good thing
the party was still at luncheon, and the north fields
quiet except for the cry of a bird. To the south the
field path was brighter, warmer and more pleasant
today than the woods, but he had had his instructions
and moodily set off down the leaf-strewn path.

It was cool here, as cool as it had been in the 'library' of the castle. Although leaves crunched under-
foot and were being swept along by a crisp breeze,
there were still plenty overhead. The dense branches
hung low and made a sombre canopy. There were ruts
along the path, some wide and deep and full of rotting
leaves, that brought unpleasantly to mind the ditch at
the Brandenburg, stained with the blood of Ingeborg
Rilke.

The path through the wood was more winding, and

it seemed to take longer to walk back to his car than it had done to walk to the castle, although he was now moving downhill. The sportsmen had, after all, roused themselves and gone out again: he could hear the crack of the guns coming from the north fields. They had lost their weather: a cloud moved over the sun, and low dark cumulus massed in the west.

He forgot them, as he realistically assessed his fate as a sergeant who had ignored instructions from his superior, behaved improperly and was the subject of a complaint by a civilian. Dismissal from the Murder Squad. Banishment from the Yard to a desk in the CID of some quiet suburban station. He began to see himself as Snow must see him, an obstinate, pig-headed young fool, wasting the Yard's time and the taxpayer's money, because the obvious, to him, was always suspect. The magician's apprentice.

He was making so much noise himself in the leaves, against the staccato sound of the guns, that when he first thought he heard a footstep, he dismissed it as fancy. But some part of his mind not swallowed up in dejection and self-reproach remained aware and a few seconds later he stopped. He could have sworn he heard a step.

It struck him as odd. There was no human habitation between the church and the river except Marley Castle, and the master and guests of Marley were walking up the north fields eastward. Had someone become suspicious of his interest in the stables and followed him? There must be a groom about. Or was his imagination playing tricks?

He paused in the shelter of a stout beech and looked back cautiously. The sun was still clouded, the woods dark. He saw no one. Imagination. He shrugged. A bad conscience was making him nervous.

He would go back to the Brandenburg and do his duty though it was probably too late to save his neck now.

The church was already in view beyond the woods when he heard a sound again. He wheeled about swiftly, his war-trained senses causing him to bend and duck his head without thought. For a moment the sun came out and light pierced through the branches. Something glistened about twenty-five yards off. Light flashed; a report sounded; a light blow struck his left shoulder as he tripped on a twig and fell, his head striking hard against the trunk of the beech. The woods were black as he went down, down into the cold, damp earth.

3

The first thing he saw when he opened his eyes in the ambulance was the pleasant, concerned face of Otto Karl. He was saying something soothing, but Capricorn's head was still one large and throbbing ache and he closed his eyes again. He was dimly aware of being wheeled into a side entrance of Marley hospital, and was badgered by doctors and nurses until he crossly woke up.

Something was done to his shoulder and someone was shining a light in his eyes. He allowed them to test his reflexes to get it over and wondered what Pritchard was doing there.

'You're all right,' Pritchard told him with a broad smile. 'Thank God, you were just hit with the edge of the pattern. They've dug the shot out of your shoulder. Only flesh wounds. You'll soon be back on the job.'

Just as well, Capricorn thought sleepily. The Chief would be beside himself. Both members of the team skulking in Marley hospital and the Yard without replacements.

He slept a little, then woke up suddenly to find it was two hours later, and he felt like himself, though still with a sore shoulder and a beastly headache.

Pritchard and another man, presumably from High Marley, were still there.

'What the devil happened?' Capricorn asked.

'Glad you're back with us,' Pritchard said, looking relieved. 'Don't worry. You'll be out in a couple of days.'

Capricorn sat up and winced. 'I'll be out today,' he said. 'Who shot me, did you find out?'

Pritchard was embarrassed. 'We believe it was Mr Karl. The whole party went out again after lunch. They all said the same thing: they thought you were off the grounds and out of range. The Captain, with Bechley, Wigmore, Fitch, and Struthers—I think you saw them in the house—were walking up the north fields towards the river. The Captain had organised the shoot more carefully, but Dankworth, who'd had a bit to drink, apparently, and Karl, wandered off from the line into the fallow fields, shooting a covey that flew towards the woods.'

'Dankworth or Karl,' Capricorn said thoughtfully.

The High Marley man spoke up. 'The gentlemen had no idea you might be in the wood. They assumed you would have gone by the field path, and then you would have been in plain view.'

He was a big, bluff country policeman, very different from the bespectacled and anxious Pritchard. His tone conveyed a certain reproach—ignorant Londoners, causing trouble.

Capricorn thought about it. Karl had seemed close enough to have heard the servant give him Fitz-Marley's message about taking the woods path. But the old man had a weak, tremulous voice; there had been laughter from the guests at the story being told. It was possible he hadn't heard.

'Dankworth should certainly have known better

than to leave the line. He said he started back to look
for runners down. But he insists he was too far off, his
shot couldn't have got near you.'

'And where was Karl!' Capricorn said, thinking of
the footfall behind him and the shot from among the
trees.

'Dankworth wasn't sure. He'd been searching and
then he saw the covey and got excited and fired. Karl
was vague but he was near the woods all right, he
doesn't deny it. If you want to prefer a charge. . . .'

'No,' Capricorn said, feeling a little light-headed
and flippant, 'Count it as open season on the Yard.
Who found me?'

'Mr Karl and the vicar. You cried out, and the vicar
ran up from the churchyard, and Mr Karl was there.
Mr Dankworth came and the three of them went into
the vicarage to telephone for the ambulance.'

So Karl had been standing by him when the vicar
came. Capricorn did not believe he had been shot
from the fallow fields. Could Karl have slipped away
unnoticed by the drink-dazed Dankworth? It seemed
a strange coincidence to have been shot by one of the
Brandenburgians. Too strange to be a coincidence, in
fact.

The High Marley man, relieved there was to be no
fuss, took himself off with civil wishes. Pritchard lingered to ask Capricorn how he was faring with the
Rilke case.

'Not much new yet,' Capricorn said, 'unless it was
one of my suspects trying to finish me off.'

He spoke humorously and Pritchard took it as humour. 'Even the most bungling old lags know it's useless "bumping off" CID men, as the Americans would
put it.' Pritchard smiled in his kindly way. 'We keep
too damned many records.'

Capricorn smiled in return. With an effort, he took down the names and addresses of the men at the shoot for his own reports, and thanked Pritchard sincerely for rushing over from Illwood. But as Pritchard turned to go, Capricorn pondered his words. What Pritchard had said was generally believed to be true, and perhaps in country stations or quiet districts it was. But among the Yard men, the Murder Squad, the Flying Squad, and in that strange new phenomenon the Ghost Squad, how much of a case in the early stages went into the records? How much just slowly burgeoned inside the policeman's head? And how many suspects might escape completely if that one policeman were done away with?

'Oh, by the way,' he recalled, before Pritchard reached the door. 'What's all that about Mrs Roth's mink coat?'

Pritchard turned back. 'You've been learning about our local troubles, have you? Not a police matter, you know.'

'I heard that Mrs Roth didn't want the police called. But I thought you might have found out.'

'Braun questioned the servants, which annoyed them. It always does, you can't blame them. And young Nora is the postman's daughter, so he was down at the station the next day. We know who did it all right,' Pritchard said, with a sigh. 'Our local thief, one Bertie Postle. With his usual brilliance he was spotted on the premises by Mrs Dermott. But as long as no complaint was made . . .' he shrugged.

'And he got rid of the goods?' Capricorn was interested.

'I found out about that too. Unofficially, for my own information. Postle's a clumsy fool and most receivers wouldn't bother with him. But I had it from a

friend of mine on the Flying Squad that a coat like
Mrs Roth's was seen on a young girl, a dancer, at the
Blue Dahlia on Gerrard Street. The girl was with
Charles Lawdon.'

Capricorn whistled and then was sorry. It made his
headache worse. 'The young fool.'

'And wouldn't I like to tell him so,' Pritchard said,
with energy. 'Silly young ass. Spoiled. Mummy's boy.
Just missed the army, more's the pity, and doesn't
know what to do for devilment. Crashed two cars.'

Capricorn remembered how Lawdon had driven
him off the road, to Snow's great discomfort, as they
first entered Illwood.

'Been prosecuted for bastardy,' Pritchard went on.
'Mummy nearly had a nervous breakdown, so his father got Braun to take him in. The family aren't that
well off, either. But our hands are tied. If I spoke to
the boy it would be actionable. The Roths would
deny everything. Lord Lawdon is one of their angels.
Used all his influence on their behalf.'

'Love or money?' Capricorn asked.

'I don't know what Lawdon's politics were before
the war,' Pritchard said slowly, his eyes wrinkling up
behind his spectacles. 'Certainly, money's involved.
He's chairman of the board of Roth's export business,
and he's a director of the real estate trust run with
Diener's money. It annoys me, because I have a feeling the youngster isn't really bad. He needs a firm
hand and something to do.'

'Your prescription sounds like a nice stretch in Dartmoor,' Capricorn said absently. 'Say, three years for
receiving stolen goods. Serious traffic offenses taken
into consideration when sentence is being passed.'

Pritchard laughed as he departed. A very decent,
kindhearted man, Capricorn thought. Snow would

think him too kind for his job, perhaps. So young Charles Lawdon was a knowing receiver of stolen goods. A bit of luxury to buy the affections of a girl. He considered this while he was trapped in his room, waiting for the doctor. Then he made a few telephone calls. His manner was genial, and he spoke of the shooting, not only as an accident, but as rather a joke on himself. The persons receiving his calls were amused and relaxed and chatted sympathetically with the invalid, and if two of the stories that Capricorn heard caused him to raise his eyebrows, no one was aware of that except the nurse who preceded the doctor.

Capricorn dealt with the doctor firmly to obtain his release, pretending he felt rather better than he did. As he came out he was surprised to see his car had been driven up beside the entrance and sitting in it was Otto Karl.

'I've been waiting,' Karl said simply. 'And when they told me you were released, I thought you might be glad to be driven back. Pritchard sent my car on for me.'

'That's very good of you,' Capricorn said, and got in, thinking somewhat wryly that it was good, unless Karl had shot him deliberately, and perhaps had something else in mind. Still, he would hardly shoot him again and throw him out of the car on the Marley road.

'The policeman from High Marley said you wouldn't be making a charge. I think he went up to the Castle to talk to the Captain. But I feel dreadful about it,' Karl said. His expression had none of his usual humour and he was surprisingly pale.

'I *know* it wasn't one of my shots,' he said abruptly. 'I shot only twice from that field. One of the shots

brought down a brace of birds and the other was
high.'

'And Dankworth?'

'He shot three times. He missed three times. He was
muzzy. I was a little—shall I say not pleased?—when
he went out again after lunch. Of course, I'm a
stranger,' Karl shrugged. 'I don't know the usual hab-
its of these gentlemen. In the morning the Captain
shepherded the party about very methodically.'

'Did you notice that Dankworth shot low?'

'No. But I must admit, I was pleased with my good
shot. It was my first. I wasn't watching Dankworth.'

His face was grim. The usually imperturbable Karl
was very perturbed indeed. The wind swept dry, dead
leaves across the windshield of the car as they rushed
through the lanes. Capricorn for the first time felt that
Karl, like Diener, was driven by some demon.

Well, Karl had embarrassment enough. His troubles
with the Home Office were not as serious as Diener's,
but he could hardly feel his position had improved
since he was suspected of shooting a policeman. Still,
no charge was being preferred, and how much did the
Home Office mean to him, after all? He had his of-
fers in America, almost certainly more profitable than
anything England nowadays could provide.

'It was careless of me to linger about the place,'
Capricorn said. 'I'm afraid I spoiled your day of sport.'

'I'd had enough,' Karl said. He smiled, with a ghost
of his usual humour. 'For a designer of weapons, I'm
not very fond of killing things, just now. I wasn't staying to the dinner. I have an appointment in London,
later.'

Capricorn thought of the charming, bubbly Randy
Clarke.

'You probably know about that,' Karl said, resigned.

He swerved the car rather dangerously as they went around a bend to avoid the body of a dead hare in the road. 'You must think I'm a callous man,' he added abruptly. 'Leaving my wife alone with the children, after she has been so good, so loyal through all the bad years, to go off and play with a model girl.'

They were approaching Illwood and he pulled over to the side of the road and stopped and turned around to face Capricorn. 'I'm not so callous,' he said. 'Randy Clarke is a good girl, in her way. But I love my wife, my family. My wife is beautiful, or was.' He looked for a moment as tortured and more unhappy than Franz Diener. 'And I look at her and I know her hair turned grey the year I was arrested. The lines around her mouth and eyes came when my appeals failed. She is thin from feeding her own ration to the children when I was not there to help her. She used to laugh—she laughed as much as Randy. Now she sighs, she cries easily, she is nervous and afraid to take our opportunity in a new land. And I look at her and think, I did this. I brought her to this. And, like a coward, I make an excuse and come to London, and I take Randy to the Blue Dahlia. And I feel young again.'

He was silent for a moment and then turned to Capricorn, a word half-formed on his lips. Then the village bus came up and, unable to pass, hooted indignantly behind them. Karl turned the key in the ignition and drove off again, very fast, saying nothing until they arrived back at the hotel.

In the quiet of the lane, Capricorn had expected him to continue, that the confidence, flowing from his shock, would have gone on to matters more significant than his domestic grief. But at the Brandenburg gates, Karl had recovered his usual composure. He gave Capricorn an ironic smile as he left him to take out his own car.

'Sorry to bore you,' he said lightly. 'Crocodile tears: you see I'm off anyway. Hope you feel better, Sergeant.'

And with a friendly wave of his hand he was on his way. Damn that bus, Capricorn thought. He wondered what Karl might have told him.

A twinge of pain in his shoulder reminded him of his wounds. It was a strange affair, that shot in the woods. A few inches—if he had not heard a sound and moved, he might have been a neatly laid out corpse by now. A shooting accident, regrettable, suitable remarks made by the host, an acceptance of the situation by the local men. Snow wouldn't be satisfied so fast, Capricorn thought, with a wave of appreciation for his dour Super, and a laugh at himself for that sudden appreciation on behalf of his own corpse.

At the thought of Snow, his emotion turned quickly to guilt. He had come to the point, he knew. Today he must ask for the warrant. He had been directly ordered now, and it must be done.

Madame Braun was at the reception desk when he claimed his key, impassive as always in black with gold and pearls. He noticed how many jobs she did, while Braun was almost always at leisure. It was Madame who ran the place, and did it well. Her hands were big in keeping with her body but they were well kept, the nails beautifully manicured with pale polish and the 'half moons' favoured by Rose, his private standard of feminine beauty. Madame, useful, elegant in her way, a murderer. Yet, he thought uncomfortably, how many of us are not, since the war began? The Fifth Commandment had been put aside for the duration.

'How long did you know Miss Rilke, Madame Braun?' he asked, on an impulse.

She looked at him coldly. 'I have made my statement to Superintendent Pritchard. Mrs Roth introduced her when she brought her here as a guest. We do not usually take unattached young women, but as Mrs Roth's protegée . . .' she shrugged her heavy shoulders.

'You have no idea of where she lived before she came here?'

'No.'

He had read her statement and knew what her answers would be. Beating a dead horse, he told himself grimly, but found himself impelled to continue.

'What did you know of Miss Rilke's associations with the other guests in the hotel—or with people outside, for that matter.'

'I knew nothing of her. I run a hotel and I have much to do.'

She handed him two slips of paper.

'If you will excuse me, Sergeant,' she said coldly, and left the desk for her office.

He looked at the messages written in Madame's spiky French hand. John Goobers, who was he? His heart sank as he identified the caller. Goobers was a functionary of his electrician. The plasterers had fouled the wiring, and it had to be pulled until the fault was discovered. The other message was even more ominous. The Chief had telephoned. He went up to his room and put a call through to Headquarters.

The Chief sounded somewhere between vexation and concern. 'Pritchard rang up. What the devil is going on down there? You were imitating a partridge in Marley Woods?'

Capricorn laughed. 'Not quite, sir. After all, I'm alive.'

'An accident, Pritchard seems satisfied. You're all right?'

'Just a headache. I tripped and hit my head on a tree,' Capricorn told him, keeping his suspicions to himself for the moment.

'Well, in that case, you can tell me why you didn't arrest Diener,' the Chief said. 'I saw Snow last night and the first thing he asked when he came round was if you'd taken care of it. As you've been dancing about in High Marley I gather you haven't done it yet.'

Here we go, Capricorn thought.

'Well, sir, Superintendent Snow was going to ask for a warrant, but not on the murder charge. The case hadn't developed that far when he was taken ill. I have some men keeping Diener under surveillance while I continue, and it still doesn't seem to me to be at that point, sir.'

'Why not?' the Chief asked. 'I understood that Pritchard had it pretty well sewn up before you went there. The lab report came in, by the way, on that warehouse full of clothes you sent them. Nothing of interest.'

Capricorn had expected that.

'There is a case could be made against Diener,' he told the Chief, 'but there are holes in it. Other people here had equal access to the murder weapon, they were on the premises at the time, their accounts of their whereabouts are as unsubstantiated as Diener's, and they possibly have motives for enmity against the girl. A good defense counsel could make us look silly unless we have more to go on.'

'Other people?' the Chief asked.

'There's our hostess,' Capricorn said, hoping that Thérèse Braun didn't listen in on the switchboard, and explained. He also mentioned the odd coincidence of Otto Karl possibly having shot him, and the hint of a motive there.

'Um,' the Chief said thoughtfully. 'See what you mean, but it sounds like pretty small beer to me. They couldn't be sure who shot you, you know. I just saw the A.C. and he knows Dankworth. Says he's always been a menace. Whatever you're working on, clear it up fast. Snow is still officially in charge; we just haven't anyone else so the A.C. said to leave it that way, and Snow says it's Diener and he wants him booked.'

'Yes, sir,' Capricorn said.

As he hung up he wondered why he had not told the Chief the extent of his suspicions about the 'accident'. Certainly he didn't want to listen to any more witticisms about a magician's fantasies. At least his Chief hadn't heard any complaints from C.C. yet. Perhaps Fitz-Marley had decided not to press his complaint, seeing that Capricorn had been shot on his land. He'd had his ounce of flesh.

A light hand tapped at his door and Nora appeared with a tray. Her open face was crumpled in concern. 'Ever so sorry to hear you had an accident, sir,' she said.

The story hadn't taken long to get about, Capricorn noticed.

'Mrs Dermott was upset and said I should bring this up, sir. Seeing you missed the lunch and tea.'

There were sandwiches, biscuits, scones, and cake as well as a large pot of tea.

'Doesn't look as though I'll need dinner.' Capricorn thanked her and smiled.

'Best to keep your strength up,' Nora told him. 'And

that's Mrs Dermott's own shortbread, she bakes that herself and she said you're to have some.'

Capricorn found he was pleased to receive a mark of favour from Mrs Dermott. She had forgiven what must have seemed his indecent curiosity but then she was obviously a woman of common sense. And she baked uncommonly good shortbread, by its looks and smell.

Nora poured his tea, and glanced around with an obvious wish to be useful. She noticed his suitcase that he'd left by the wardrobe. 'Would you like me to take the suitcase to the basement, sir?' she asked. 'Lots of the guests do that, it gives you more room.'

'Thank you,' he said, 'but please don't bother. I won't be here that long.'

'I see, sir.' Nora sounded disappointed.

'And you don't have much here, do you? Not like Miss Rilke. She *did* have a lot of stuff. And all so lovely, it was.' She gazed thoughtfully at the space where the over-sized wardrobe had been, now replaced with a more modest affair.

As Capricorn drank his tea and half listened to her chat, he recalled the day he had been sorting Miss Rilke's things. He had been about to remark something, and then Snow had spoken, and it had gone out of his mind. What was that? he wondered.

He couldn't remember. It puzzled him, and he pursued the thought while he ate one of Mrs Dermott's scones, and it was quite finished before he even realized that it had been delicious. Whatever it was hung in the back of his mind, tantalizing as a sneeze that refuses to get itself over and done with.

'Really lovely,' Nora repeated with a sigh, stroking her palms together with an abstracted air as if she were feeling some fine thing.

And he remembered. Of course. How stupid of him to have forgotten. It was very strange, mysterious in fact. Nora was right. All of Miss Rilke's things were 'lovely,' new or almost new. And not only the clothing she had at the Brandenburg, but the things he had seen at Randy Clarke's. She had brought nothing with her when she came to the hotel; Lise Roth had made that clear. Miss Rilke had borrowed her nightdress. But Capricorn had seen the garment in which the girl was killed.

He had not lived with a group of travelling women in his childhood without learning something about stuffs and styles. And Mrs Raintree, the wife of the vicar at Chuffield, and her daughter Rose had made their own clothes, and he remember the young Rose feeling a length of cloth and commenting on its fineness and softness or rejecting it as coarse. He thought of the nightgown, coarse, skimpy and somewhat frayed, that was Ingeborg Rilke's shroud.

When he first examined the garment with Snow, they had been interested in the tears and gaps, the blood and tissue left by the ghastly battering, the laboratory reports of chemical analyses. Fashion had not been in his mind. But Ingeborg Rilke had been a fashion model. All her things, bought by her admiring lover—or one of them!—had been to suit. Then where the devil had she found that wretched garment to die in?

'Nora,' he said, looking up, 'Did you ever see Miss Rilke with any old clothes? Anything not fine and pretty like the things that were left here?'

'Why, no, sir,' she said, staring. 'There wasn't anything she had I wouldn't give a week's pay for. Even her stockings were all real silk.' She heaved a tragic sigh, and looked down at her legs, clad in sturdy lisle.

'But when she first came?'

Nora frowned. 'Well, now you remind me, she did look real queer at first. But she only had one outfit and she soon got rid of that. I remember because she threw it in the wastebasket and Mrs Dermott made me show it to her. "Waste not, want not," she said, but the things were so old they were no good to anyone and we gave them to the rag and bone. Miss Rilke got all new things, good ones, and then when she started at the model school her things got really gorgeous, and never so much as a ladder in her stocking. The least bit wrong with anything and out it would go, but Madame Braun had me take her all those things. Said she gave them to poor refugees,' Nora told him with a sniff of disbelief.

Her voice grew dreamy. 'The day before she was killed she wore a chiffon blouse with full sleeves, oh, it was lovely. She tore it on a twig on the terrace, and I was going to pluck up courage and ask if I could have it myself, but then the poor lady got killed.'

Capricorn, who had been stirring a second cup of tea, sat quite still. The late afternoon sun struck through the window to lie in a pool of light on his bedside table, and he stared at it as though mesmerized, without seeing. Mentally, he reviewed the items he had packed and sent to the lab. Then he rose and found a duplicate of the list in his kit. It was a long list covering three pages, but there was no blouse with a torn sleeve.

Everything in the room had been examined and re-examined. He had gone over it himself. The tiniest tear in a garment would have to be noted. The list contained a white chiffon blouse with full sleeves and sparkling buttons, and a navy blue blouse of the same pattern with bronze clips. But no tear.

'Tell me more about the clothes Miss Rilke wore that day,' he said, 'The colours, if you remember.'

'Of course, sir. She had on linen trousers and the chiffon blouse to match, in sort of red-gold colours like leaves. Smashing it was. And suède shoes to match as well, with flat heels only lovely. You could see they weren't utility.'

'Thank you, Nora,' he said. 'You've been very helpful. By the way, did you happen to notice if Miss Rilke changed for dinner that night?'

'Well, yes, sir. I mean I noticed, sir, but she didn't. After I turned down Mr Diener's bed for the night, I was going back through the lounge, just before dinner, and I noticed particular because she usually changed, like Mrs Roth and Lady Cecily. Mrs Roth had changed into a blue dinner dress but Miss Rilke was still sitting next to Mr Diener just as she'd been since the Captain left at tea-time. She looked funny, as if she was cold or something, but it was warm.'

She clapped a hand to her mouth. 'You're not going to arrest Mr Diener, are you sir? All the staff is sure he couldn't have done it. He's such a nice gentleman.'

He smiled at her. ' "Nice gentlemen" have been known to do murder,' he pointed out.

'That's what my Jim says,' Nora replied gloomily. 'The fellow I go out with. He's jealous, that's what I think. Mr Diener, he's interesting and Jim is dull, like. Country people are slow,' she explained, 'after you've mixed with all sorts, like I have.'

'Steady, perhaps,' Capricorn suggested. 'A very good quality for a husband.'

Nora blushed.

'But I'm not arresting Mr Diener.'

Oh, you're not, his official self commented, silently, but in a nasty way.

'Of course, Superintendent Snow is in charge,' he concluded.

She gave him an anxious nod and departed.

Blast that arrest, he thought. This whole case had been handled backwards. Because of the assumption of Diener's guilt, the most glaring inconsistencies had gone unnoticed.

He took his pen and made notes.

None of the garments described by Nora as having been worn by the victim the last day of her life had been found. Instead her corpse had been discovered clad only in a nightdress that would have disgraced an orphanage. Where had the nightdress come from? Where had the clothes gone?

Here was another link in the chain of mystery that had begun with Price. Price said that she had asked him to take a suitcase from the Brandenburg. She had spoken as though she expected to be elsewhere by morning. Yet nothing had been done about that possibility. Lise Roth had said she left the girl that night with Diener. Mrs Dermott's observations seemed to bear that out. Diener said she left with Lise Roth. Whichever one was lying, it could no longer be assumed that Ingeborg Rilke was on those premises all night until her death in the morning.

The more he thought about it, the more of a puzzle it seemed. Certainly she could have left the hotel unnoticed at any time before midnight. But she had not used Diener's car and no taxi had been called; the only taxi service in Illwood was from Bill's garage, and Bill had been questioned by Pritchard. There was no bus service to or from the village after eight p.m. And so if Ingeborg Rilke had left the hotel, either she met someone with a car, or she walked. She could have been driven by someone from the hotel, but the porter had said no cars were taken out that night after Diener's car returned from Marley Castle. No, Pritchard could not be blamed for assuming that Miss Rilke had stayed in the hotel.

Capricorn dropped his pen and gazed out of the window into the fading light. The nights were drawing in. No one was on the lawn playing croquet. He remembered the scene the first day he was there with the Roths, Braun and Fitz-Marley playing while the ditch beyond was still stained with Ingeborg Rilke's blood.

His head ached badly. The stuff the doctor had given him had made him muzzy. He leaned back in the comfortable chair the hotel provided and drifted into a dream where he was back at Aunt Dolly's and his head was being beaten with a golf iron by the sadistic admirer of the compulsively roaming Sylvie, while in the background Tod waved seditious pamphlets and shouted his allegiance to his commissar, the Führer.

Then Tod was riding a point-to-point, a nightgowned Sylvie crept down a staircase and slid down castle walls. He was back in Pritchard's office with the sweet scent of flowers and the telephone rang and rang. He woke reluctantly, surprised for a moment to find himself in his room and that it was Manning and not an irate farmer who was calling.

His head still throbbed, but his mind had cleared, and before he acknowledged Manning, he knew who had killed Ingeborg Rilke, with an idea of how it was done. Unfortunately, he didn't know why and there seemed no way on earth of proving it.

4

He had not paused to turn the lamp on, and the room was almost dark. The memory of his dream was still with him, and he could easily have imagined he felt the presence of the dead girl. As they spoke, Manning's voice was different from its familiar, chuckling tone, more serious than Capricorn had ever heard it, even in the midst of war, hushed and grave.

'I'm not refusing you,' he was saying, 'only asking, do you really feel it's necessary, must you have it to go on?'

'It's more necessary than ever,' Capricorn said. 'It might save an innocent man from execution. But what's the trouble?'

'I don't know,' Manning said. 'That's the devil of it. All I know is, after I spoke to you this morning, I got on my friend's back to hurry things up a little. Just to make sure, I made an arrangement for tonight for dinner. It was the strangest thing,' he said, sounding puzzled. 'This morning everything was normal. But when I met him tonight he was positively frightened. Said he couldn't tell me anymore. Much too hush-hush. *Really* hush-hush.'

'The war's over,' Capricorn said, considering.

'That's what I said,' Manning retorted. 'But no go. You know as well as I do, Merle, that most of the stuff under the Act is nothing anyway. Stamped by somebody as secret and stays that way. But my bird swore to me that this is such a dicey business that even after the thirty-year limit it won't be released.'

'So that's it?' Capricorn said, with a cold feeling of dismay.

'No,' Manning said, 'I'll push on, if you want it. I can handle my little bird, but if it's that hot, what's the use? You won't be able to use it in open court.'

'That's not for me to decide,' Capricorn said. 'But if we know the truth, we won't be trying the wrong man, even if we can't get the right one.'

Manning was silent for a moment.

'And that's not all,' he said, with some reluctance. 'I don't know what it's about yet, but I was definitely given the impression that anybody who is known to know about this, if you see what I mean, is *persona non grata* Upstairs. So you won't be able to mention me or my little bird. And you might find yourself suddenly in Coventry.'

Capricorn whistled. He thought rapidly and his face set into the expression that caused his aunts to exclaim:

'You're obstinate, Merle.'

'Find out for me anyway,' he urged. 'Anything you can. I'm sure I know who did it, and I have an idea how it was done. But the why—a lot of whys are missing. I'll keep you out of it,' he promised, wondering exactly how he was going to do that.

'O.K.' Manning sighed, 'I can see two, no, three promising careers going down the drain. But O.K.'

'One more thing,' Capricorn asked, 'But this is easy. Just an address of a lady under MI5 surveillance. Hope she's still in the country.'

He gave Manning the details, thanked him heartily

and rang off, and immediately asked the operator to connect him with Mrs Dermott, who fortunately lived in the hotel. She agreed to receive him and told him where she could be found.

He came out into the corridor, blinking a little at the light, and bumped into Charles Lawdon who was leaving his room.

Lawdon's young, ingenuous face looked concerned.

'Sorry,' he said. 'Did I hurt you? I heard you had an accident. I hope you're all right,' he added, rather shyly.

'Quite, thank you,' Capricorn said. 'My apologies, I was wool-gathering. I haven't thanked you yet for helping Superintendent Snow.'

'Oh, that was nothing,' Lawdon said. 'I just ran into him. That is, I don't mean I ran into him—'

'No,' Capricorn was amused. 'We haven't put that one down on your tally. But you were kind. There is one thing I wanted to ask you, by the way. Do you mind if I ask you now? It won't take a minute.'

'Go ahead,' Lawdon said, looking very uncomfortable.

'In the statement you gave Superintendent Pritchard you said that you'd hardly noticed Miss Rilke. You'll forgive me, but isn't that a little strange? She was an attractive young woman after all, and you were both up here on the same floor.'

He glanced around. This end of the corridor had a very quiet private air, compared to the more public space, near the wide sweep of the stairs, at the front.

Lawdon had recovered himself. 'Oh,' he said easily, 'it was in a way of speaking. I meant interested. I wasn't interested. Though I didn't notice her at first. She was just like somebody's aunt.'

Capricorn remembered the photograph.

'And even though they smartened her up, she was always sort of—' he searched for a word, 'sort of a rabbit. Timid. Nothing to say. And,' he hesitated, 'I suppose you know. There was . . .' he nodded towards the staircase leading to Diener's quarters. 'And old Braun sneaking in.'

He shrugged. Apparently the young man was fastidious in his way. 'I like a girl that gives you more of a run for your money,' he said.

Capricorn thought briefly of angels who feared to tread and dismissed those celestial creatures as being unsuited for the business of detection.

'The kind that insist on mink coats?' he asked.

Lawdon blushed, and then looked mortified about his blushing. 'I was all sorts of a fool,' he muttered. He started to rub his right foot against his left ankle, caught himself and stopped. 'I mean, I didn't know, at first. It just seemed very cheap. Though I had trouble getting that,' he added gloomily.

'What did you pay?'

'A hundred pounds.'

He avoided Capricorn's eye.

'And didn't you think it strange that you were offered a garment worth many times that sum?'

'It was secondhand,' he said.

'I'm sure the man you bought it from had kept the bill,' Capricorn remarked ironically.

He regarded the shamefaced young man.

'This isn't an official inquiry,' he told him. 'You're lucky. No complaint was made. But if I were you I'd keep away from that sort of thing. It must have embarrassed your father.'

'Oh, my father,' Lawdon shrugged. He had the mutinous air of a young man to whom fathers were a natural enemy.

'I did feel rotten, when I knew. I asked Josie to give it back, to get straight, but she wouldn't. She's a gold-digger,' he said frankly. 'But in a way, so's that Mrs Roth.'

Young, but not dense, Capricorn observed.

'I mean, she soon got that sable coat from Diener. And *she* wouldn't have given it back.'

Capricorn did not care to argue the point and let the young man go, not certain whether his lecturing had had an effect. But he forgot Lawdon quickly, with more important matters on his mind, and went downstairs to the ground floor in search of Mrs Dermott.

It was a semi-basement room of good size, and after the softly shaded light of upstairs it seemed ablaze with electricity. A sewing machine and a large linen basket indicated that it was used for work as well as sleep.

It looked very much like its occupant, Capricorn noticed with amusement. Not here the delicately tinted walls, the thick carpet, the graceful though comfortable furniture vaguely reminiscent of Queen Anne, chosen by Thérèse Braun with an eye to English taste. Mrs Dermott's room was whitewashed, the floor boards polished, with a small rug by the side of the bed. The solid oak furniture was almost certainly her own, together with the crêpe-trimmed photographs of two young men, one in the uniform of the First World War and one of the Second. Husband and father? Mrs Dermott was unlucky.

There was also a framed reproduction of *The Monarch of the Glen*, a steel engraving of Balmoral Castle, and beside the bed a tartan-covered tin. On the chest of drawers there was a fresh white cloth covered with a small collection of sea shells.

Mrs Dermott rose from her sewing table as he entered and faced him with a look that would have been suitable for a Scottish martyr.

'What do you want of me?' she said.

'The truth,' Capricorn replied simply.

'Ah hiv told you the truth.'

Capricorn noticed that she sounded more Scotch when she was agitated.

'You have. But not all of it. Think,' he urged her. 'A person who is innocent is helped by a full disclosure of the truth. Even if for some reason, probably misguided, he doesn't want it known. Only the guilty gain by a confusion.'

She gave him her frank, direct look, a world away from Lise Roth's flutterings. For a woman like that to have such loyalty to a German, just two years after the war's end, meant that Diener had made a deep impression on her. Certainly her respect would not be won by a merely free-spending guest.

'Mr Diener couldna have killed the girl,' she said. 'He is a *gud* man. He only wanted to help her. He was sorry for her. He's sorry for a lot of people. Some deserve it,' she added grimly. 'Some don't.'

She was silent for a moment.

'Did you know he has a special fund to help soldiers who were crippled in the war? The first time I heard his name was when my cousin Andrew got a grant from the Diener Fund. Poor Andy, he lost his legs at Dunkirk but he can run a machine now and earns five pound a week.'

Capricorn reflected for a moment on this as coming from a munitions maker. Conscience money, he supposed, but useful just the same.

'And he supports the War Orphans' home in Marley. And every stray dog and cat he runs into. Even one of the wardens from a prison he was in who came down with rheumatic fever. Mr Diener is a very kind man.' Her face was flushed.

'I'm sure you're right,' Capricorn said. 'But it won't prevent him from being tried for murder if I don't get to the bottom of this business. You know more than you've told me. Now, let's have it. Who is the lady, who is not a lady, that Mr Diener is protecting?'

She looked at him sternly, but her fingers were crumpling her apron.

'Mr Diener trusts me not to talk about his private business.'

'Mr Diener is right to trust you,' Capricorn said gently, 'but he is very wrong to trust certain other people. Now, if the person involved is who I suspect it is, that person intends to leave him in a very difficult situation that he might not be able to escape from.'

Mrs Dermott considered this and Capricorn didn't rush her. She took her time, and he stood quietly, listening to the tick-tick of the big clock on the chimney-piece.

At last she spoke. 'Ah couldna prove anything,' she said slowly, 'but I'll tell you. I've seen a powder box left by his bedside. A gold powder box with blue stones.' She looked at him meaningly. 'And once a handkerchief under his pillow. I put it in with her laundry and she didn't know she'd left it. A fancy lace thing with an "L" in the corner.'

Capricorn thanked her heartily, with rising excitement and was about to rush off, when she detained him with a strong grip of her bony hand.

'You'll no be arresting him now?' she demanded.

'You've confirmed what I suspected,' he said. 'It accounts for some of the oddities in Mr Diener's behaviour. It's not the whole story, but I've enough to be on my way. I'll do my best.'

She gave him a stare as he took his leave saying plainly that his best had better be good enough. He hoped fervently not to disappoint her. Certainly he would waste no time.

His next object wasn't far away. Diener was in the cocktail bar with the Roths and Braun and the attendant constable. By the goggle-eyed stare of the constable, Capricorn gathered that he had fallen victim to Lise Roth's charms.

She was dressed for the evening in an ankle-length dress of cream-coloured silk with a blue scarf around her shoulders and was a sight to make any man pause. Capricorn paused. Even knowing what he did about her made no difference to that first tug at the heart. Her eyes sparkled like her sapphire earrings and her laughter floated pleasantly towards him.

Diener, who had apparently recovered his spirits, was directing Braun in the preparation of a punch bowl.

'The important thing is the proportion,' he was saying. 'One bottle of brandy to four Liebfraumilch. And then the two bottles of champagne but only poured on just before you serve.'

For once he was talking in English. The constable who was supposed to be watching him only took his eyes from Lise Roth to gaze fascinated at the drink. Diener was addressing him as well as the others, and Capricorn wondered how long it was possible to keep any guard or policeman near this man without his drifting into becoming a guest.

The grey-looking Roth was supercilious. 'All that fruit,' he grumbled. 'It only spoils the taste of the wine.'

'Not if you do it like this,' Diener said, trium-
phantly, producing a large, covered crystal bowl from
behind the bar. 'If the fruit is in the brandy for
twenty-four hours beforehand, the acidity will be
gone. Once it is mixed, of course, you must drink it
sofort.'

Braun drew the corks on the Rhine wine with a
flourish and poured it in the bowl, while Diener happily popped the champagne.

'I'm sorry to intrude on your party,' Capricorn said,
'but I wonder if you could spare me a moment, pri-
vately?'

Diener smiled. 'Can't I offer you a glass first, Sergeant?'

'I won't keep you more than a few minutes,' Capricorn said, 'And you will be able to return to your
guests.'

'Ah, always correct,' Diener said, with a conspiratorial look at the constable, which Capricorn managed
to appear not to notice.

Diener flung his arm around him in a friendly way
as they walked off to his rooms, causing his wound to
throb slightly. But Capricorn was more uncomfortable
in thought than in body. Diener had become *used* to
his situation. He accepted the constable as he had accepted his gaolers, and managed to banish the reality
of the situation from his mind. He must have had a lot
of practice at that in the last few years. He was whis-
tling softly, not 'Gloomy Sunday' but some cheerful
melody that Capricorn could remember his father
singing to his friends, many years ago, the Serenade
from *The Student Prince*.

Back in Diener's rooms, tidied up by Mrs Dermott
and looking more cheerful with a blaze of golden autumn flowers in a huge vase by the lamp, Capricorn

hated to dispel the happy mood, but there was no time for compunctions.

'What can I do for you now, my friend?' Diener asked with a good humour that was perhaps natural to him, and only in part stimulated by the alcohol he had got through that evening.

'You've recovered from your peppering, I see.'

'Yes, thank you,' Capricorn said. 'This is more a matter of what I can do for you. You know that the statement you gave is enough to land you in the dock. I don't know all the reasons you are making such a mystery, but I know some. I know, for instance, why you think you can't be found guilty if and when you are tried. I am here to tell you that you're wrong about that.'

'Nonsense,' Diener said, still cheerful. 'My dear boy—you don't mind my calling you that, you could be my son, you know—'

A cloud passed over his face as he remembered the fate of his dead child, but it was quickly wiped away. Yes, Capricorn thought, he was a man who had learned not to dwell on unpleasant realities, perhaps to the point where the real world itself was something to be shunned.

Suddenly, uncomfortably, he remembered the madman conjured up by such diverse persons as Pritchard, Braun, Randy Clarke, and Lise Roth to explain the murder of Ingeborg Rilke.

'There's Pritchard's maniac,' Snow had said after meeting Diener.

What was madness but the determination to escape reality? Had he come this far, Capricorn wondered, just to prove himself wrong?

'You can never condemn me,' Diener said, with confidence. 'You can only arrest me and put me in

gaol. I would not like it, but that is all you could do.'
He looked at Capricorn in rather childish triumph.

'Why do you keep up this charade?' Capricorn asked,
exasperated. 'A girl was killed. I suspect that you
know her killer. Why should you protect a murderer,
and at your own expense?'

'You don't know that I'm protecting anyone,' Diener
said, turning away. 'What difference could it make, in
any case? The girl cannot be brought back.'

'A killer is on the loose,' Capricorn said bitterly. 'A
man who has killed once, can kill again.'

Diener's back was still towards him. 'And yet,
surely,' he said, 'murder is the crime least likely to be
repeated. There are tensions, pressures in a man's life,
perhaps, which lead to murder, that could never be
repeated again.'

Once more, Capricorn felt chill. Was Diener speaking for himself? An apology for his own deed? For all
that Capricorn's investigation had revealed, that his
imagination had knit together, none of it really pre-
cluded the murder being done by Diener. It only
pointed to another possibility, with the motive for that
possibility still obscure.

A wind blew through the open window. It shook
the petals of the chrysanthemums loose until they lay
in a golden pool in a circle of lamplight. Once again,
Capricorn saw in his mind's eye the image of Ingeborg Rilke's mutilated body in the golden ditch.

'You found her body,' he said. 'You saw what was
done. Should such a man escape?'

Diener turned towards him. 'It was horrible, dis-
gusting,' he said, his forehead deeply scored by his
frown. 'But I have been made aware of much horror.
The world is full of it. Can you bear to think of one
millionth part of the agonies being suffered in the

world right now?' he demanded. 'The disease and disaster inflicted by nature, the ravages of men? Famine in India. Prisoners in the Arctic. The driven populations of Latvia and Estonia—let us not talk of horror.' He gazed downward with an expression that belied his words. If he knew the killer, he was not as hardened as he wished to seem. Yet, he made it clear, he would reveal nothing.

'But you assume too much,' he said. 'I don't know who killed that girl. Her life was a terror; her death the same.'

Capricorn turned on another lamp and looked at Diener steadily.

'You might not know who killed Miss Rilke. My Superintendent has asked for a warrant for your arrest.'

Diener's face was impassive.

Capricorn could not tell him what Lise Roth had said in her statement. Such an action would be contrary to the Judge's Rules. But he could break that impassivity.

'You are relying on an alibi that you could produce in court,' he said. 'The one that you have gallantly refused to give to us. You believe that your alibi will be upheld, if necessary, by the lady you are protecting. I must tell you, Mr Diener, that Lise Roth has booked passage for herself and her husband on the *Paloma* and plans to leave the country next week.'

Diener's face went sickly white. His big body flinched and he stared for a moment until he pulled himself together. 'You're lying,' he said. 'You're trying to trap me.'

'We are not allowed to entrap witnesses,' Capricorn said. 'If you want to be sure, you could telephone the Silver Star Line.'

Diener believed him. It was obvious in the tremor

of his hands, the greyness of his lips. Suddenly he seemed twenty years older.

'Do you want to tell the truth now?' Capricorn said.

Diener sank down in his big chair. His shoulders were bowed, his hands dangled between his knees. He looked exhausted, with an expression that Capricorn had not seen before, even on men about to be executed, a hopelessness, a weariness not of the body but of the spirit of the man.

'What does it matter?' he said. Even his voice had lost its resonance. The lamplight shone on his fair hair, showing it to be mixed with silver. His face was partly shadowed, the visible eye looked sunken and the eyelid drooped. This is the way he would look, Capricorn thought, as an old man.

'What does anything matter now?' He stared at nothing.

He responded to no further questions; he seemed as deaf as the dead. Capricorn withdrew, feeling like a murderer himself. There was no help to be had from Diener, and he had only shaken his own previous certainty.

It was very dark on the porch, the moon and stars obscured by cloud. A light rain was falling and as he walked up outside the house to the front the drops dashed cold against his face. Through the glass terrace he could see the punch party in the cocktail lounge. Bereft of its host, it was still going along merrily.

Even the grey-faced Roth was jovial. Lise Roth was smiling up at young Charles Lawdon, who had joined the group, while Braun solicitously filled her glass. Only Madame Braun who watched from the doorway was frowning. Charles Lawdon whispered something to Lise Roth. The sound of her laughter came to Capricorn light, mocking. The cold rain slid under his collar and down his neck. You're going to lose this one, he thought suddenly. It was his first failure, and the taste was bitter.

5

There was a note waiting for him when he went inside. A telephone message: would he call Manning. His heart beating quickly, he telephoned the number and Manning was on the line.

'I managed your last request easily through channels,' he said. 'You're in luck. The fair Marquise is living at Claridge's under the protection, shall I say, of a Turkish banker. He's away most of the time, of course, and I understand the lady is quite friendly. Enjoy the hunt,' he chuckled, like himself again, and hung up.

Suddenly very much cheered by this one bit of good fortune, Capricorn moved fast. It wasn't until he was halfway to London that he remembered his dinner, and was thankful for Mrs Dermott's good tea. And though he hadn't proved anything by her revelations, he reflected, at least she had cleared some of the cobwebs away.

When he arrived at his destination, he found the Marquise was out. Impatient, while he was waiting, despite the hour, he put a call through to the police at Cobleigh and made inquiries about Mrs Lucy Weeks. They were helpful and gave him the information he wanted straight away. Too keyed up to wait until morning, he spoke to the startled matron in the suburbs of that city. Mrs Weeks was cautious and

only after ringing off to confirm his identity with the
local police, and perhaps to get rid of her husband for
a while, would she talk to him at all. She sounded like
a strong-minded woman, with none of the soft charm
of Lise Roth, not at all what he had fancied to be
Diener's 'type'. But perhaps his Lucy had changed.
Seven years in a suburb of Cobleigh with an ordinary
English husband might have been sobering for a girl
who had been the wild young mistress of a rich foreigner.

Coldly but clearly she answered his very personal
questions, only as an alternative to getting a summons
to appear at the trial. She tersely bade him goodbye,
hoping, he felt certain, never to talk to a policeman
again.

By the time he was finished with Mrs Weeks, the
Marquise had arrived, fortunately alone. Very different from the Englishwoman, the Marquise was willing
enough to talk. She only shied away from the aspects
of his questions that seemed degrading to herself, but
her dislike of and indignation against her former lover
proved stronger than anything else. She ended by telling the truth with a detail that almost made Capricorn
blush. He concluded, after he had thanked her and
departed, that the insult to her pride vexed her more
than the injury to her person. Remembering his Aunt
Dolly's blond lodger, he sighed for the vulnerability of
women.

His mind was running ahead sharp and clear and
despite his injury he felt full of strength. He rang up
Illwood station but to his annoyance, Pritchard had
gone home. Capricorn found him there, explained all
that had happened, and asked his assistance for the
next actions to be taken. He heard the sound of a
female expostulating in the background. A wife, he

thought, as he so often did, was a hindrance to a policeman. Got in the way of his doing his job. A detective was like a soldier in the front line. He shouldn't be held up by domestic considerations.

Pritchard was relieved, worried, helpful, and foot-dragging in turn. Capricorn chafed at the last, and Pritchard pointed out mildly that it was one in the morning, and although he personally had no objection to being woken from his sleep, the people that Capricorn wanted to see might feel otherwise.

'By the way,' he added, with an attempt at casualness, against the wails of an infant coming over the line, 'the Captain has filed a complaint against you with the C.C. I told the C.C. how decent you had been about the accident but he said one thing has nothing to do with another. He's an old bastard,' Pritchard relieved his feelings despite the presence of his wife, 'and to him Fitz-Marley isn't just an ordinary irate citizen, you know. The Fitz-Marleys are still lords of the manor to a lot of people round here. Anyway, the C.C.'s getting on to Headquarters. Thought you should know.'

'Never mind that,' Capricorn said, forgetting it as he checked Pritchard's time-keeping against his own watch. 'I suppose you're right, blast it. Have to wait until morning.'

All those countrymen would be in their beds. Much as he'd like to haul them out, it was not the way of the Yard. It was the SS who'd specialized in that, he remembered.

'I'll be in your office at seven o'clock then.'

'Seven,' Pritchard agreed. There was a further crackling of opposition from the other side of the bed which both men ignored. Capricorn, in a fever of impatience, was sure he would never sleep that night.

However, by the time he made the long drive back to
Illwood and roused the night porter to let him in, he
was ready enough for his bed. His head still ached
and his shoulder smarted. The night porter was a long
time fussing with the key.

'Have they always had these damned gates?' Capricorn asked the porter, who seemed hardly strong
enough to pull them open. Capricorn gave him a
hand.

'Yes, sir. Thank you, sir,' the man answered, for the
help and a tip. 'I understand they've been here since
the property was first built.'

He looked up at the eagles on the gate-post, looking
menacing by moonlight. 'Not those,' he added. 'They
were put on by the first Germans who bought the
place, they say. The old Graf and his sons, the ones
who changed its name to Brandenburg House. Before
that it was just Marley House or Marley Manor, more
natural-like, if you ask me.'

Capricorn went up to get a few hours' sleep, reflect-
ing on locks and keys. He remembered how his father
had despised those objects and thought how misleading they could be. In their act The Great Capricornus
would be searched enthusiastically by members of the
audience, trussed like a turkey and handcuffed. Then
he would kiss his young son farewell, before being
lowered into a vault, to the delicious horror of the
spectators. It was during the kiss, of course, that
young Merlin would pass his father the key with
which he undid the handcuffs and loosened himself at
his leisure. Smiling, the policeman closed his eyes.

It seemed just moments later, though it was about
an hour and half, when the gates were creaking again.
Young Charles Lawdon? A voice and a laugh pleasantly familiar—surely not! But it was. Otto Karl was

being very indiscreet; he had brought Randy Clarke back with him. The day's doings must have disturbed him a hell of a lot for that family man to abandon caution.

Voices, and more voices. Footsteps in the hall: Otto Karl and the charming Randy.

'But you said there would be food.' She was laughing, but her voice was loud and clear. She must have awakened half the people on the floor. Karl's voice, a low murmur, and then the steps receded. Where would Karl find provender at that hour, Capricorn wondered, in the delicious quiet and solitude of his room. There was something entrancing about a problem that was no concern of his. For another couple of hours, he had nothing to do but rest.

It was a thought that sometimes comes even to detectives from the Yard, but, as with Capricorn, they are never surprised to find it is untrue. When a tap sounded at his door, Capricorn knew resignedly that whoever it was would not go away. The door opened, a grey figure was outlined against the shaded light from the hall, and he even managed to be pleased to recognize that it was Manning.

The grey ghost advanced. 'Thought I'd better come and talk to you.' His voice was hushed. 'The night porter didn't know your room. I'm afraid I had to wake up the housekeeper to track you down.'

Capricorn switched on the bedside lamp. He swung his long body out of bed with some excitement. The busy Manning hadn't come down to Illwood with a small bit of information.

Manning closed the door behind him carefully. Capricorn gave him the comfortable chair and pulled one over from the desk for himself. While he found his dressing gown, Manning took out his cigarettes and would say nothing until he lit one for himself and one for Capricorn.

'Wasn't the kind of thing to tell you on the 'phone.' The Special Branch man was back in that uncharacteristic serious mood. It seemed particularly strange to Capricorn, who had known him to risk his life with a casual air and a joke.

'Glad I got here,' Manning said. 'Wasn't sure if I was driving or flying. Been drinking double whiskies all night.' He rubbed his head in some vexation, as if trying to get rid of the alcohol.

'I knew how to get what I wanted from my little bird, he has the weakness, but he's the kind of drunk that watches like a hawk to make sure you drink even. Can't fool him, either. He can count your drinks until he goes under the table.'

'He sounds like a fine repository for the nation's secrets,' Capricorn said drily.

'Well, you can't say he's the exception that proves the rule,' Manning retorted.

He looked very tired. They both considered some famous topers they'd known in the Service, and Capricorn sighed.

'Sometimes you wonder that we won at all,' he said.

'We won what we won,' Manning said, with an inflexion that reminded Capricorn of Diener. 'Maybe the Germans had more drunks than we did. Or more fools. That's part of what my bird was telling me tonight. It's a tale,' he sighed.

He looked at Capricorn's bed with a certain longing, and his friend wondered if he'd be able to keep him awake long enough to tell it. Then there was another knock on his door, and to Capricorn's surprised 'come in' it opened to admit Mrs Dermott, fully dressed, brushed and starched, bearing a tray smelling marvellously of coffee.

'Seein' yer working all night I thought you might like a drop of something. Coffee,' she said sternly to Manning, whose whisky-laden breath had not escaped her notice.

'It's very kind of you but you shouldn't have troubled at this hour,' Capricorn said, with a feeling of remorse, as Mrs Dermott seemed to work about sixteen hours a day as a general rule.

'I'd been woken anyway,' she said with a sniff. 'There were those that were looking for lobster and wine.'

Randy Clarke, of course. Karl had brought her back with the promise of some of Braun's delicacies.

'There's something to eat as well in case you're hungry. You had no dinner tonight,' she reproached Capricorn.

'What a totally admirable woman,' Manning stared as the door closed behind her. 'I think I'll marry her if she'll have me.'

'Too much sense to marry a policeman,' Capricorn rejoined as he poured the coffee.

The two weary men drank the strong black brew gratefully and Manning began his story.

'I only got bits and scraps and you have to try to put it together to make sense—or nonsense, whatever you think. My friend would say little, take it back, turn it round, and the drunker and more indiscreet he got the more it was confused.'

While they ate he tried to explain the confidences, the evasions, the daring revelations instantly retracted and covered over with euphemisms and expressions of doubt.

They pushed their plates away, Capricorn refilled their cups, and they smoked cigarette after cigarette as Manning talked. The smoke drifted about like a cloud around their heads in the dim light of the heavily shaded lamp. They might have posed for a portrait of 'The Two Conspirators,' Capricorn noted with a tiny part of his mind while the rest struggled with the strange things that he heard.

'Incredible,' Manning was saying. 'But there were so many incredible things. God knows, you and I never got filled in on the big picture, but even from what we stumbled across there were things that went wrong that couldn't go wrong, ballsed-up messes that were never explained. Especially in SOE. You remember the business of the Dutch paratroopers.'

Capricorn nodded grimly. There were still questions being asked about that at the Hague. It had not only been the Dutch, either. Hand-picked men had been dropped, with great difficulty, behind enemy lines to engage in sabotage and aid resistance movements, time and again to find the Germans ready and waiting.

'Not,' Manning said bitterly, 'that this is going to explain anything like that. Just the opposite,' he brooded. He drank some coffee with a gulp as if trying to clear his mind.

'Look,' he said. 'One of the reasons I came is because you're not going to like this. No help to you. It puts your theory up the spout. It was your German that killed the girl, it seems certain. He had quite a motive, you'll find out. Much stronger than a mere disappointed lover.'

Capricorn's first thought was that he didn't believe it. Manning didn't know what he'd learned from two ladies the evening before. None the less he found the words depressing.

'You'd better get on,' he said calmly.

'But get on with what, that's the trouble,' Manning fretted. 'Perhaps my bird made it up to seem important. Wouldn't be the first time an agent let fantasy run away with him. Because it sounds like fantasy,' he said with great gloom. 'Did you ever wonder,' he went on with seeming inconsequence, 'if we'd lost the war, who, in England, would have turned Quisling?'

'Too busy with the problems we actually had,' Capricorn, ex-agent and policeman said, then reflected that perhaps that wasn't entirely true.

'Of course,' Manning said. 'Still, it seems remarkable, looking back, when you think of the number of sympathizers the Nazis had, that there were almost no traitors? Amery—who wasn't normal. A few prisoners who wound up in the British Free Korps. Joyce.'

'Who wasn't British,' Capricorn said.

'No. But he'd applied for a British passport,' Manning answered. 'Just as your friend Franz Diener had applied for British citizenship. Don't think that hasn't been on his mind. You see, it wasn't just bureaucratic muddle that kept him in prison so long.'

Capricorn frowned. 'But what could Diener have done? He was in camps and prisons since 1940. What could that have to do with Ingeborg Rilke?'

'My friend thinks,' Manning said slowly, 'that Ingeborg Rilke knew what he'd done. He'd lived with this thing, in fear, for more than five years. Then he has this mouse of a woman by his side for nine months. A man has to talk to someone. She was the one person who seemed to him to be safe. Not the type to go blabbing about.'

'About what?' Capricorn said, almost in a fever of anticipation.

Manning knocked the ash of his cigarette, exhaled, sat back in his chair, and regarded Capricorn from half-closed eyes. Agitated as he was, Capricorn could not help noticing how Manning, as usual, seemed to belong just where he was. He might have been a country gentleman, a little tired from a day of sport, enjoying a somnolent hour, in any day of a placid life time.

But what he said had nothing to do with placidity of any sort.

'The trouble is,' he said 'when a war is won, the winners are the heroes.'

Capricorn waited.

'It sounds obvious, but you see what I mean. X is in charge of Y department. We won the war. Therefore, it is assumed, our Y department was better than the enemy's. Therefore, our X was brilliant. QED.'

'There are known facts,' Capricorn countered.

'Yes, there are. But what led to those facts, who was responsible, how can you know? After all, if we hear from anyone, it's our X. The X that was in charge of the German Y department, well, he's dead. Or tried and imprisoned at Nuremberg. And any documents that happen to exist get stamped Official Secret for thirty years, at least. Actually, I think we've destroyed most of them.'

Manning blew a long column of smoke and gazed into it thoughtfully. 'There was a group that tried to make contact with the Germans, you know that. Some splinter group of Welsh Nationalists, not the main party. It was supposed to have been infiltrated by German spies. And there was a story about The Link.'

'But The Link was admittedly pro-German,' Capricorn remarked. 'They were interned in 1940. Even Domville,' recalling the former head of Naval Intelligence who had been swept up with the rest. 'That was MI5's baby.'

'The Welsh nationalists involved came from your friend Diener's doorstep,' Manning offered. 'Those mountains with some unpronounceable name where he had a great place. It wasn't clear where they got their money, but Diener, with his Nazi family connections, was obviously suspect.'

Capricorn listened with all his attention.

'That much is definite. The rest. . . .'

Manning shrugged. 'Sometimes I think the great wars of the future will be between different departments. Instead of Britain against Germany,' he grinned, his usual mocking self, 'it will be the equivalent of SIS against MI5. Rather like the *Abwehr* against the *Verbindungsstab* or Stephenson's lot against the FBI.

'Anyway,' he went on, taking pity on Capricorn's hardly restrained impatience, 'there are claims going about that we had penetrated the German system so thoroughly, that it was actually our men directing the Germans.'

Capricorn's eyebrows shot up.

'Yes, I know,' Manning went on. 'A few discrepancies do come to mind. The story goes you have to lose some to win the most. Things go wrong. We only controlled their British section. And, as you know, they had three separate systems. Our people weren't coordinated, to say the least. And then there were the Americans blundering about.'

'Not the only ones blundering,' Capricorn said, remembering the bitter complaints of the Americans when he was in liaison.

'No, well, now there are people claiming credit for all sorts of things. The fellows over at NID, for instance. Didn't have much to do with them myself, and I don't know.'

'Nor I.'

'No. But the story is being put about that it was an NID man with the help of someone from our shop who engineered the adventures of Mr Horn.'

Capricorn whistled. He recognized the pseudonym used by the Number Two man of the German Reich when he had parachuted over Scotland, certainly one of the most mystifying acts of the war. Hitler had said Hess was mad. The British had said he was mad. The concept of madness, so often convenient . . .

'So he says. A writer fellow, with a lot of imagination. He *says*,' Manning eyed Capricorn, 'that since the whole of The Link had been imprisoned, he set up a dummy "Link" and made contact with "Mr Horn." He also suborned his astrologer, and between fixing up the stars, and sending messages of encouragement and invitation from the newly reconstituted Link, and some Welshmen under his control, he lured Mr H. to these shores. He complained later that the Churchill government made nothing of his great coup, and was very disappointed about the whole affair. So endeth that lesson.'

'But what could that have to do with Diener?'

'Here we get into a more familiar area—total muddle and doubt,' Manning told him.

'Diener was believed, you remember, to have association with the Welsh Nationalists, and possibly, through his Nazi brother-in-law, with The Link. At the time all this happened, he was in a camp with quite a few of the Welsh and some Link members. Not in the same house, he was sharing there with some

other Germans, Karl and Roth. I believe the Englishman Fitz-Marley was there with them. But they were
close by.

'You have to remember that the false Link was NID
and SIS's game. The real one was MI5's pigeon. NID
and SIS, naturally, told MI5 nothing about it. Somehow
MI5 got to believe that some one, or more than one,
from that camp was in touch with Jerry. In fact,' he told
Capricorn bluntly, 'my friend says they damned well
were and that NID's story is a shower of shit. On the
other hand, they're not about to make a stink themselves, seeing they were in charge of the damned place,
and it seems incredible it could have happened at all.
At that time the internees were totally cut off from
everything. No radios. No newspapers. Nothing.'

'How were the messages supposed to be going out?'

'Wireless transmitter—maybe some human agency,
but it was never pinned down.'

'It seems impossible, but even supposing they could
have rigged up something—and how could they have
got the parts?—why should they?' Capricorn was per-
plexed. 'The invitation to Mr Horn was a hoax, we
assume. No one actually invited him.' Manning looked
away but Capricorn continued. 'Suppose it was a
stunt of NID's and/or our shop—let them have the
credit—how would the Germans in the camp have
known about it?'

Manning inhaled slowly. 'My friend didn't know
any more than you do. If the Germans or the Welsh
had managed to build or conceal a receiver, they
might have picked up some of the messages going
back and forth and been deluded themselves. My
party believes that a group in that camp were genu-
inely involved. Perhaps they were contacted by a dou-

ble agent through our lot and put through their paces.'

'Double agent?' Capricorn said nastily. 'You mean ours and the Germans? Or NID and MI5?'

Manning laughed.

'Maybe because my party's from the other shop, he doesn't believe NID's story at all. Just thinks they're taking credit for something that happened. Your guess is as good as anyone's. Whatever the truth of it is, if MI5 was suspicious of Diener before you can imagine how they felt afterwards. They couldn't prove anything. No radio equipment was ever found.'

'But why him?' Capricorn asked. 'You said there were some of the Welsh in the same camp, and some of the real, known Link members.'

'MI5 had snouts in the camp,' Manning said. 'They couldn't give them much to go on, but the snouts said Diener knew about it all right. They were certain something was going on in that house. It was searched and turned upside down, but no luck. All Five could do was to split them up, but they've had their collective malevolent eye on your boy ever since. They'd never let him stay in England, for all that Lord Lawdon has tried to do with Upstairs.'

'But it seems absurd for such a man to be involved in a mad escapade like that,' Capricorn said.

He got up and paced around the room for a few moments before resuming his uncomfortable seat.

'Why would he endanger his life to help a German government that he despised?'

'Assuming that's true,' the cynical Manning replied, 'you must realise, you are looking at the situation from the viewpoint of after-the-war. "Mr Horn" had said he wanted to make peace. The internees didn't know

much, but you remember at the beginning of the war
things looked very bad. A man who knew as much as
Diener, knew what it was going to take even to make
the effort against Germany, let alone to win. He probably thought he was doing the world a favour. After
all, nobody thought badly of Dahlerus, who tried it
two years before.'

Capricorn grimaced. Manning's words made a certain sense. Diener was no admirer of the way the war
had ended in reality. He thought it was the *Götterdämmerung*. What might he have done to avoid that?

'And as far as the risk of being caught,' Manning
continued, 'he could've been pretty sure of himself.
After all, he *wasn't* caught. And it's another aspect of
the difference in point of view from '41 to '47. He
didn't know then what we were going to do with him.
He'd been arrested and imprisoned without trial. For
all he knew, we could have killed him as well.'

'All the same,' Capricorn said, lighting another cigarette, 'it's a lot of assumptions that aren't really justified. Just suppose that someone in that camp, even in
that house, was dickering with the Germans. Why did
it have to be Franz Diener? You said yourself, there
was Paul Roth, who had been a banker to the Nazis
for over a decade. And there was Karl, who seems a
pleasant, sensible sort of fellow, but that '41 point of
view you talk about must have been the same for him
as for Diener, and with an extra edge because he
wasn't a rich man, all he had was his brains as a designer of weapons. He must have realised that his best
years were passing him by, wasted while he was rotting in a gaol. And certainly it would be nothing for him
to build and take apart a receiver and transmitter. He
could probably manage with hairpins.'

'It could've been both of them,' Manning said, 'except that the Powers-that-be don't have their knives sharpened for Karl, so they don't think so. Diener seemed much bigger game, of course.'

He looked reflective. 'It could have been a sort of innocence on his part. He might have thought by arranging the peace he would have an influence for good.'

Capricorn, rather wishing he did not, remembered the conversation between Lise Roth and Diener about *Einfluss*.

'We have had too much influence.'

Manning stretched. 'Of course, it's no use asking me. The Powers move in their mysterious ways their wonders to perform. Perhaps they know more than my little bird turned up, though I don't think so. Oh,' he said, very tired and rubbing his eyes, 'I did forget something damning. There is actual physical proof of a spy in that camp because photographs were taken when it was in rather a shambles near the beginning. They had a great pile of herring that was used for their food, just lying in the open, rotting, with flies— The photographs turned up in Germany and were used for anti-British propaganda.'

He and Capricorn looked at each other. They were both policemen and a solid fact meant more than the greatest pile of suspicion.

'The sum total of it all is,' Manning concluded, 'that everybody wants to forget the whole thing. No nasty questions about who, what, where and when from the *hoi polloi*. They want to get your boy out of the country, and then they'll bury the bones and make an end of it. This business with the girl had got them very fussed. They are convinced he killed her rather than let her leave him with what she knew. But they're not much looking forward to the trial.'

'That's absurd,' Capricorn said. 'I told you, she was the most close-mouthed girl I ever knew of. Besides, I'll bet my next year's pay that that girl was killed by a sadist. There was nothing like that in Diener's sex life. I just checked. And you would be surprised to know—'

'Nothing would surprise me,' Manning said. 'But he wouldn't be the first man to be roused to sadism by a killing. And you said yourself the girl was changing. Made bold by success. Remembering she'd been a human being once with fancies for odd things like licorice. She'd spread her wings and he didn't know how high and far she'd fly.'

'Diener wasn't living with her,' Capricorn protested. 'He was having an affair with Lise Roth. She probably only took the girl there as a red herring. To protect her status as a virtuous matron. The girl was a scarecrow at that time.'

'And she changed.'

Manning hauled himself to his feet. 'It ought to be getting lighter,' he said, nodding at the dark window. 'Damned summer time. I must be going. No, he had the name, he had the game, no doubt. A man with that much time on his hands could handle more than one woman.'

'He protected Lise Roth when he made his statement.' Capricorn was stubborn.

'Would it have made any difference?' Manning, usually in concurrence with his friend, sounded as doubtful as the Chief.

'Think, even if he sullied the lady's fair name, did it mean he couldn't have slipped out and killed the Rilke girl? Lise Roth wouldn't say even if she had missed him. Besides, old Roth knew about the game in the camp. Who knows what he might have done if he were made a public laughing stock?'

'One of the reasons I came,' Manning said, looking down at the mutinous Capricorn, 'was so that you could back off this limb you've crawled out on, before it gets lopped off. Don't think you'd fancy the conjuring business again,' he said with a grin.

Capricorn shuddered. He thanked Manning, who took his leave. Capricorn felt guilty, knowing that his friend had an exhausting day ahead. But he was deeply disquieted. He saw the figure of Diener, as he had seen him that first time, standing at the window against the fading light. What was it he had been saying?

'Damned if I do and damned if I don't.'

He rose unhappily and turned, restless, to his own window. The night was still black. The moon had set; there were no stars. Inside, the remains of food, the dirty plates, gave the room a slovenly air. The smoke hung, a curling pall over the lamp.

'Damned if I do and damned if I don't.'

Manning had closed the case. The same case, after all the fuss, as Superintendent Snow's. Capricorn returned to bed but not to sleep. For a long time he stared into the darkness, his mind whirling. He went into a kind of waking nightmare where indeed he was out on the limb of a tree that was chopped off, he was dismissed from the Force and reduced to following in the train of the Merlinos, a reluctant conjurer.

Pritchard, Snow, and Manning. Between them they had built up a case against Diener that seemed impregnable, a veritable fortress of fact. But even as the waves of anxiety washed over him, strong enough to make him toss and turn, fighting the sheets as if they were an enemy, he became aware of another small solid reality beneath his concern. And that was his own belief that they were all wrong. That was why he could not back down; and that was why he was going forward, no matter the cost. One white night or many made no difference. A man had to act on his own beliefs, he thought, very tired, or else he was less than a reluctant conjurer; he was nothing at all.

Having decided, the waves of anxiety still beat against him, but with lessened force. He threw back the covers, and lit yet another cigarette, his mind clearing as he gave up all effort to sleep. Yes, he thought Manning wrong. The facts were true, but the interpretation unsound. The fortress of fact that had been built seemed now to be like one of The Great Capricornus's creations: the boxes in which one 'saw' ladies being cut in half; the coffins apparently so solid from which he then escaped.

At last Capricorn lay down, to rest a little before it was time to go. The citadel of fact was all very well, but it had been built on the wrong ground. He had to go ahead, take the last and most dangerous risk, and hope for one tiny bit of luck to prove where that citadel belonged.

6

Filled with more obduracy than optimism, Capricorn was at Pritchard's desk at the appointed time, before Peabody would be out and about. Pritchard telephoned and made the appointment. The farmer was agreeable, if somewhat puzzled.

He met the two detectives in a room in his house that had been turned into an office, where he was puzzling over a quantity of forms with the aid of electric light and a pair of spectacles. He remembered making the complaint that now interested Capricorn. His man had reported that the trespass had taken place on Friday night, but he himself had been busy with an early crop on another property a few miles distant and he had not had time to inspect it until the morning he called Pritchard.

As soon as it was light enough the three men tramped over the ground, Peabody pointing out, as nearly as he could recall, the place where the tracks had been made. Owing to the dry spell that week they had still been clear on his inspection. Yes, they could have been made by one horse. The rider had been either very skilled or lucky not to have hurt himself at night on the branches of the thickly clustered trees. The area extended from about a hundred or two hundred yards from the lane near the Brandenburg all the way down to the easterly flank of the orchard.

The trees were wet in the morning mist and heavy with apples. A few windfalls lay in the path among the rotting leaves. Peabody branched off here and there, not quite sure now, with the tracks covered and muddied, just where they had lain, but they came at last to the orchard's end, at roughly the point he recalled the offending rider having gone.

'Did you notice where the tracks went from here?' Capricorn asked.

Peabody had not. Beyond that point were the Marley woods, damp and dismal as the orchard but without its fine crop of fruit, in which he had no interest.

'Was there any sign that the rider doubled back to Illwood?'

Not through the orchard, the farmer told them, but he had not bothered to search beyond his own land. The rider, or riders, might have gone through Marley wood over to High Marley, or circled round the wood over pasture land back to the village, taking a westerly route, but he had no way of knowing.

Pritchard looked unhappy. He felt this to be hardly conclusive of anything, especially since the complaint had been lodged against the riding school which had not denied that the trespass was very likely done by one of its pupils. The young riders were constantly in trouble for similar offenses. Determined, Capricorn went on with his plan, and drove the reluctant Pritchard through the grey morning over the High Marley and up to the stables of Marley Castle.

Two horses' heads protruded over the loose boxes and stared suspiciously at the strangers. In a stall an elderly man was squatting beside a black stallion, holding the horse's hoof between his knees, carefully rubbing liniment on a joint. Pritchard introduced himself and Capricorn, explained their business, and brought out a photograph of Ingeborg Rilke.

The stallion whinnied excitedly. The man continued stroking his fetlock, calming him down, and pointedly ignored the photograph. He remained dumb to Pritchard's questions and shot the policemen a look oddly like that of the horses.

Pritchard, annoyed, spoke of taking him down to the station at High Marley. The groom mumbled that 'the Cap'n was down to a meeting at the New Town and they could ask him.' He added, half under his breath, that he didn't know anything and a man couldn't tell what he didn't know.

Pritchard grew restive, but Capricorn, smiling and agreeable, seemed to relax, more and more, into an indolent curiosity. He stared about him, admired the bay and the chestnut, and exclaimed particularly over the black stallion. It was exceptional, with a proud head, superb shoulders and slim flanks.

'He's all right now,' the groom replied, frowning. 'Got a nasty swelling last week.' For a moment he forgot his suspicions, reminded of a grievance. 'The Captain rode him too hard,' he confided. 'In a temper, that's what. Usually, he's careful with Midnight.'

Capricorn was all amiable concern. Diplomatically, he expressed sympathy for the horse without criticising its owner. Then, as though he had all the time in the world, he leaned against a post with his hands in his pocket, and looked up at the sky. He speculated, at some length, on the chances of the weather clearing. It was good luck the Captain had had such a fine day for his shoot, he added. Probably the first shoot he'd had in a long time. People lived quietly these days, since the war.

The groom blew his nose on a large handkerchief and nodded. That they did. Not that he knew much about what went on in the castle. He lived in High Marley and only came up in the day. The Captain, he could always take care of the horses himself, if needed.

The photograph Pritchard had shown him was the one of Ingeborg Rilke in her 'maiden aunt' period. Capricorn took it from him and idly compared it to the *La Belle* cover.

'Amazing, isn't it,' he murmured, to no one in particular. 'Women, they're beyond belief. It's the same girl,' he explained, showing both pictures to the groom.

'I'll never believe that,' the groom answered, firmly.

He was quite friendly now, but he still insisted he had never seen either of those ladies. Of course, the stables were a good bit off from the castle and he didn't notice all the comings and goings. If the young lady had been a rider, of course, he would have known if she—he looked at the photographs again, puzzled—or they had visited, but so many young ladies now were not. Miss Mayne, who'd been engaged to poor Major Fitz-Marley, she was a fine horsewoman and he had known her well.

Capricorn let it go. Casually, he asked how long ago the stallion had been injured. What day had it been, last week, if the groom could recall? The man remembered that the Captain had had him out one morning before he came up to work, but as to which morning it was, he couldn't say. Nor did any of Capricorn's questions help. The man wasn't stubborn; he didn't know. One day, he explained, was much the same as another. It was about a week ago, that's all he could tell.

Pritchard looked at Capricorn, part disappointed, part relieved, obviously anxious to go.

Capricorn lingered. 'Well, you've done a good job,' He nodded at the stallion's foreleg. 'No sign of swelling now.'

The groom nodded in satisfaction. 'Farley's liniment. Nothing like it, if it's properly used. The bottle was almost gone so I said to the Captain, "I'll walk to the town and get it myself," I said. "No use leaving that joint to stiffen up, van or no van.'"

'No van?' Capricorn said softly.

'No. That van it went dead the day before over by Illwood and the Captain, he'd been in a roaring temper. So he'd took Midnight and rode like the devil and I have to go traipsing back to town no sooner nor I got here. But he's fine now, look at him.'

He stood and regarded his charge proudly. The stallion lifted its head and whinnied again, softly now, and allowed the groom to stroke his high arched neck. Capricorn looked on, happy enough to stroke both of them. He met Pritchard's gaze, and knew that, if he still wasn't sure, at least he would be helpful.

It took some persuasion and considerable time before Capricorn was armed with a search warrant. Pritchard had a case of nerves concerning what would happen if they found nothing, which seemed to him the most likely result of their search, but he proceeded stoically. He informed the High Marley police of what was going on, but at Capricorn's request he took extra men from Illwood to help in the search. Illwood, Capricorn thought, was not quite so much, these days at any rate, part of the Fitz-Marley fief.

Even with the warrant, the policemen had trouble gaining access to Marley Castle. They banged and rat-

tled on the big main door for about twenty minutes
before the old man reproachfully opened up. The
search had been planned in Pritchard's office, and, ig-
noring Herne's protests, the men moved methodically
through the few occupied rooms, hoping they
wouldn't need to go through the rest.

Capricorn and Pritchard went through the small library, while Herne twittered and expostulated, standing by them and wringing his hands. All they found
was more of the same kind of papers that Capricorn
had already seen, workaday records to do with the estate, jumbled up with Nazi propaganda of the crudest
sort.

The only possible objects of interest were bunches
of keys, some small and modern, some old, large and
rusty, and one so big, heavy and imposing that The
Great Capricornus might have used it in his act to
catch the eye of his audience. Capricorn put them
away to check on later. This was too much for Herne,
who said he was going for the police, and gazed out
forlornly into the main hall that was being ransacked
by a team of blue-uniformed men.

Both detectives felt uncomfortable. Senile. If they
had to take testimony from him, of course, it would be
worthless. Capricorn soothed the old man. When he
was quiet, Capricorn went ahead anyway. He showed
Herne the two photographs of Ingeborg Rilke and
asked if she had ever stayed at the castle. But Herne
was even more suspicious than the groom and determined to give no information at all. He knew of no
ladies who had stayed in the house since Mrs Fitz-
Marley died. The captain may have had guests, he
wouldn't know. The Captain gave few dinners, and
Herne went to bed early, as did his wife.

A sergeant from Illwood looked in to say that all the

rooms in use had been gone over except one, but that room was a bedroom and there was an old lady lying on the bed. Herne was upset again and Pritchard had to quiet him. They looked in on the room, a strangely Victorian spot in the otherwise bare household, filled with china, bric-a-brac, red plush curtains, rugs, footstools, cushions, stuffed armchairs, a wash basin with jug and pitcher. Mrs Herne was asleep, and after a quiet conference, Pritchard told Herne they would leave her room until she woke.

While the old man was grateful for a moment, or at least less angry, Capricorn asked him to show the unoccupied rooms. Herne was clearly reluctant, but Capricorn produced the bunches of keys and in an ordinary tone of voice, with no trace of hurry or suggestion of the unusual, asked which key went where. It was quite beyond him, he added, to puzzle it out.

Herne took a bunch of keys from his hand, smiling patronizingly, and said that of course, one had to know the castle. He turned and lead the two men on a tour, pausing to point out anything of historical or family interest, in a practiced manner, remembering from years before, perhaps, when he had shown interested guests around the building. Time was slipping back and forth in his mind, and soon he seemed to have forgotten that the two men in country clothes were policemen at all.

They were shown room after room. As the lived-in quarters, except for the Hernes', had been almost medieval, Capricorn had had visions of damp stone, gaping walls, broken staircases, rooms bleak and strange. The reality was much duller. Many of the rooms they looked into had once been arranged for comfortable living, with plaster, paint, furniture that was now piled up against the walls and covered with dust

sheets, huge rolled carpets, and layers of thick dust
over everything that rose as they entered, proclaiming
clearly that no one else had disturbed those rooms for
a long time.

They tramped on, the number of rooms seeming
endless, and all under the unbroken pall of dust. The
only variation was the difficulty in entering, as many
of the old locks were rusted and jammed. On the top
floor they looked into servants' quarters that surely
had not been occupied since the First World War, and
Herne, limping but still giving his lecture on castle
life, fumbled with one more lock on one more door.
Again, the lock was stuck.

It hardly seemed worth the trouble, but Capricorn
took the key, brushed it off, and tried again. The lock
still wouldn't budge. He took a small object from his
pocket that made Pritchard raise his eyebrows. Plac-
ing it in the lock, he tried it gently, poked about for a
while, scraped and blew in the keyhole, and tried
again. The door opened to his touch.

'The old nurseries,' Herne said. 'The Major and the
Captain were the last to use them.'

Even the Captain had been a child. There was a
rocking horse, an old Meccano set. Cups on the chim-
ney piece; best rider, sixteen and under class, Illwood
and Marley Agricultural. Children's books. A pile of
old copies of *Boys' Own*. Cricket bats. Tennis rac-
quets. An old boxing glove.

'That was the Major's,' Horne said. 'The Major, he
was the great one for sports. Swimming, boating.'

'And the Captain?' Capricorn asked genially, looking at a heap of old wires and junk in a corner. 'What
were his interests?'

'Oh, the Captain—he was more mechanical,' Herne
said, peering around through his thick glasses. 'When

he was a little boy he loved the Meccano. And when he was older he was always tinkering with something. Took all the clocks apart once and the Colonel was very put out. And spent all his money on wireless valves and such things. He had catalogues and wrote up to London, and him just a lad.'

Pritchard was looking over at Capricorn as he examined the mess of stuff, wondering why he was wasting time. Pritchard's frown had deepened with each successive frustration, and he was restless, seized by a growing desire to leave.

'Radio parts,' Capricorn said. 'Very clever. A transmitter. An amateur enthusiast, eh?'

'Yes, sir.' Herne smiled, pleased to hear the Captain praised. 'Mr Frederick—the Captain that is—he was one of those amateur wireless operators when he was only a boy. But it was the building he liked best,' he said, back in a rosier time and looking happy. 'Liked to build things and take them apart. The Colonel used to grumble about the money he spent, a boy his age, for the parts, sir, but Mrs Fitz-Marley took his side, there's no harm in it, she always said. Better than collecting birds' eggs like some boys—that used to upset the poor lady dreadfully. She had a bird sanctuary on the grounds.'

Herne's forehead puckered, grieving with the dead woman over the fate of stolen eggs, the present and its troubles momentarily displaced. It seemed natural to him when he was thanked and tipped, as he had been in his role of caretaker and guide years before, and he led the way back downstairs hindered only by his rheumatism and bad sight, his fear of his companions quite forgotten.

Pritchard glanced at Capricorn doubtfully as they descended. Capricorn had told him as much as he thought necessary of Manning's confidences, and Pritchard had realised the reason for Capricorn's interest in the transmitter.

'It's not proof of anything, you know,' he said in an undertone. 'Certainly nothing to do with our case. It *may* mean something to do with that other business but—where are you going?'

Capricorn sped back to the old nursery, and collected a sizeable heap of the old radio equipment. He bundled it into a rag rug from the nursery floor, and holding it over his shoulder, made his way down the steep flight of steps to catch up with the others.

'Turn again, Whittington,' Pritchard said, as he caught sight of him. 'Though I doubt you'll end up as Lord Mayor of anything.'

His rueful look changed to apprehension and then to alarm as they reached the main hall and were confronted by the bristling, scarlet-faced figure of Fitz-Marley himself.

'Pritchard,' he barked, 'what the hell is the meaning of this? I had word from Illwood something was going on. I've already spoken to the C.C. I'll have you out of the Force. Get your men out of here. I suppose it's that damned actor from London behind this.'

Gossip travelled fast in the country, Capricorn thought. He put his bundle down and approached Fitz-Marley, whom he overtopped by more than half a foot, and looked down at him.

'Sergeant Capricorn, at your service,' he said.

Fitz-Marley was carrying a stick. His arm tightened and for a moment Capricorn thought he was going to strike him. So, apparently, did Pritchard, because he moved between the two men.

'Get out,' Fitz-Marley said in a low tense voice. 'Out.'

Pritchard produced the warrant.

Fitz-Marley ripped it up without looking at it.

'You got this under false pretences. Lied to the magistrate. Perjured yourself. If you think I'm going to allow this you are very much mistaken. My solicitor is with the magistrate now and I expect them here in a few minutes.'

The devil you do. Capricorn almost said it aloud. If there were to be a legal argument over the warrant the search might be stopped. The quick look that he and Pritchard had given some of the rooms so far was merely preliminary. And there were the grounds to be gone over. He looked at the arrogant figure before him and thought, I'm damned if I'll let you get away with it.

A rap sounded at the door and old Herne was there amazingly fast to admit a phalanx of impressive-looking gentlemen. Pritchard was white. Fitz-Marley smiled, a thin-lipped smile with his strong teeth gleaming as if in triumph. Capricorn was poker-faced. For a moment it might have been a tableau of opposing wills, but Capricorn had no intention of remaining still.

'You will excuse me, Captain, while you talk to your lawyer,' he said firmly. 'But we must continue our search.'

One of the important-looking men came towards him with a document in his hand, which Capricorn managed not to see as he strode away. Pritchard's eyebrows went up hopelessly, and he looked as though he wanted to shrink.

'Just keep on there, you men,' Capricorn called firmly to two constables who were peering down the stairs from the floor above in some perplexity.

The elder stood irresolute, while the younger, he

who had been castigated by Superintendent Snow for his sleepy looks at the Brandenburg, glided back into the Captain's bedroom, which he had already searched, with some idea of taking refuge. There wasn't much to search. A military-style bed, a wardrobe with a few clothes, a small chest. All had been turned out and there was nothing of the sort he had been ordered to look for.

The only other piece of furniture was a heavy oak settle that stood under the window against the wall. It looked so heavy, and it was so flush with the wall that the two constables hadn't bothered to pull it out. Now, with an idea of looking busy, and rather than show his face out there in *that* row, he pulled at the bench.

It moved out abruptly from the wall. Something glimmered as it fell to the floor, something that had fallen over the back of the bench to remain hidden and forgotten. Not much of anything, he thought, turning it over in his hands . . . or was it?

Downstairs a great argument was going on. The Captain was trying to have the Scotland Yard sergeant thrown out, the constable saw with a thrill of horror. The men were all standing around and arguing, the Captain was shouting, and the tall sergeant was going on with the search as if he were alone, taking down some of the weapons from the wall, and examining them and seeming to weigh them in his hands.

The constable started downstairs. One of the gentlemen took hold of the sergeant's arm. Sergeant Capricorn looked up and saw the young policeman descending.

'Just a moment, sir,' Capricorn said softly to the man attempting to restrain him. 'I think the constable has what we were looking for.'

He went towards him and took the garment the young man had found. Later on, it was some consolation to Snow, who was not about to overpraise his own sergeant, that it was not Capricorn who had found the vital piece of evidence. He had had a march stolen on him, Snow said derisively, by 'the laziest copper in Illwood.'

It was a small thing after all, easily overlooked, even by the man who had hastily whisked together all the girl's clothes left in his rooms and destroyed them. A wisp of cloth, fine enough to draw through a ring, yet as Capricorn drew it out, under the eye of all the watching men, it was obviously a girl's blouse, fine, delicate, the colour of dead leaves, a perfect thing of its kind, except for a tear on one of the full, loose sleeves.

Fitz-Marley stared. Capricorn went to where he had left the rag rug, and dumped its contents at Fitz-Marley's feet.

'What's left of your transmitter and receiving set,' he said. 'An interesting achievement.'

There was quiet in the hall. For a time Fitz-Marley continued to glare at Capricorn. His face was ashen. In the silence the ticking from a great old clock in the centre of the hall sounded ominous and somehow intolerable.

Fitz-Marley spat out one word. 'Conjurer!'

Then he turned his back on the assembled group and marched off into his library. A small man, Capricorn thought. Did England really ever have to fear the like of him? Then he thought of the men in the dock at Nuremberg. They, too, had seemed small men, showing no sign of personality commensurate with the evil they had actually committed. Still, the Captain, disloyal, peppery, eccentric, vicious as he was, did not seem the stuff of which dictators were made. His dream would never have come true; he would not have been the leader, an English Führer.

'Shouldn't we . . .' Pritchard began, moving to follow him.

'He can't get out of there,' Capricorn said, with the interior of that room, with its one high window clear in his mind. 'Give him a minute.'

Without directly meeting the gaze of anyone, he was aware of a certain appreciation from the group of men huddled near the door. The Captain had been a soldier and was from an old army family respected in this country. After the sound of a shot came from the other room, there was an audible sigh of relief.

Song and Shifting Afterpiece

It was late in the afternoon before Capricorn and
Pritchard were finished and on their way back to Illwood. The Chief at the Yard had been advised, the
Chief Constable had been consulted. Snow had been informed, and Capricorn already had written up his
notes. Pritchard, thoughtful as always, had telephoned
Diener and dismissed the man on duty at the Brandenburg. The important people had dispersed with a
quietly thankful air about them. The only real grief
shown for the Captain was from old Mr and Mrs
Herne, who had wept for young master Frederick.

The skies had cleared, but Pritchard sat thoughtful
as Capricorn drove, frowning and hardly aware of the
sunset that glowed full and red through the almost
leafless branches of Marley Wood.

'What made you think of the Captain in the first
place?' he puzzled. 'He was the last—I'd never seen
him with the girl. Had no idea he knew her as more
than an acquaintance.'

'I had a strong hint when he tried to kill me,' Capricorn answered drily. 'I knew it wasn't an accident, and
that meant Karl or the Captain. The Captain seemed
to have an alibi, but I checked with the four men
who'd been in the north fields. Wigmore said something that made me wonder and I got it out of Fitch

that the Captain had slipped back to the house for a few minutes—something about Herne and the dinner.'

Pritchard looked glum.

'I don't think they deliberately withheld that when you took their statements,' Capricorn added. 'It probably was so unimportant to them it slipped their minds. They certainly knew he didn't shoot me by accident and murder was the last thing they would suspect. Fitz-Marley thought I was on his trail for the "Horn" business because I mentioned something from Five's file on Paul Roth. But it was when I passed the stables that something dropped into place on the "how". Before that—'

He pulled over to allow an oncoming horse and cart to pass. The animal proceeded placidly, the driver gave them a nod of thanks, then the clip-clop of the horse's hooves was submerged in the sound of the motor as Capricorn moved off.

'And Lise Roth had told me about his horses,' he said ruefully. 'But who thinks in terms of horses now?'

'I should have,' Pritchard said, even more downcast. 'I knew about his stables. But as you say—who thinks in terms of horses? His estate van was broken down; he had to be driven to the castle. I never thought of his riding back.'

'Like you, I just didn't believe that Diener committed that murder,' Capricorn said, reminding Pritchard of his good judgement and cheering him up. 'Nor did I believe in a madman—though I suppose Fitz-Marley was that, in a way. The thing that puzzled me was her apparent dropping out of sight for nearly two years. I didn't believe it had really happened. Lise Roth was obviously lying. And when you think she was the girl's confidante, and was released about the same time— you can see how that narrows down the possibilities.

It was someone the Roths knew, and someone free at that time. It let out Diener, but not Karl.'

'But the Captain—she was so plain, then—' Pritchard said.

'Roth and the Captain had become friends, and after their release, the Captain was introduced to Mrs Roth. He was a womaniser with strong sadistic leanings. Lise Roth introduced her homeless, poverty-stricken friend who was also terrified and complaisant. The girl had always been in gaol. She merely went to one more.'

'But she was free,' Pritchard said. 'Why would she accept. . . .'

'She'd never known anything else,' Capricorn said bitterly. 'To her the world was nothing but sadistic men, harpy-like women, and prisons.'

'But nobody knew she'd been there,' Pritchard said, worrying over it, as if there might still be some strange mistake.

'Nobody that spoke up,' Capricorn amended. 'The Captain was a man to pen his women up in any case, but with Ingeborg Rilke—he would never take her in public. He was ashamed of her. She had to be hidden, she was too pathetic, and shabby. That's what gave him away,' he said, remembering. 'His meanness was his undoing. She'd spent the night with him, of course. That's why she was wearing that shabby old nightgown; it was one she'd had in the camp and had left behind in the castle. It puzzled me for a long time. Since she'd known Diener, all her things were good and new.'

'She left Fitz-Marley for Diener,' Pritchard said.

'No,' Capricorn shook his head. 'She would never have had the courage or sense to leave him. Lise Roth, who seems to be a procuress by nature, introduced

Fitz-Marley to the Marquise. He fell for her charms and threw Ingeborg out to sink or swim. I daresay the girl went to Lise Roth. By that time, Diener had been released and his love affair with Mrs Roth was under way. It was a good move for her to take the girl to the Brandenburg to cover her own tracks. She did it so well that everyone was convinced.'

'I always thought the Captain a stupid man, rather ridiculous,' Pritchard said slowly. 'But I never thought of him as dangerous.'

'He was dangerous only to the helpless,' Capricorn said, 'but you have to remember, he wanted to make us all helpless.'

As they approached Illwood, a red Aston-Martin came roaring up, nearly driving them off the road. This time Charles Lawdon stopped. Capricorn regarded his cheerful, healthy young face and remembered how in desperation he had almost suspected him.

Lawdon was actually apologizing. He did it quite nicely and looked at Capricorn with interest. 'I say, you found out who killed that girl, didn't you, poor devil, the girl I mean, not the killer. Got old Diener off the hot spot. Glad you did. He'd been very decent to me.'

He turned red under Capricorn's gaze. So it wasn't only for Lise Roth's personal pleasure that Diener had bought her the sable coat. Young Charles, Capricorn reflected, was about the age Diener's son would have been, if he had lived.

Pritchard gave the boy a paternal glance. 'Don't you have anything else to do but to drive about being a menace to the public, as well as the police?'

'No,' Lawdon said simply.

'Would you like to work?' Pritchard asked.

'Yes, if I could find something. But not politics or business,' he said hastily. 'I don't care much about money but something exciting.'

'Try joining the police,' Capricorn advised, half seriously. 'That should fill your order. And we're short of men.'

Lawdon looked at him thoughtfully. 'I might just do that,' he said. He grinned. 'Father would have a fit.'

His car zoomed off but soon slowed down to a more sedate pace.

'What have you done?' Pritchard said, in mock despair.

'It might actually work,' Capricorn said. 'Do you want to go to the station?'

'I'll come up with you to the Brandenburg,' Pritchard said. 'There are still a few things I don't. . . . Why did the Captain decide to kill the girl that night do you think? I can understand, with her getting more independent, he might have regretted letting something slip, here or there, but what precipitated it that night, I wonder?'

'He'd been thinking about it, I expect, for some time,' Capricorn said slowly. 'Brooding over it. The others worried about the Joyce case, and talking, talking, talking. And he was jealous of Diener. Diener had Lise Roth, and the Captain was very attracted to her. His Marquise had left him in short order, not without telling him a few unpleasant truths. And although he hadn't wanted the Rilke girl, she had become attractive in the eyes of other men and she obviously worshipped Diener. She had only feared the Captain, and he knew it. So when Diener had that very public quarrel—Fitz-Marley was there, remember—it may have seemed like his chance.'

'Get rid of the girl who might be dangerous, and a man he hated at the same time,' Pritchard said.

'Yes. Of course, Diener would have an alibi in Lise Roth, but Fitz-Marley could have blackmailed her, if necessary, to keep silent. He knew her, you see. There was the matter of the treachery in the camp. Fitz-Marley would not have gone to death alone. If he implicated Roth and Diener, Mrs Roth might have ended up a shorn lamb. He was safe enough. She would never take a risk like that to save the life of her best friend.

'It was all so easy,' he went on, with a sigh. 'All he had to do, before he left, was to order Ingeborg to come to the castle that night and to tell no one. And she did. She couldn't ask for the car and so she walked. Three miles through the woods, to her death.'

'I'll never understand that,' Pritchard said, shaking his head.

The Brandenburg came into view, mellow and pleasant in its green setting.

'Why did she want to leave Diener's protection?'

'It wasn't Diener himself she wanted to leave. She must have had some idea of escaping from the whole sorry mess. Braun. Diener and Lise Roth. Hiding herself, perhaps, somewhere in London. I expect it seemed possible when she was with her model friend in town. A very confident young woman. But away from her the confidence melted. She could stand up against the wrath of her good friend, but not against the demands of her enemy. Her gaoler snapped his fingers; she went.'

As they approached the gates Capricorn looked up at the heavy black eagles put there by the family from Brandenburg, the first Germans who had bought the place from the Fitz-Marleys. For a moment he was back in Germany again, back to the victims he had seen released from camps and the terrified subjection of the women to their guards.

'How did he manage the gates?' Pritchard asked.

Capricorn took the big key, that had seemed like a piece of stage property, from his kit. 'I think he had the key,' he said. 'There had probably always been a key to that gate in the castle. Though the lock could be opened in a minute by anyone who really tried.'

He got out of the car and tried the key in the lock, demonstrating to Pritchard how easily it worked.

'No rust,' Pritchard said, examining the key. 'He'd cleaned it up. He couldn't have known, though, that Diener would leave the porch door open.'

'No. That club was a weapon of opportunity. He didn't need a weapon. He probably intended to strangle her long, thin neck.'

Pritchard shook his head. 'Almost any of those weapons in the castle could have knocked her out, I suppose.'

'Or even a stick,' Capricorn said. 'Well, we don't have to trouble looking for that.'

'He enjoyed that killing,' Pritchard said, with the most unforgiving tone of which he was capable. He fidgeted in disgust. 'The nerve of the man, just cantering along through the night with an unconscious woman across the saddle.'

'Not so much nerve,' Capricorn answered. 'It was a chance in a million that anyone would be in Marley Wood at that hour. And he could have made up any number of tales. Out for a ride and found her wandering. Sleepwalking, perhaps. The girl herself wouldn't know he'd intended murder. He was safe. Mad, but only nor' nor' westerly.'

'Hm. He fakes signs of struggle in the ditch, walks

away, locks the gate and rides back to Marley,' Pritchard said. 'And no one the wiser, if his horse hadn't
bruised his leg. Or if you hadn't come down on the
case.'

He looked at the young sergeant with respect.

'Superintendent Snow's case,' Capricorn said, smiling. He saw Diener approaching and slipped away.
Pritchard was Diener's friend, and entitled to any
thanks that might be forthcoming. As he ran up the
stairs, his mind registered the fact that Diener, safe
now to go to America, to begin again, had not looked
suddenly rejuvenated. He still bore the mark of the
years that had come upon him so suddenly with the
knowledge of Lise Roth's treachery. Unlucky in love,
he thought absently, collecting his things. Diener's wife,
his mistress in Cobleigh, Lise Roth. And the girl who
had worshipped him had been only his pathetic ward.
He had given protection and friendship and never felt
the glow of her love.

Capricorn looked round the room, bare again, with
his things neatly packed. No trace of Ingeborg Rilke
here. Her ghost was laid.

He had spoken to Manning already in the afternoon, an extremely relieved Manning. He had told
him of the miniature camera that they had found in
Fitz-Marley's pocket. Manning had speculated why
the Captain had never gotten rid of the thing.

'Perhaps he still had a use for it,' Capricorn had replied, tartly.

'Well, it'll all be tidied away now,' Manning had
told him. 'No more said and done than necessary. And
you haven't bloodied your head. Might even get some
credit.'

His Chief had indicated that. There would not be
any sudden promotion, the Yard didn't work that way.

But in the fullness of time, as more Superintendents were appointed, his name might be considered, not unfavourably.

All in all he was having a pleasant professional moment. Madame Braun took the news of his departure calmly, but with the greatest sign of pleasure he had seen on her mask-like face Nora bade him a sad farewell and Mrs Dermott sought him out with a look of strong approval, and shook his hand. Smiling, he wondered for a moment how two such strong-minded ladies as Mrs Dermott and Madame Braun got along in one house. Very daring, he asked her.

'She knows her job,' Mrs Dermott said. 'A hard worker. But I doubt I'll be staying on. When Mr Diener goes, I shall look for my own place in London. I have my man's pension and a bit saved. No more live-in jobs, I'll just work in the day for one or two gentlemen.'

Capricorn thought wistfully how it would be, if his flat ever came into being, to have her for a housekeeper. He told her so, gave her his card, and asked her to keep in touch.

'Ah will,' she said. 'When ah get settled, ah'll have you in mind.'

He heard Diener's voice in the lounge as he came down, talking to Pritchard. Tho others had melted away. The Roths were probably packing for the *Paloma*. Braun was keeping out of the way, leaving Madame behind the bar. Was Karl still closeted with Randy Clarke? He needn't be nervous anymore, Capricorn reflected. He could stay in England if he wished. The dead were about to bury their dead.

'But aren't you happy to be going to the United States?' Pritchard was asking. 'To begin again, a new company—'

'What difference does it make?' Diener said, sighing. 'Oh, it's better, I suppose, than to be in prison. But in the long run, what is the good to build, to plan, to start something to last fifty, a hundred years? The United States that you know will not survive. The Marxists, the Communists or whatever they call themselves then, will have won there. The Americans will not know how to fight. Look how easily they won the war—to lose it to Russia and China. You think they will be able to save their own homeland?'

Whatever Pritchard answered was lost in Diener's flood of words.

'You will see. Gradually they will take the universities, train the teachers—remember Cambridge in the thirties? Already they have the cinema.' He gestured towards the television set that he himself had placed on the bar. 'They will take that, believe me. The radio made Hitler possible.' His face darkened. 'What monstrous Führer will be projected by that screen?' Like all his questions, it was merely rhetorical.

'They will take over the newspapers, the magazines, their men will write the books, they will infiltrate the lawyers and the judiciary. The people will be enslaved—certainly if Russia defeats them, perhaps without a war at all. No,' he sighed over his drink. 'It is the *Götterdämmerung*. There is no escape.'

'Perhaps you'll feel more hopeful once you are away from here,' Capricorn said as he joined them. 'In a different country, with a new life.'

Diener jumped to his feet, and tried to thank him, in German and in English. Capricorn insisted no thanks were necessary. He was to drive Pritchard back to the station on his way to London—the thought of filing his report made him happy—and so he sat down and joined them for a moment. Such was the glow of his spirit, he even accepted the offer of a drink.

'I imagine you'll be leaving for the States very soon,' he said.

'Oh, I'll go there,' Diener said. 'But I may not stay. With the world the way it is, perhaps I shall retire. Find some place where life is still pleasant, a few German friends to talk to, where there is some Rhine wine, a terrace, a view. Roth has told me so long about Buenos Aires—it might be a good place for an old man.'

'Buenos Aires?' Capricorn said, in great surprise. Could Diener still love Lise Roth, after everything?

Diener smiled at his surprise, in understanding. 'Perhaps we all betray each other, at the last,' he said.

He had forgiven her, Lise Roth. Well, forgiveness is a Christian virtue, but not like this, Capricorn thought. Surely, not like this. He felt full of rebellion at Diener's too easy, submissive charity. A man, he thought, should have more pride.

The two men looked at each other in comprehension and regret. It was time to leave, Capricorn thought and rose, tall and proud, the CID man, his case over, crowned with success.

Madame Braun was still behind the bar, and there could have been no one at the reception desk, for a visitor came peering round the door alone—a strange visitor for the Brandenburg, short, squat, her henna'd hair cascading in many ringlets down to her purple velvet cloak, her finest garment, trimmed with a hundred ermine tails.

'Merle, you silly twit,' his aunt's voice boomed. 'Oh, there you are. Bin looking all over for you. Having a booze-up, eh?' She beamed on the assembled company.

'Aunt Dolly,' Capricorn said, resigned. 'How nice to see you.'

'Bin trying to get you,' she said. 'Got news. The man called up from the flat and said he rang you but you was out. They want you to go and look. Something about the plaster done or the floors, I forget. So I caught the train and came to tell you. I fancied 'aving dinner some place posh,' she said. 'Because I've done it, Merle.'

Her face was a red glow of satisfaction. 'Booked our turn on television. We signed the contracts today. It was a friend of Tod what done it, though we don't want Tod with us. But they'd like a man, for the women, see. Someone worth looking at, like us girls. You'd be just the article if only you'd give up that silly police lark, Merle. What you want to do it for anyway? Your poor mother must've been frightened by *The 'ound of the Baskervilles*.' She frowned and began to look angry.

Diener answered for him. 'The police aren't all so bad,' he said, amused, with an expressive look at Capricorn. 'They can be quite useful.'

Capricorn, who was longing to get back to the Yard, could only offer her congratulations and dinner and make his apologies to Pritchard.

Diener had been watching Dolly with interest. 'Miss Merlino, isn't it?' he said. 'I've seen you many times, at Cobleigh Music Hall, before the war. You haven't changed at all.'

Dolly beamed in delight, and Diener begged her to be seated and called for Braun's best wine. They talked of old times with such content, that it ended with Diener pressing her to stay to dine with him while the policemen went about their business. Dolly seemed quite happy with the substitution.

'I'll send your aunt home with Price,' Diener promised, and waved goodbye to Capricorn in front of the hotel—a man condemned now to a strange exile, sunken, diminished, but still gracious, still chivalrous to women. From the bar came the brassy sound of Dolly singing one of her favourite ballads, with its own irony.

It's the same the whole world over,
It's the poor what gets the blame;
It's the rich that gets the pleasure:
Isn't it a bloomin' shame?

Capricorn left Pritchard at the station, but before they parted Pritchard assured him that Diener had not known Fitz-Marley was the killer, although he had had his suspicions, and had been tormented by them. One of the reasons he had kept to his rooms was to avoid seeing the man.

'Of course, he should have been more frank with us but there were compelling reasons,' Pritchard said, apologetically. He was misguidedly loyal to Mrs Roth and his other friends, but he was innocent.'

He smiled widely in relief and said goodbye with sincere thanks. A truly good man, Capricorn thought, as Pritchard disappeared into the station in the fading light, to his flower beds, and quiet routine. Perhaps almost too good, too trusting for a detective. Snow would certainly think so. Would Snow have considered Diener innocent? He thought not.

The road to London was almost free of traffic and he sped along with not even an owl tonight to distract him. Snow would say that withholding information in a capital case was an offense that should have legal consequences. Withholding information about dealings with an enemy in time of war . . . was inno-

cence? Capricorn moved to ease the pressure on his
shoulder. He himself had drunk with Diener. Snow
would not have done that.

But Snow had always been a policeman. Snow had
not lived in the strange world of spies and counter-
spies. If Diener were guilty of a crime in failing to betray Fitz-Marley's treason, what of the Service itself
that had apparently arranged the whole exploit?
They, too, had kept their knowledge and let Fitz-
Marley walk out, a free man, to resume his life as the
leading landowner of Marley and a public figure.

And if SIS had run that whole operation as they
claimed, was Fitz-Marley technically a traitor? Treachery may have been his intention, but did the law take
cognizance of the intention or the deed? Capricorn
shook his head, as he left the country behind him and
made his way through London to the Embankment and
the Yard. Strange and puzzling questions, perhaps only
to be dealt with by lawyers in the courts, yet the Service
could not have afforded a public trial.

He left word that he would be using Snow's office,
wanting a little more quiet than he would find in the
room he shared with other sergeants.

As he finished up some paper work, Snow's certain
judgement troubled his mind. Patriotism, treason
seemed simple matters to Snow. But in that other
world it was not so simple. Capricorn's pen hung in
his fingers, and he stared at the paper before him, not
seeing. He thought of the Service claim that they had
run all the *Abwehr* agents in Britain. He knew what
that meant. To keep an enemy agent 'operational' he
had to be fed information, so lightly called 'chicken
feed' in the Service. But a good agent had to produce
good information. The more German agents the Service ran, the more good information they had to give

away. A 'good trade' looked all right on paper. But information dealt with real things, live men and women who ended up as dead ones. Agents, always considered 'expendable.' Planes, ships, troops—what would the public think of that? How did you explain to the widows and orphans? That an accountant might say that the 'bottom line' was a net plus? If it were. . . .

Capricorn, who had worked in liaison with the Americans towards the war's end, remembered their growing hostility to the Service. Hoover himself refused to work with them eventually. He preferred MI5 who seemed to him more sober and reliable. Innocence in that world was hard to define.

The puzzle absorbed his mind, diminishing the pleasure of handing in his report. He received three telephone calls that pleased him. The first was from a moved and grateful Herr Krause, who had been notified of events as the girl's next of kin. His usual flow of words for once was halted and he stammered out his thanks, adding, 'My brother, the *Rechtsgelehrter*, I thank you for his sake.'

Capricorn appreciated that.

In lighter vein was the call from Otto Karl, on his way back to Cobleigh and his family, repentant, he told Capricorn, for his sins, but laughingly admitting they had been great fun.

'By the way,' he asked, 'are you the von Braun of the detectives?'

'Alas, no,' Capricorn said, 'Just a nuts and bolts man.'

It was Karl's humour, he reflected, that had made him so unlikely in the role of Ingeborg Rilke's murderer, even when the evidence seemed to point his way. That, and his affair with the ebullient Randy Clarke. Capricorn smiled. He could not see that British sunbeam attracted to a sadist. The third call was from the sunbeam herself. She was frankly glad that her friend's killer was dead, and expressed her appreciation to Capricorn by suggesting he come one day and visit her.

He thanked her and promised to see her again. A charming girl, he thought and smiled to himself. Of course, you'd never be sure she wouldn't take the milkman in with the milk. . . . He couldn't help comparing her with his friend Rose and felt a little melancholy at his loss of that lady, as he often did, when he had time.

But as he headed for home through the darkening streets his mind reverted back to the problem that had troubled him enough to take the joy from his triumph. Who was innocent? At Nuremberg they were trying that very question, but it was ending in the age-old way. The vanquished were found guilty, though some of the victors had committed the same crimes. As Diener had pointed out, a war begun to save Poland from Germany, had ended with Poland being given to Russia. A strange and turned-about war, at the last. Who was innocent?

A picture of the sad, strange face of Ingeborg Rilke floated once more through his mind, a reminder of all that had been destroyed.

A child ran in front of the car, happily chasing a ball, and he stopped abruptly. Well, he thought, resigned, our children can still play in the streets. He heard a woman's voice calling from a nearby house. The lights were on, the curtains left undrawn, and the inside looked warm and cosy. Englishmen were still in their homes, not working as slaves in foreign lands.

He paused for a moment, his foot still on the brake. At the end of the war, Capricorn had been asked to stay on in the Service, but he had chosen, after all, to return to the Force. There the questions were simpler. There were known rules and the boundaries were clearly marked, policemen and villains, hunters and hunted, no grey zone in which the enemy turned around to stare at you with your own face.

Sighing he pushed the accelerator and made for home, even if it was only Aunt Dolly's. Aunt Dolly . . . she was still probably being wined and dined by Diener. What was it she had come to tell him, apart from her celebration of her professional good luck? The plasterer was done or was it the floors? He couldn't remember. In spite of his weariness and pain he drove back towards what he thought of as 'his' square.

It was quite dark when he got there but the street lamps were lit. He peered up at his windows. Could it be? They were clean, positively shining, the splashes and dirt all washed away. He opened the front door with his key and touched the switch. Miraculously, the place was flooded with soft light.

He stared. The walls were light, smooth as satin and rose nobly to the ceiling with its fine old plasterwork restored. The floors were dark and gleaming. He walked from room to room, rejoicing in his new, modern kitchen, the well-fitted bathroom—daring, he turned a tap and hot water gushed forth in rich abundance. There was the bedroom over the silent garden, the square room that would be his study, the long living room, gracious with its double arches.

Peace, quiet, space. He looked around him and felt a great surge of joy and thankfulness. One man, at least, had come home.

Bestsellers

☐ **COMES THE BLIND FURY** by John Saul $2.75 (11428-4)

☐ **CLASS REUNION** by Rona Jaffe $2.75 (11408-X)

☐ **THE EXILES** by William Stuart Long $2.75 (12369-0)

☐ **THE BRONX ZOO** by Sparky Lyle and
  Peter Golenbock $2.50 (10764-4)

☐ **THE PASSING BELLS** by Phillip Rock $2.75 (16837-6)

☐ **TO LOVE AGAIN** by Danielle Steel $2.50 (18631-5)

☐ **SECOND GENERATION** by Howard Fast $2.75 (17892-4)

☐ **EVERGREEN** by Belva Plain $2.75 (13294-0)

☐ **CALIFORNIA WOMAN** by Daniel Knapp $2.50 (11035-1)

☐ **DAWN WIND** by Christina Savage $2.50 (11792-5)

☐ **REGINA'S SONG**
  by Sharleen Cooper Cohen $2.50 (17414-7)

☐ **SABRINA** by Madeleine A. Polland $2.50 (17633-6)

☐ **THE ADMIRAL'S DAUGHTER**
  by Victoria Fyodorova and Haskel Frankel $2.50 (10366-5)

☐ **THE LAST DECATHLON** by John Redgate $2.50 (14643-7)

☐ **THE PETROGRAD CONSIGNMENT**
  by Owen Sela $2.50 (16885-6)

☐ **EXCALIBUR!** by Gil Kane and John Jakes $2.50 (12291-0)

☐ **SHOGUN** by James Clavell $2.95 (17800-2)

☐ **MY MOTHER, MY SELF** by Nancy Friday $2.50 (15663-7)

☐ **THE IMMIGRANTS** by Howard Fast $2.75 (14175-3)

At your local bookstore or use this handy coupon for ordering:

Dell **DELL BOOKS**
P.O. BOX 1000, PINEBROOK, N.J. 07058

Please send me the books I have checked above. I am enclosing $_____
(please add 75¢ per copy to cover postage and handling). Send check or money
order—no cash or C.O.D.'s. Please allow up to 8 weeks for shipment.

Mr/Mrs/Miss_____

Address_____

City_____State/Zip_____

"The Hollywood novel by just about the hottest screenwriter around." —*Wall Street Journal*

TINSEL

by William Goldman
author of *Marathon Man* and *Magic*

William Goldman—Academy Award-winning screenwriter of *Butch Cassidy and the Sundance Kid* and *All The President's Men*—has written a shattering, nationally-best-selling novel. He has seen and learned a lot of Hollywood's best-kept secrets. In *Tinsel,* he tells a story only an insider could.

"Scathing, witty, merciless, and a fast enjoyable read. The film colony may squirm, but the rest of us will lap it up."— John Barkham Reviews

"No-punches-pulled slashes at the business. Complete with names named." —*Kirkus Reviews*

A Dell Book $2.75 (18735-4)

At your local bookstore or use this handy coupon for ordering:

Dell	**DELL BOOKS** TINSEL $2.75 (18735-4) **P.O. BOX 1000, PINEBROOK, N.J. 07058**

Please send me the above title. I am enclosing $ _____
(please add 75¢ per copy to cover postage and handling). Send check or money order—no cash or C.O.D.'s. Please allow up to 8 weeks for shipment.

Mr/Mrs/Miss _____

Address _____

City _____ State/Zip _____

Comes the Blind Fury

John Saul

Bestselling author of *Cry for the Strangers* and *Suffer the Children*

More than a century ago, a gentle, blind child walked the paths of Paradise Point. Then other children came, teasing and taunting her until she lost her footing on the cliff and plunged into the drowning sea.

Now, 12-year-old Michelle and her family have come to live in that same house—to escape the city pressures, to have a better life.

But the sins of the past do not die. They reach out to embrace the living. Dreams will become nightmares.

Serenity will become terror. There will be no escape.

A Dell Book $2.75   (11428-4)

At your local bookstore or use this handy coupon for ordering:

| **Dell** | **DELL BOOKS**   COMES THE BLIND FURY $2.75   (11428-4) |
| | **P.O. BOX 1000, PINEBROOK, N.J. 07058** |

Please send me the above title. I am enclosing $ _____
(please add 75¢ per copy to cover postage and handling). Send check or money order—no cash or C.O.D.'s. Please allow up to 8 weeks for shipment.

Mr/Mrs/Miss_____

Address _____

City _____ State/Zip _____

BY REASON OF INSANITY

Shane Stevens

author of *Rat Pack* and *Go Down Dead*

"Sensational."—*New York Post*

Thomas Bishop—born of a mindless rape—escapes from an institution for the criminally insane to deluge a nation in blood and horror. Not even Bishop himself knows where—and in what chilling horror—it will end.

"This is Shane Stevens' masterpiece. The most suspenseful novel in years."—Curt Gentry, co-author of *Helter Skelter*

"A masterful suspense thriller steeped in blood, guts and sex."—*The Cincinnati Enquirer*

A Dell Book $2.75   (11028-9)

At your local bookstore or use this handy coupon for ordering:

Dell	**DELL BOOKS** BY REASON OF INSANITY $2.75 (11028-9)
	P.O. BOX 1000, PINEBROOK, N.J. 07058

Please send me the above title. I am enclosing $_____
(please add 75¢ per copy to cover postage and handling). Send check or money order—no cash or C.O.D.'s. Please allow up to 8 weeks for shipment.

Mr/Mrs/Miss_____

Address_____

City_____State/Zip_____

Presenting Dell's
Alfred Hitchcock series
for those who dare to read them!

☐ **MURDERER'S ROW** $1.95 (16036-7)
☐ **DON'T LOOK A GIFT SHARK IN THE MOUTH** ...$1.95 (13620-8)
☐ **BREAKING THE SCREAM BARRIER** $1.95 (14627-0)
☐ **DEATH ON ARRIVAL** $1.75 (11839-5)
☐ **NOOSE REPORT** $1.50 (16455-9)
☐ **MURDERS ON THE HALF SKULL** $1.50 (16093-6)
☐ **BEHIND THE DEATH BALL** $1.50 (13497-8)
☐ **WITCHES' BREW** $1.25 (19613-2)
☐ **A HANGMAN'S DOZEN** $1.25 (13428-5)
☐ **SCREAM ALONG WITH ME** $1.25 (13633-4)
☐ **HAPPINESS IS A WARM CORPSE** $1.50 (13438-2)
☐ **KILLERS AT LARGE** $1.50 (14443-4)
☐ **MURDER GO ROUND** $1.50 (15607-6)
☐ **SLAY RIDE** $1.50 (13641-5)
☐ **THIS ONE WILL KILL YOU** $1.50 (18808-3)
☐ **12 STORIES FOR LATE AT NIGHT** $1.50 (19178-5)
☐ **STORIES MY MOTHER NEVER TOLD ME** $1.25 (18290-5)
☐ **13 MORE THEY WOULDN'T LET ME DO ON TV** $1.50 (13640-7)
☐ **STORIES TO BE READ WITH THE LIGHTS ON** $1.50 (14949-5)
☐ **SIXTEEN SKELETONS FROM MY CLOSET** $1.25 (18011-2)
☐ **14 OF MY FAVORITES IN SUSPENSE** $1.50 (13630-X)

At your local bookstore or use this handy coupon for ordering:

| **Dell** | **DELL BOOKS**
P.O. BOX 1000, PINEBROOK, N.J. 07058 |

Please send me the books I have checked above. I am enclosing $_____
(please add 75¢ per copy to cover postage and handling). Send check or money
order—no cash or C.O.D.'s. Please allow up to 8 weeks for shipment.

Mr/Mrs/Miss _____

Address _____

City _____ State/Zip _____